the Queen
and the
HANDYMAN

"For Peggy,
for your future
happiness!

In Jesus' love,
Maria Rattoon
August 2011

the Queen and the HANDYMAN

Maria Tatham

TATE PUBLISHING & Enterprises

Published by Tate Publishing & Enterprises, LLC
127 E. Trade Center Terrace | Mustang, Oklahoma 73064 USA
1.888.361.9473 | www.tatepublishing.com

Tate Publishing is committed to excellence in the publishing industry. The company reflects the philosophy established by the founders, based on Psalm 68:11,
"The Lord gave the word and great was the company of those who published it."

Book design copyright © 2011 by Tate Publishing, LLC. All rights reserved.
Cover design by Blake Brasor
Interior design by Sarah Kirchen

Published in the United States of America

ISBN: 978-1-61739-972-5
1. Fiction / Fantasy / General   2. Fiction / Fantasy / Historical
11.05.16

For my husband, Tom.

Acknowledgments

I owe a huge debt to my very patient and helpful husband, Tom. To those friends who read and critiqued drafts: Bobbi Book, Betty Canterbury, Dr. Gwenyth Hood, Regina Mocey-Hanton, Jean Steffens, and Kathy VanCleve. To my friends Susan Dorman, who gave me editorial advice, and Eunice Tschappat, who spoke a word in season that helped me persevere. To all my teachers, but especially the late Dr. J. Harvey Gossard, former Dean of Winebrenner Theological Seminary, who gave his students a well-considered introduction to the Reformation period. To my cousins for their encouragement: Mimi Martinez, JoAnn Tomazinis, Rosemary Zinkhan, and the late Arthur Torelli Jr. To my father-in-law and his wife, Bill and Sally Tatham, for their generosity in many things. To our pastor and his wife, Dr. David and Linda Lindeblad, for their loving support. To my editor, Aubrey Kinat, for her help in focusing as I polished this. And to those writers who first took me to other worlds, including the world that is unseen: C. S. Lewis and Frank Peretti.

Also, I wish to say to all who read this that, during her lifetime, my mother, Helen Torelli Thomas, was a constant source of encouragement.

There is always a debt a writer owes to people who show up as characters in their stories. I want to acknowledge all the Trimble-like men I've known, especially Tom, who made Trimble real to me.

And thank you to my former pastor, Dennis E. Jones, and his wife, Pamela, who appear in these pages as if simply changing into seventeenth-century dress, as Bishop Jerome and his wife, Cami.

Be careful of the way in which you think of the dead. Think not of what might have been. Look steadfastly and you shall see the living glory of your well-beloved dead in the depths of heaven.

Les Miserables, Victor Hugo. Translated from the French by Charles E. Wilbour, the Modern Library

By faith Abel offered to God a more acceptable sacrifice than Cain, through which he was commended as righteous, God commending him by accepting his gifts. And through his faith, though he died, he still speaks.

Hebrews 11:4 (ESV)

Table of Contents

Prologue: Destiny

Far away in the Eastern Wilds, where there was a power that sought to unmake the will and feed on the mind of a man, a king fell in single combat with a powerful sorcerer. Angels descended to claim the king's soul. The sorcerer despised them, the heaven from which they came, and God himself. The king's wife, the mother of his small daughter, though far from him in the west of the kingdom, felt his pangs and knew he had died. She and the child lived on as if in a happy lie...

Part One:
Her Quest (and His)

Deception

Supper at the tiny castle at Zuphof was always informal unless there were important guests. With Christmas over, and in the first iron-grip of winter, there were none. Marta's courtiers were laughing and chatting as they indulged in bubbly and holiday leftovers.

It was the anniversary of her father the king's so-called heroic death—the fourth of January, the year of our LORD 1622 (of the Zupian calendar)—and the courtiers were taking turns flattering his "sacred memory." As usual, Marta's mother was absent from the feast. Marta was quietly fuming as she studied the courtiers in light of something she had just discovered.

Her chancellor, the Earl of Ester, raised his goblet, his gray goatee waggling as he said, "To the king!"

The others followed his lead and raised their goblets. "To the king!"

Wine was splashed and spilled, and someone yawned and produced a belch of such incredible proportions that even Trimble, Marta's paunchy faithful family retainer, would have been proud.

Marta's ladies-in-waiting, Kikki and Betsy, glanced at her and smiled. She returned their smile weakly, feeling a twinge of pity for them. They didn't suspect that an ax was about to fall, and they were right in its path.

The earl went on, "Among his many extraordinary gifts, the king had a peculiar talent for adventure."

True, Ester! Marta thought. *And very sly, your double meaning!*

Countess Gallina, with a napkin tucked into her high-bosomed bodice, looked like a chicken whose wattle wiggled as she declared, "He had a *genius* for it! No one—*no one*—was like His Royal Highness!"

These compliments would have been welcome if her courtiers hadn't been such barefaced liars.

The earl turned to Marta with a question. She couldn't make sense of what he was saying because she was so angry.

He smiled as he waited for an answer.

She found her voice at last. "It's time to stop pretending," she said.

He set down his goblet and with an appearance of frank good humor asked, "I'm sorry, Majesty, but I don't understand."

"You've deceived me," she said. "You and everyone else! I am simply letting you know—and warning you—that I now know the truth."

"Majesty, please understand!" The earl went as white as the tablecloth, his goatee waggling furiously. "We meant well! At the time, you were a child who needed to be protected from the facts."

"I'm no longer a child."

He inclined his head. "Of course not."

"And the deception has continued."

The courtiers began to murmur. Their murmurs grew louder, and the countess was even so bold as to stare at Marta as if Marta was somehow at fault.

Marta tapped her goblet with a knife, her hand shaking as she gripped it. "I'm deeply displeased. I cannot stress this *too* much. You would all do well to be silent."

The earl's expression changed to one of barely-concealed resentment.

"The discussion is over for now," said Marta. "But later, I will have questions for *each* of you."

As she said "each of you," she glanced at Kikki and Betsy. They blushed and lowered their eyes.

Shakily, she laid the knife across her plate, then tossed her napkin onto the table and stood.

The earl pushed his chair back and rose. The other courtiers followed suit, and the room cleared like a walkway swept of leaves by an icy wind.

The two persons who remained with Marta now approached her: the young, steely and thin, newly-appointed bishop, Jerome Wenzel and his small, blonde, winsomely stout wife, Camila. They appeared embarrassed, as if they were the last two healthy branches of a tree that had been heavily pruned.

"Your Majesty—" Jerome began but faltered.

Marta held up a hand. "I understand that you knew nothing about this."

Jerome's dark brows lowered, and Camila slipped her hand into his and squeezed it.

"That isn't quite true, Majesty," Jerome said. "I've known. I've been wondering how to speak with you about it."

Marta studied him. "Thank you, Bishop! Honesty is rare."

"We're praying for you," Camila offered.

Jerome's keen gaze held Marta's. "Allow me to give you some advice. Think hard, and pray long before acting on what you've learned."

The next morning, Marta escaped outdoors with Kikki and Betsy into the bracing, wintry world, heading for the pond on the castle grounds. She was trying to divert herself, to wait on God for her answers, to be the proverbial sparrow in his loving hands. As she skated, her thoughts circled with her, around and around her problem: the longstanding nature of the deception, the near impossibility of trusting anyone as a result, and her father's possible plight. The letter, which had given her the gift of truth, and which she now carried with her everywhere, seemed to be burning a hole in her pocket.

She glanced over her shoulder and saw her ladies flounder and pull each other down. Kikki was plump and hailed from warmer Sapore. Betsy was hampered by specs that slid down her nose—at the moment, these were skittering across the ice.

Marta had retrieved them for her and was skating away when a wrinkle in the ice sent her sprawling toward a snowdrift at the edge of the pond. The world went white and very cold.

Strong arms pulled her up onto the blades of her skates. Most of the snow dropped away from her rumpled clothes but some slipped down her collar. As she shivered, she found herself looking into the eyes of Trimble. They were large eyes, a bit droopy at the outer corners, their color a lovely blue. At the moment, they were filled with concern and amusement. She blushed and shivered again. Just another embarrassing moment for the queen! She didn't know whether to cry or laugh.

"Preoccupied, mistress?" Trimble asked, the corners of his mustache lifting.

She brushed off her dove-gray coat and tucked a wheat-colored braid under her feathered, black cap. Trimble always behaved with the utmost respect, and yet he had a knack for nudging her back onto the path of humility. But though she was embarrassed by her tumble, his expression was kindness itself. What a picture he was with his cheeks and nose so rosy! He was a comforting soul, and someone in whom she might possibly confide. Should she confide in him? Once her father's valet, now the head handyman at the palace—he was almost like one of the family.

But how did he happen to be *here*? Earlier he had been hammering on the dais for her coronation. Ah! Through a gap in the hedge bordering the grounds, she watched as his son Timka skated the canal with a yard of sailcloth to catch the wind. She sighed. How wonderful to be so carefree! She had once been carefree.

"...Eh?" Trimble was saying.

She was startled. "Oh—sorry! I was noticing Timka."

"I was noticing you." He gently smiled.

"That's kind, but please don't worry!"

"You should have been told long ago!"

She frowned. "*You* might have said something. I trusted you! You aren't only a servant but a friend—and Father's friend as well!"

He looked away, his jaw clenching. "I thought it wasn't my place to speak. I was wrong." He met her gaze. "Will you forgive me?"

She tried to lighten his load of guilt by sounding glib. "Of course! But I have to ask if there's anything *else* I should know?"

He slowly shook his head, his expression sympathetic. "There's still much that remains a mystery."

Marta sighed and looked away. Kikki was shuffling toward her, and Betsy was off the ice and walking, wobbling in her skates, along the shore toward the summerhouse.

"They've announced lunch!" Betsy called.

Marta squeezed Trimble's arm and said, "We'll talk again."

The corners of his mustache lifted, but only slightly and a bit sadly. He saluted and then turned away to watch Timka.

Kikki reached Marta and smiled, showing dimples. With a glove of red suede, she stuffed a chestnut curl under her bonnet of mink.

"*Ah!*" she yelped as her skates slid out from under her, and she made a grab for Marta's arm.

"Don't pull me, or we'll *both* go down," Marta said, steadying her. "Take my hand, and I'll get you to shore."

They headed for the summerhouse. Snow was falling again, straight down as if from an enormous sifter, all around in every direction.

"You make skating look simple." Kikki laughed and added, "*Most of the time.*"

Marta was amazed at her—she didn't seem the least bit ashamed. She followed her lead, acting as if nothing had happened to change their relationship. Confrontation could wait.

"If you'd grown up here," she said, "*you'd* be skating circles around me."

"That would be nice!" Kikki sighed. "Though I'm glad I grew up in Sapore—beautiful Sapore!"

"Homesick, friend?"

"Yes—for Father," Kikki said, then gave a little gasp and covered her mouth.

Marta said nothing about this *faux pas,* just smiled.

There was an inch of fresh white on the steps of the summer-house; they climbed them, gripping the railing. Kikki tottered over the floorboards and plumped onto a bench, then unlaced her skates and chatted with Betsy. Neither spoke to Marta, but both smiled. They seemed more sorry for her than guilty.

As Marta sat to remove her skates, she thought of Kikki's father, Vincenzo, prince of Sapore. He was one of the nicest men she knew, a true gentleman, and kind and charming too—that indefinable Saporian charm that warmed one's heart.

Vincenzo's son—Kikki's brother, Bartolo—was the same sort of man. Marta had no brother; she had loved but lost Bartolo; and her own father, King Peter—what had happened to *him?*

The three were enjoying lunch by a cheerful fire in the castle's Winter Parlor. For the first time, Camila had been asked to join them—a last-minute suggestion by Kikki and Betsy, who knew that Marta esteemed her and probably hoped to have her there as a buffer between Marta's anger and them.

They were enjoying tomato bisque, a fondue of cheese with toasted bread to dunk, and a salad of leaf lettuce grown in the greenhouse. Marta's dog, Keyah—a tawny, perk-eared, long-haired spitz—lay across her slippered feet.

Camila ate simply and eagerly without minding her manners or forgetting them. As the mother of a large family, she most likely dined in disorder, managing squabbles, tears, and spills. But all of her actions, even eating, seemed to be in simple and trusting response to divine commands—in this case, to enjoy herself.

Marta found her comforting. She was the daughter of the former bishop, John Kolpos. Her mother had died when she was small, and she had been sent to live with an aunt. After that, Marta had rarely seen her. She had married Jerome, the official preacher at the Cathedral of Blessed Gregor, and when her father died, Jerome had succeeded him as bishop. Now Marta saw her regularly, but not as much as she would have liked.

Jerome and Camila had adopted several children—some who needed special care—from among the poorest of the poor. As a result, the couple was a favorite topic of gossip at court. Many of the courtiers disapproved of the adoptions and disliked having divine service interrupted by the sometimes-rowdy children and their attentive mother. They considered Camila and Jerome their inferiors as a result of their unusual family situation. Though aware of this, Jerome watched over the courtiers with diligence and wisdom, with Camila at his side. And though they looked down their long noses at her, Camila was always kind to them.

As Marta watched her interact with Kikki and Betsy—listening to the sound, not the sense, of their chatter—she began to fret, ate a little too quickly, and hiccupped loudly.

"Bless you!" said Camila.

"As I was saying, Majesty, I hope the mail can get through," Betsy said. "Ferdy has promised to write."

"You've had one letter from him already this week," Marta said a little absently.

Betsy smiled shyly as she dipped a crust of bread in fondue.

Camila dunked her bread and then nibbled, her eyes alight with interest. "And who is Ferdy?"

"Ferdinand—Ferdinand de Lanz, my fiancé," Betsy said.

Kikki coated a crust generously, licked her thumb, and then said, "How well do you know his family, Betsy? You've never mentioned this."

Betsy sat a little straighter. "Fairly well—not intimately yet."

"Mm." Kikki raised an eyebrow.

Marta glanced at Kikki, hoping to end the discussion, but Kikki forged on.

"His father, Borg, is—sorry, Betsy, but there's really no nice way to say this—an adulterer." Kikki looked concerned. "Are you really sure about Ferdy's character? I'm asking because I don't want to see you hurt."

Betsy set down her spoon and, with fire and ice in her glance, glared at her. "Of course I'm sure!"

"Well, then!" Kikki sighed. "We must trust your judgment."

Helping herself to more bread, Camila glanced from one to the other.

Betsy exploded. "Kikki, you should *assume* the best about him—and *me!* Honestly, you always behave as though *you* know better!"

"I'm sorry, but it's difficult when—" Kikki began but stopped when she saw Marta glance her way. "No, you're right, Betsy—I *should* assume." She lifted her bowl to drink the last of her bisque. "Ferdy does seem nice and is rather good-looking."

Marta said quietly, "I'm happy for you, Betsy."

Camila looked thoughtful. "People can be very different from their families. Perhaps that's the case with Ferdy."

Betsy smiled at her.

Kikki frowned.

Knowing that Kikki wanted to say more, Marta raised her crystal goblet, with its ruddy sherry, and said, "To Ferdy and Betsy! May they live long and happily together!"

Betsy blushed with pleasure and tipped her goblet.

Kikki graciously raised her own.

Camila sipped and then set her drink down.

They left the table for the fireplace. Kikki settled on a high-backed bench with cushions, and Betsy gathered her skirts to sit on a footstool. Marta stood by the fireplace, where Camila joined her as if wishing to be helpful.

Betsy pushed up her specs and gazed at Marta mournfully, while Kikki stared at Marta eagerly. They seemed to be waiting for some mention of Marta's trouble in spite of the part they had played in it.

Marta swirled the sherry in her goblet, staring at it. Keyah, looking chunkier than she was because of her long hair and gorgeous ruff, trotted to the hearthstone and lay down, gazing at her with bright, uptilted eyes.

Camila stooped to pet Keyah, while Kikki and Betsy darted little glances at each other—glances that said they'd noticed that Marta was having another drink.

Observing their silent interchange, Marta set her goblet on the mantelpiece.

There was a pause, and Kikki blurted, "Well, are you going to tell us about the letter?" She raised the hem of her gown and drew her legs up. "Or do you truly feel you can no longer trust us?"

"*Can* I?"

"I know we deserve that, but yes, you can! Can't she, Betsy?"

"Yes!"

Camila gave Keyah a final pat and straightened. "Perhaps I should go so you can speak privately."

Betsy looked worried at the thought of Camila's departure.

"No, Camila—stay," Marta said. "You too are a friend."

Camila smiled. "Please, call me Cami."

Marta smiled. "All right, *Cami!*" Her smile faltered. "What would you think, Cami, of friends who lied to you?"

Kikki and Betsy sat as still as statues.

Cami tilted her head as she considered Marta's question. "I wouldn't necessarily think less of them or assume that they thought little of me. I would seek the reason *why* they weren't honest."

Cami caught the eye of each of the women in turn. "If you are speaking of Kikki and Betsy, Majesty, *ask* them, without becoming angry—meekly. The fault may not be all their own."

Marta blinked. So this was honesty! She felt as if she had disembarked from a rolling, storm-tossed galleon onto solid ground.

"All right," she said with quivering lips. Then she faced Kikki and Betsy and said, "How could you deceive me, friends? Why *did* you?"

"How? Why?" Kikki caught her lip in her teeth. "Oh, that we *hadn't!* But Marta—think! How could we reveal a secret your mother was keeping?"

"I understand that, Kikki, but it was still wrong!"

"We were afraid of causing trouble," Betsy said.

"There was trouble already."

A tear slipped down Betsy's cheek. "Forgive us!"

Marta gently nodded. Cami slipped away to the bench and perched in the corner opposite to Kikki, her soft countenance beaming on them all.

"So are you going to tell us about the letter, Majesty?" Kikki went on.

"We won't tell *anyone*," Betsy said.

"Don't make promises you can't keep, Betsy!" Marta said.

"Why don't you read the letter to us?" Kikki suggested. "Surely Cami—the wife of your bishop—may hear it too?"

Such a request from anyone but Kikki would have angered Marta, but she merely shook her head in amazement.

"We've been almost as ill-informed as *you*," said Betsy.

Cami looked on as if expecting something like this and as if nothing in human nature could surprise her. Marta wiped her eyes, drew the letter from her pocket, and sat on the bench between her and Kikki.

Betsy pulled the footstool closer. As Marta began to unfold the letter, Betsy grasped Marta's hand. "First, please allow me to say something! And I believe I speak for Kikki too. Though we have never experienced anything like this, we understand how painful it must be!"

"And confusing," Kikki murmured.

The three embraced.

Laughing with joy at being able to unburden her heart, Marta said, "I've cried so much that by now my nose must look like *Trimble's!*"

Cami laughed. "Yes, Trimble's *nose!*"

"Read, friend!" Kikki cried.

"Yes, Majesty!" said Betsy.

Marta cleared her throat, then read aloud, "'Your Majesty, Queen Marta Louisa of Zuphof, your letter in which you proposed a visit to our abbey has reached us at last. Your courier escaped an encounter with bandits and is recuperating here. Both he and the letter survived—God be praised!

"'I answer in some perplexity. While we would rejoice to receive you, we cannot do so under a pretense. His Highness, our beloved King Peter, isn't buried here. As his death is almost certain, I wish I could say he was, for that would mean there were no longer troubling questions about his fate.

"'I'm disturbed to learn that someone lied to you. If it was your mother, I beg you to forgive her and try to understand. She has probably suffered more than any of us know.

"'If I can be of further help to you in this or in any other matter, ask and you will find me, your devoted servant, Matthew of Maiberg, Abbot of Blessed Philip the Bold's, Madrigal. PS: The brothers pray daily for the House of Happstein and the reunification and peace of the kingdom.'"

Marta folded the letter and returned it to her pocket.

Kikki took Marta's hand. "I'm so sorry you had to learn this from a letter!" Her tears fell. "It's hard to understand your mother's motive. Perhaps she felt it was somehow better for you *not* to know."

"Kikki, I forgive her but don't wish to have her actions condoned."

"What will you do, Majesty?" Betsy asked, her eyes huge behind the lenses of her specs.

Marta studied Betsy's serious face, and Kikki's so full of genuine affection. She forgave them, yes, but somehow couldn't bring herself to tell them everything.

Confrontation

She had been fitted for a gown of red and gold, indigo and emerald, with a train that fell in a sweep from her slender shoulders. In May, she was to be crowned, an event she dreaded—the royal rubberstamp on her management of tiny, beleaguered Zuphof. To the north and south, neighboring duchies, which had rebelled and seceded, were encroaching, gobbling up rich dairy land and timberland and annexing village after village. On the eastern frontier, the outlaw—Lord Alexander Drugen—held sway.

Marta keenly felt her own inadequacies, so before assuming the reins of government, she'd planned to journey to the abbey to pray in a place endued with her father's memory. In October, she had written to the abbot announcing her plans, and her courier had set out. She wasn't surprised to learn he'd gotten into trouble on the road. According to all the stories, there were worse things than robbers in the passes leading into that fabled realm. Some said the way led past the den of a dragon—a *wyrm* with wings as vast as storm clouds.

She was standing at the foot of the stairs with Kikki and Betsy, asking them to pray for her, for she was about to speak with her mother about a change in plans in light of what she'd learned. She turned away from them toward the broad sweep of marble. Keyah began to run up ahead, but she told her to stay. Then, taking a deep breath, she raced upward—past the dynastic portraits and varnished woodwork and frosted panes of the arched casements—to the dim corridor, where guards were dozing in tipped-back chairs. She woke them as she knocked at the doors of the Royal Apartments and slipped inside.

On the dim winter afternoon, Carissima was working on needle-point by candlelight, leaning forward in a chair that faced a taut canvas stretched on a freestanding frame. She was dressed in a dark gown with a delicate ivory-colored ruff at the neck—the garb of mourning after all these years. Her black hair, silver at the temples, was arranged in a plain chignon. On her brow, over the frown line, lay a simple coronet of silver with one dark-looking garnet.

She gestured to a chair near her own. Marta sat on the edge, watching her finish a stitch and then anchor the needle in the fabric.

"I've been told what happened at the feast," Carissima said, her gaze forthright but afraid. "Have you come to scold me too?"

"Of course, not, Mother! But I do need to speak with you."

Carissima leaned forward and put her hand over Marta's. "I pray you will find peace, darling."

Marta couldn't help but laugh a little. "When you—and everyone else—lied?"

"I ordered them to do this." Carissima sounded as if all she had done was completely reasonable. "You mustn't blame them. I knew the truth would only make you suffer more."

Marta withdrew her hand. "I was always told he died. Now I learn he may be *alive?*"

"That's not how you must understand the abbot." With trembling hands, Carissima smoothed the skirt of her gown. "Yes, I know about his letter, for he wrote to me as well." When she raised her chin, there were tears in her eyes. "While there was no definite confirmation of your father's death, there were very credible rumors."

Pity tugged at Marta's heart; she spoke gently: "What was done in light of these?"

"The Earl of Ester made the trip to question Lord Drugen." Carissima paused to search Marta's face. "Please don't look at me that way!

I understand how you must feel about the earl, but I believe his word is to be trusted."

Marta tried to remain calm. "How can he be trusted when he lied to me for years? Does he find lying *easy*—?"

Carissima's delicate nostrils flared. "Marta!"

"Mother, I'm not implying that *you* find it easy to lie—please don't think that! It's just that because Ester lied, I'll never be able to believe him again. And chances are, he has hidden something from you!"

Carissima cocked her head, ashamed yet defiant. "He has said that Drugen told him your father visited then left and that their discussions ended amicably with promises on his own part."

Marta rose from the chair to pace. "Drugen wasn't to be trusted. He may have killed Father and paid Ester to be silent."

Carissima's eyes widened. "I've never heard you speak so *cynically!*"

"What else was done, Mother?"

Carissima shoulders drooped a little. "Those knights who hadn't accompanied your father made a thorough search." She sighed. "Everywhere they went they heard the same story. Your father died in some unknown conflict, and his knights likely shared his fate." As she looked Marta in the eye, she seemed to be hoping that Marta would be satisfied by this.

"You seem to have given up so easily!"

Carissima's tears fell. "Marta, that is unjust! I did *everything* I could to discover what happened. If your father were alive, wouldn't he have gotten word to us long ago?"

Ashamed, Marta offered her a handkerchief. "But, you see, he might not have been able to at first, and that might still be the case."

Carissima shook her head sadly, grew calmer and reached out to Marta. As Marta took her hand, she braced herself for a storm.

"I don't need your permission, Mother," she said firmly, "but I want your blessing. I intend to take the knights and search for Father myself—beginning at Lord Drugen's."

Carissima's eyebrows rose in small, frightened arcs. She withdrew her hand from Marta's. "A young, unmarried woman alone in the wilds for weeks on end with a dozen rough men?"

Marta threw up her hands. "They are my *servants*, Mother—knights who are sworn to protect me."

Carissima's tone was adamant. "It's unthinkable!"

Marta hoped to be convincing but had no airtight argument. "It's quite reasonable."

Carissima's hands clenched in her lap. "You have no idea of the danger!"

Marta blurted: "*Whatever* it is, I can face it for Father's sake!"

Carissima fell silent. Marta sat back on her heels, staring into space and imagining the danger *and* the success. Watching from a nearby hilltop as her knights stormed Drugen's fortress. Riding with them through the broken and burned gates to see her father at a tower window waving his hand and smiling.

"Marta, did you hear me?" Carissima was saying. "Don't speak of this again! If you attempt to go, I'll do everything in my power to stop you—including confining you."

"You forget that *I* am queen!"

"Not quite yet!" Carissima's tone was filled with urgency. "Marta, I've talked with the bishop, and he agrees that you shouldn't act impulsively."

Marta made no reply. Carissima's words sank into her heart—down, down to the place where the rest of her pain was hiding. Weeping, she kissed Carissima's damp cheek and then escaped to her own room.

There, she threw herself onto her bed and sobbed. By the time her tears stopped and she opened her burning eyes, the light in the room had changed. The snow had stopped, and the clouds had parted. A slanting beam of golden sunlight was pouring through the window of the balcony door over the carpet. It looked as solemn and still as she felt.

She sat up, took her journal from the bedside table, and went to her desk. The inkstand was full, and the quills were sharpened. For a moment, she rested a nib on her lips, then dipped it in ink and scrawled:

My heart is full—there is much to tell! Mother has lied, and she and I have lived that lie. Everyone has lied, I've discovered. I look about me at friends and find conspirators. The lie was woven into every aspect of life, and now, with a single word from one honest soul, all that I've known and trusted has been smashed to pieces.

Father may be alive. He isn't a dead hero but simply a man who never came home. God forgive those words! I still believe the best about Father, but—oh, the torturing doubt!

And Mother. I must forgive her, I know, but how far can I believe her? Is, as she says, the likeliest thing the true thing? Did he indeed die, but we just don't know when or where or how? Or is he living another life without us—forgetting us?

At the remembrance of his boyish face, which made me laugh whenever I beheld it, a knife enters my heart. I stagger with my hands on the hilt but can't remove it—

She paused and then scribbled:

Perhaps I may still save him! If so, life will remain comprehensible.

Determination

Marta was sitting on the floor in her room. Night had descended, and the curtains were drawn across the balcony doors. A fire was blazing, and the candles were lit. She had locked the door leading to her room and was still in evening dress, though supper had ended hours ago. Her wide skirts were settled around her as if she were the center of some blossom fashioned from satin, lace, and jewels.

On the floor, in a semicircle of neat piles, her things were ordered: undergarments, changes of clothes, quills, inkhorn, paper, her journal, Psalter and New Testament, and a jar of lotion to protect her hands and face. There was a small stash of provisions and a flagon of wine mixed with water.

Keyah lay on the end of the bed on a cushion made for her. Her dark eyes twinkled in the firelight, but they looked sad, as if she knew of Marta's plans, knew that soon her mistress would be leaving, perhaps never to return.

Marta leaned to stroke Keyah's head, saying, "Do you think it's foolish, little friend, to attempt the trip with only a hired guide?"

Keyah moved a paw and blinked.

"Well, foolishness is my birthright, Keyah—the family *talent*, it seems."

Keyah raised her head.

Marta sighed. Doubt was pestering her. She pressed a pair of gloves palm to palm and laid them on top of a folded shawl. The bishop, who was a trustworthy man, had said when she'd confided in him, "You'll forgive me, Majesty, if I don't approve?" His look had been grave. "It's always foolish to act all alone, especially when ignoring counsel and warnings. I am not acquainted with the man you seek—Lord Drugen, isn't it?—but I know something about him that makes me afraid for you. You need to be *afraid*."

She had said, "What about my faith in God's protection and provision for this venture?"

"It isn't faith but presumption! Send mature men of sound judgment who can discover the truth and act on it."

She didn't want the bishop's careful wisdom and resented the fact that he held out no hope that her father might be alive—he had smiled with pity when she had expressed that hope. But still, she worried that such a godly man *must* be right.

She had made him promise to keep her secret. He had agreed to but had looked displeased and concerned.

He had then tried to stop her with a healthy dose of guilt. "You'll be leaving your ship-of-state to be wrecked on the rocks of *Ester's* ambition."

This reproach couldn't be reasoned away. Marta bit her lip as she rose carefully to her knees in her beautiful gown to open her portmanteau and satchel.

Keyah jumped off the bed and onto Marta's skirt, poking a curious snout inside the satchel.

"Nothing for you!" Marta said, hugging her.

Keyah turned her head to lap Marta's mouth and nose, and Marta held her tightly.

Her father could be *counting* on her! More difficult quests had been attempted and achieved. *Love* would lend her wings. She could manage, despite the weather and without her knights. She would go—she would find him!—even if the wilds were filled with all the dangers and devils of bygone days!

Dangers and devils? Such thoughts were foreign to her. She took pride in being modern, in reasoning bogeys away. Yet perhaps they *existed* and she was about to meet them face-to-face! Whatever the case, she would go, even if the bishop were right!

Having changed into her traveling clothes, she was lying fully dressed on her bed, her elegant but impractical boots standing at the ready beside it. The fire was burning low, and the candles had been extinguished. She stared at the faintly glowing ceiling, pondering.

She had been seven when her father left. He had been a funny sort of king with a taste for quests—a poet and a musician. Music was part of her memories of him. She recalled his guitar playing and his dancing. How well he and Carissima had danced! When Marta was a tot, he had swooped her up into his arms so she could dance *with* them. This impression of love and life had left an indelible mark on her.

Everyone made music then, keying the hurdy-gurdy or strumming the lute, bawling tavern songs, or singing the Psalms. Music had filled the streets, pealing from the huge bronze bells of the Cathedral of Blessed Gregor, martyr of Spoot, and floating out open windows as scratchy violin lessons or off-pitch family ensembles. Even Carissima sang then.

Now the streets were strangely quiet, except for the cry of gulls and moan of the sea beyond the breakwater. It was as if the earth itself were mourning the king and the end of all happy times. She must remedy this—bring *hope* home to Zuphof! Before she married—if only she could marry Bartolo—she would do what she could to save her father, mother, and kingdom.

In her father's absence, his enemies had been daring and success-ful. Little remained of the Kingdom of Zuphof but the Royal City. The city was old, and its orchards, pastures, and canal were enclosed by a crumbling wall and guarded by a dilapidated drawbridge he had promised to fix. The ancient port was now used mostly for fishing.

To the west lay the Zonderzee—a cold, stormy vastness, teeming with kipper and herring and the great slow beasts of the sea. To the east were scattered villages and the seemingly endless fens stretch-ing to wild foothills and formidable mountains—where Drugen did whatever he wished—and creatures out of some fairytale or night-mare roamed.

The Royal City, which once had been splendid with hundreds of pennants flying, was now depressing, even on a fair summer day. In the dead of winter, it was too much even for the stouthearted. It seemed to have crawled out of the ice-bound bay. Its houses looked as if they were shoving one another in their attempt to keep their places on the windy streets. Its roofs were greenish from constant dampness, drizzle, sleet, and snow. She must bring her father home; he must rule and make things right! Then she would marry—if only it could be Bartolo!—for the good of the kingdom.

For now, all her thoughts must be focused on finding her father, though no one else was hopeful, though she was the only *fool!* So behind Carissima's back and without her blessing and all alone, she would go.

She hadn't told anyone but the bishop—only he could be trusted to keep her secret, though unwillingly. She couldn't risk the con-cern of Kikki and Betsy, or Trimble and Tinka, his wife. She couldn't enlist her men-at-arms, who would be torn by their loyalties and tattle to Carissima.

So, concealing her identity, she would ride alone to the village of Stootna and hire a guide. Her purse was fat, and her heart was strangely unafraid. But leaving the castle without being seen wasn't going to be easy. So just before dawn on the morrow, while all were deep in dreams—even the guards on duty—she would shut Keyah up in her room and fly!

She peered out of the castle gates and onto the cobbled street, gripping her horse's reins and looking through the eyeholes in her velvet mask—something to protect as well as disguise her. She was bundled in a closefitting, velvet hat with a feather, merino scarves, a belted fur coat, and the elegant but impractical boots.

"Hush, Toivo!" she whispered and then led him onto the drawbridge.

As usual, the dilapidated draw was down, spanning the moat, but for some reason, the portcullis was up. She had planned to swear the guard to secrecy, but there would be no need. He must be catching his winks someplace warmer.

Reaching the far side, she removed the burlap—with which she had muffled Toivo's hoofs—and grasped his reins, climbed to the sidesaddle, and turned his nose due east.

It was then that she heard a curious commotion, a sound like the runners of a sleigh slicing over the ice, accompanied by the pound of boots.

She turned her head. Trimble came into view, drawing her covered conveyance. He managed to brake without being run over, laid the shafts down, caught his breath, and then said, "I know you feel you must go, mistress, but...you can't go alone!"

He straightened his knit cap and gestured toward the sleigh. "Tinka packed some things you'll need. Yes, she knows I'm going—we decided together. Your father would want me to. You're only a young woman, and the world is full of danger—"

Marta held up a hand. "No need to convince me! I'm grateful. I couldn't risk telling you and had planned to hire a guide at Stootna."

"Hire a guide and go out with this *stranger* to the wilds? Thank heaven I didn't miss you!"

"Do you know the way to Drugen's?"

"I was there once, long ago. You just keep heading east."

She dismounted. He removed Toivo's saddle and secured it on the hooks at the back of the sleigh. They loaded her things beneath the seat and in the hollow under the scroll dash. He had brought a bucket and brush for Toivo, and she had brought some feed, his feed-bag, and blanket. Places were found for all their gear in cubbyholes and pockets.

At last, he got Toivo into harness between the shafts, then helped Marta into the sleigh and climbed in beside her.

"Ready, mistress?" he inquired.

"Ready!"

"I brought this." From under the dash he brought forth a battered scabbard in which was a sword of antique make. "Did you remember to bring a weapon?"

"A pistol that belongs to Father."

"Excellent! Off we go!"

He took the reins and lightly flicked the lash. Toivo started off, and the sleigh gained momentum and raced along. Toivo seemed exhilarated as he skirted a curve at a bold pace and swung down onto the open road.

"I hope you realize what you're getting into, *butterball,*" she said. "We're doing this against the best advice. And it's a long, difficult trek."

"A long trek, is it?" The corners of Trimble's mustache lifted. "And how would you know, *skinny?*"

"I've read books and studied maps."

"Well! That should be helpful in crossing the fens in dead of winter and traveling impassable mountains!" He glanced at her. "Are you sure you won't turn back? Speak to your mother again, and convince her to let the knights attend you."

Marta shook her head. "I've tried. She simply won't listen. She has threatened to lock me up."

"She'll send the Royal Guard to fetch you back."

"I turned their horses out of the stables—that should delay them."

"They aren't the smartest bunch anyway."

"When and *if* they catch up, they'll *have* to heed me. I'm their queen apparent. *Ergo,* Mother's reach is limited."

Trimble frowned. "When you speak of your mother, always speak with respect."

"I know...I *do!* I simply meant *I* could handle the guard. They can come along or go back."

They rode in silence for a time, then he said, "I like a journey—I always have."

"Really? I think of you as such a homebody."

"I am, but I'm not."

He reined Toivo in and pointed the lash. Daylight was shining over the rim of the far hills, illuminating the icy fens and a line of windmills with their sails at rest. A star shone in the purple that still lingered above them.

He took a deep breath. "Onward, mistress!"

"Onward!" she cried. "Together, we'll find Father and bring him home."

He raised a hand and blew a kiss back toward Zuphof. He had turned up his coat collar; it was a suitable coat for him—dirt brown with green flecks.

"God bless their foolish hearts!" He shook his head. "More should have been done at the time to learn what happened to the king. Though who am *I* to judge?"

He gently elbowed Marta. "You can still turn back. When you marry, you and your husband can send a deputation to search the kingdom and beyond. As you said, the journey to Drugen's will be long and difficult."

"Are you really saying, Trimble—be honest—that there's no point in going because Father is dead?"

"It's just that Drugen is such a villain, and the king was only a simple *gentleman*."

Marta reddened with anger. "The king is much more than *that!*"

"Of course," said Trimble. "But—forgive me—being the man he was, rather than arresting Drugen, he would have given him the opportunity to repent." Toivo had slowed to a walk, so Trimble snapped the traces. "That would have been to the king's credit, but Drugen might have perceived it as weakness and struck him down."

Marta studied Trimble's profile, amazed at the amount of thinking that went on under his funny cap.

"It's simple," she said. "He may still be alive."

Toivo's sturdy gait continued unflaggingly. He was a smart little chestnut, fleet and stout, his tail as long as his legs, his flaxen mane and forelock wild in a wind that was filling with flurries.

Marta's gaze flicked from him to Trimble, who seemed to be studying her clothes with an appraising eye. She lifted a hand in its mitten with the embroidered gauntlet to touch her velvet hat with its pheasant feather.

Trimble *cluck-clucked* as he shook his head. "Pardon me, mistress, but I hope you brought some sensible togs."

She pursed her lips. She didn't want to think yet about losing her finery for the plain things packed in her satchel. She was also putting off thinking about other unpleasant things, such as how and where to answer the calls of nature.

They continued, plowing through or flying over the highroad, beside a ditch filled with ice-covered cattails. On the far side, windmills—used to pump the fens when they flooded—stood like sentinels. Ahead, sprawling over the only rise, Stootna hunkered, familiar from Marta's short tenure as a student in its famous girls' school.

Girls' school—that seemed a lifetime ago! Before that, she had been tutored at the castle and, after that, polished up at Mademoiselle Polinard's Finishing Academy. It would be nice to have a year at university.

She was jolted out of reverie by Trimble saying, "I should have gone with the king but felt he didn't need the likes of me. The best men went with him—that's why there are so many turnip-tops running things now."

He shook his head, repeating, "I should have."

She tried to think of something kind to say and then remembered what she had heard. "Wasn't Tinka going to have a baby? Weren't you going to be a father for the first time?"

He smiled but then grew serious again. "I was also afraid of somehow failing the king in his venture."

"You could never fail anyone, Trimble."

"Oh, ho—*couldn't* I? I should have gone later when he didn't return."

"You're going now. That is what matters."

He stared at the road, his expression gloomy. In a moment he reached into the pocket of his coat and brought a letter out. "I forgot this. The bishop's wife—that nice little gal—asked me to give it to you."

Pleased and curious, Marta took it from him. "*Cami* knew you would be going with me, and going *today?*"

He smiled. "She and Tinka are friends."

Marta tore the letter open.

Your Majesty, dear Marta:

It feels as though we've been friends for a long time, so I'll be frank. I don't like to gossip, but you need to know what kind of man you'll be dealing with. A friend of my father's knew Alexander Drugen. Drugen seduced this man's daughter—his only child. When Drugen abandoned her, she killed herself.

We'll be praying, but you must do your part to keep safe. Be prepared to deal with someone unlike anyone you've met. Don't try to match wits with him, and don't let him make you angry, for he will try to do this, I'm sure. There must be more to your father the King's story, and Drugen must be hiding something. Trust yourself to the Lord and to the kind man who is sacrificing so much to go with you.

I must end here. I'm so tired I can barely hold up my head. I was up all night with Jan, who has a sore throat. Please pray for him! He often gets one, and then an earache. Poor child!

In the love of our Lord, Jesus Christ, I am your sincere friend,

Cami Kolpos Wenzel

Marta turned to Trimble. "Do you know what this *says?*"

"I think so." He slid a chubby finger under his cap and scratched. "Years ago Cami's father helped a friend to bring a civil suit against that *villain* Drugen. She's probably warning you."

Marta gaped. "Did the friend win his suit?"

"No, and not only that, not long afterward he died in a so-called 'accident.'"

The wintry scenery slipped by. Marta watched it without seeing it. More than once Trimble had called Drugen a "villain." Cami's letter showed that his assessment was fair. Marta treasured Cami's warning and the bishop's now that she was away from the safety of home. The warnings now seemed more real. She folded the letter and placed it within the pages of her Psalter, where she would see it and hopefully remember to pray for Jan.

She said, "Cami must be worried. Before we go much farther, I need to post a reply."

They passed some cottages, frozen laundry leaning in the wind, cows huddled in the corner of a paddock.

"Shall we stop at Stootna?" Trimble asked. "You could write to Cami and get a good night's sleep before going on."

"I'm not sure I want to, now that there's no need to hire a guide." She chewed her lip, wondering what to do. "Perhaps this is best. But how do I keep from being recognized?"

His tone was cheerful. "You can manage if you're careful. I know of an inn near the livery. People you know would never think of staying there."

He reined Toivo in.

Marta shielded her eyes to take in the familiar sight. Evening was falling, casting a crazy shadow of Toivo and the sleigh toward the houses and cathedral, town hall and jumble of buildings huddled in snowdrifts within a golden haze. The roofs looked as if they were frosted with sparkling icing. She began to imagine a roaring fire, hot bath, and cozy bed.

Yes! Yes, they would stop! If anyone recognized her, by the time Carissima learned about it, she and Trimble would be long gone.

"All right, Trimble!" she said. "By the way, did you know they make delicious lobster chowder in Stootna? Not as good as Tinka's, of course."

He wiggled a finger in his ear. "Don't expect any fancy fare, just a hot meal and a place to lay your head."

He urged Toivo forward, and Toivo trotted on with a whinny of pleasure.

"I've been wondering," said Trimble. "Did you leave a note for your poor mother?"

"No."

"We could post one from Stootna, along with the letter to Cami."

Marta turned her head away. She knew that she should at least *try* to lighten Carissima's burden of worry, but this was humbling. "All right, Trimble. Thanks for the nudge! But I won't be leaving a forwarding address."

She noticed his furrowed brow. "However, I *will* remember to say that you and Tinka didn't encourage me to do this. That you came along simply to keep me safe."

He batted his eyelashes. "Would you ask her to keep a special eye out on Tinka and Timka?"

"Of course!"

"Let's hurry then! I smell supper."

Discovery

The Bucket & Ladle Inn crouched on a side street with its back to a narrow mews. Not far from it the Cathedral stood, its bell tower soaring into the twilight. As Marta and Trimble zipped by the inn on the way to the livery, Trimble pointed it out.

"You're not used to such accommodations, I know." There were circles under his eyes, and his nose and cheeks were red. "I've stayed there. The food is plain but good."

She yawned without covering her mouth. "All right, as long as it's warm and *somewhat* tidy." She slowly blinked as a pedestrian jumped out of their way. "We'll have to get going early tomorrow, you know."

He smiled. "I'll be up before you."

"What story shall we tell if someone asks about us?" She smiled, anticipating a joke.

"Hm." His mustache twitched. "You're a foreign dignitary fleeing from a murderous coup. And of course, I'm your humble lackey!"

She laughed, until she remembered that this would be the way things would have to be for quite a while.

As they rode into the yard of the livery, she sighed with relief. She was shivering all over. A stable boy appeared, gawked at her finery, and took hold of Toivo's bridle. Trimble paid him for one night's stay for Toivo and the sleigh, then helped Marta disembark. Her hand trembled in his, and her legs wobbled. He took her arm and helped her negotiate the stable-yard filth and frozen puddles. Reaching the street, they headed for the inn.

They decided to enter through the back way. The mews behind the inn had a wall topped with broken bottles and kept by a gatekeeper who admitted them for two pence. From the eaves of the surrounding buildings enormous icicles drooped. Wash-water and slops dumped from the backdoors and windows had turned to ice and made walking treacherous. Day was fading fast. Everything looked especially bleak after their brief interlude of fun.

Opening the inn's squeaky back door, the smell of stewing pork and the noise of barnyard fowl greeted them. They picked their way along a corridor cluttered with crates of live chickens, and cabbages, carrots and potatoes, past a steamy kitchen into a sort of lobby.

While Trimble spoke with the innkeeper, she went to the small fireplace to warm her hands. The mantelpiece was silted with soot and dust. Above it, hung crookedly, was a landscape of Zuphof's canal in winter. She smiled at the happy-faced skaters, then let her gaze travel up through the crowd of diminishing figures to the horizon. There, the skaters' eyes were wide, and their mouths were gaping in horror. Against the sky, partly obscured by speckles of soot, was the silhouette of a flying dragon.

A hand gripped her shoulder, startling her. "Mistress? You're on the second floor—which is good because you're near the water closet. I'm down here in the common room. I'll take your things up if you can manage the candle." He held out a lighted candle and she took it, shaking a little.

The innkeeper bustled away down the corridor, giving orders for their supper.

Holding the candle in one hand and gripping the rickety railing with the other, Marta preceded Trimble up the stairs. She had to climb carefully on the toes of her boots for the steps were both steep and shallow. Trimble's knees cracked, and cracked again. Except for the light of the candle the stairwell was inky. Its shadows seemed to darken her hopes. On the second floor she turned onto a corridor with him. Close by was the water closet. From under the door a stinky draft wafted. She sighed. At least the arrangements were *inside!*

They reached a door painted with a "7." Trimble handed a key to her and she unlocked it. Shadows shrank back into the corners. The room was cold, the window was shuttered, and the ceiling sloped over the narrow bed. There was no fireplace, only a chimneystack that passed through it on the way to the roof.

"Take heart!" Trimble said, depositing her satchel and bag on the only chair. "Supper will soon be here."

He bid her goodnight and closed the door, saying, "You'll be safe, but I'm downstairs if you need me."

After she had been waiting for an hour, and had visited the small water closet, a maid brought a supper tray.

"God bless you!" Marta said to her.

The maid bobbed a curtsy and left.

As soon as she was gone, Marta demolished the stewed pork with its fluffy dumplings, and downed the delicious brown beer. She did this fully dressed since the only source of heat was the warm bricks of the chimneystack.

After peeking down the corridor to the right and left, she made a last trip to the water closet. Then she set her New Testament on the bed, undressed, laid her clothes over the chair, dressed for bed, jumped in it and pulled the cold covers up. *At least it's clean,* she thought. *Thank you,* LORD*!*

By the light of the candle she read the passage from the Gospel of Luke, in which these words of Christ are recorded: "What shall a man give in exchange for his soul?" She considered this question as she closed her New Testament and prayed. It was the great question, and she pondered it reverently, thinking of her refusal of Bartolo's proposal of marriage.

Then she snuffed the candle and pulled the covers over her head. The smell of candle smoke tickled her nose then passed away. Except for the LORD, she was all alone in the dark.

Tun! Tun!

She stirred in her sleep.

Tun, clang! Tun, clang!

Tun, clang, bawl! Tun, clang, bawl!

She sat up in bed and banged her head on the ceiling. "Ouch!" Her breath froze in the air.

The sparse furnishings were just visible. Dawn! Crouching, she slipped her feet out from under the covers and shivered. It was the Sabbath, and they were already ringing the cathedral bells.

She ran tiptoe over the cold floor; leaned against the warm chimney bricks to pull on her hose and boots; raced to dress. She left her ridiculously lovely gown and gorgeous mittens on the chair; she would pay the innkeeper to send them to Cami for safekeeping along with the letter. Then she donned a plain chemise and a sensible skirt and bodice. Her fur coat, scarves, and mask would still do, with the addition of other gloves she had brought that were lined with curly lamb. She thought for a moment. It was hard to relinquish her frivolous feathered hat, so she kept it, smiling. There was no mirror to check her appearance—oh, well! Grabbing her bags she hurried toward the water closet. After a quick visit she would go down and wake Trimble.

A door creaked open and a man who hadn't shaved looked out into the corridor, saw her, and slowly smiled.

Annoyed and frightened, she put her nose in the air. His "Hoity-toity! La de dah!" pursued her as she hurried to the water closet. Quickly she threw the bolt on the door and listened. The sound of boots on the floorboards approached, paused, then started down the stairs. As she waited to hear them descend and pass on, she put a hand to her face and realized she was crying, touched her forehead and found she had a goose-egg.

She finished in the closet then stood for a while hugging her bags and staring at the door. What now? She probably shouldn't go downstairs. Trimble might not be up, and the man might be there. She went back to #7 and threw her things on the bed.

As she waited for Trimble to knock or the maid to appear with breakfast, she circled the narrow space and prayed. At last she grew calmer and noticed things. On the wall near the window, a picture was nailed, a print of Blessed Gregor the Martyr of Spoot, her kingdom's patron. On the nail, dangling over the picture was an old rosary made of ivory. The artist had depicted Gregor as supremely fearless as he gripped the sword that would become her father's. The wyrm that Gregor had battled looked more like a cow with pointy teeth and stunted wings. Curlicues of smoke were puffing from its nostrils. In downplaying the awfulness of the wyrm, the artist may have been quieting his own fear of horrors that might be real.

With a *whoosh* the wind passed over the roof, rattling the tiles as if huge wings had swooped by. She looked up. Were dragons and wyrms merely creatures from legends, or real predators? If real, were they now extinct?

Reaching for her writing things, she kept her fears at bay by doing what needed to be done. She scrawled:

Mother,

By now, you know I'm gone. Please understand, and please don't interfere! (I won't be so foolish as to ask you not to worry.) I intended to hire a guide, but Trimble discovered my plan and came along to keep me safe. Would you please be kind enough—I know you will be!—to watch over Tinka and Timka?

My love to you,
Marta

51

Then she quickly penned:

> Dear Kikki and Betsy,
>
> By now, you know I've gone to find the King. Please look in on my mother, and try to keep her calm.
>
> Fare thee well, and pray for me! God keep you both—and Ferdy!
>
> Marta
>
> PS: Betsy, please let Keyah sleep in your room, for she'll be lonely. Thank you!

She paused to gather her thoughts then wrote:

> Dear Cami,
>
> You cannot know what it means to find friends who will be entirely honest with me. I'm so grateful. I take your warning and the Bishop's seriously, but I have to do this.
>
> Thank you for your prayers! Greetings to your husband, and a kiss and a prayer for Jan and the others!
>
> With affection,
Marta

She set this aside and chewed her fingernails. After a few moments she threw caution to the wind to write one last important and very difficult letter. She crumpled her first attempt and started again.

> From Marta Happstein
> To Bartolo Piccolo

Dear Bartolo,

Putting the past—the wonderful but sad past—behind us, may I rely on your kindness and the longstanding friendship between our families to request your aid?

Following are the details of recent events…

I can ask no one else. Your sister knows nothing of this request.

Today, my servant and I leave Stootna for Alexander Drugen's fortress in the Eastern Wilds. Our interim destination will be Biklava. I won't expect a reply, Bartolo; I'll expect you and those knights you appoint to the task at Drugen's.

With gratitude…

She lingered over this letter as if lingering with Bartolo. She almost kissed it but instead prayed that it would go swiftly to the only man, besides Trimble, who could now be of help to her.

Someone pounded on the door. The backs of her hands tingled. Trimble announced himself and she opened the door to him.

He immediately noticed her goose-egg. "What happened? Have you had some trouble? I meant to check on you before falling asleep, but—"

The sight of his funny face and tatty clothes filled her with profound relief. "Don't fret, Trimble!" She gingerly touched her goose-egg. "It was only a minor skirmish with the ceiling over the bed. Can we get going? Do you have a match so I can seal my letters?"

He smiled. "Did you write to your mother?"

"I did!"

She sat on the bed. He rummaged in a pocket for a match and struck it. She sealed her letters with wax and her signet ring, handed the letters to him, and tossed her writing things into her satchel.

She stood with the satchel over her shoulder and grinned. "I have to say, I've never been so glad to see someone."

He looked pleased as he hurried her out the door and banged it shut behind them. "We can leave your letters with the innkeeper to post tomorrow."

She explained about her fancy clothes. "If it weren't Sunday we could take care of mailing things ourselves."

Sighing, he shifted the bags on his shoulders. Was he unhappy about traveling on the Sabbath? He always kept it with all his heart.

"I know how you feel about the Lord's Day," she said. "Forgive me for this!"

He nodded and held out a hand to show that she must lead the way.

The livery yard was empty and quiet. While Marta waited, Trimble searched around and at last pounded a fist on the stable doors.

The doors opened. A bearded man in a canvas coat and a hat with earflaps appeared. He spoke with Trimble. Trimble suddenly threw up his hands. The two embraced in a rough and rugged way, then spoke again. The man glanced at Marta. Trimble took him by the arm and led him toward her.

"Let me speak with her first," Trimble said to him.

The man stopped and turned his back to them, while Trimble came to her.

"Are you ready for a shock?" His eyes searched hers. "It's your father's champion, Gurnemanz."

Her heart skipped. "But how can that be?"

Trimble motioned to him. He approached slowly as if reluctant to encounter her, and yet he knelt before her. Despite the bitter cold he removed his hat.

"Whoever you are, please get up!" she said. "Someone may come along and notice us."

He rose and folded his hands over his lean belly.

She studied him, feeling wonder and fear. "Is it really you, Gurnemanz?"

Gurnemanz met her gaze. "Yes, Majesty."

She shook her head in amazement. "But how do you come to be here? Why aren't you with the king? Where is he?"

"That won't be easy to explain," he said. "Even if I manage to, you may not believe me."

She looked at him eagerly. "You must try!"

He flashed a quick smile then said in a tone filled with conviction, "As you know, I accompanied the king to Drugen's. There, we met with trouble of an unexpected kind. Drugen has an extraordinary power over others. I know this will sound grandiose, but it's true." He shrugged as if to say that couldn't be helped. "I began to fear for my soul. I broke my pledge to the king and abandoned him."

Marta wanted to strike him. She raised her hand and it trembled in the air, while he stood meekly awaiting the blow. Slowly she lowered it.

His gaze was sympathetic. "I understand. But allow me to paint the picture for you. At Drugen's, we began to change—all of us, even our master the king. We constantly quarreled and blood was spilled."

He drew nearer. "If Drugen had simply wished to kill the king— if that was his sole intention—he could have. It would have meant a fight. We would have given him a taste of steel. We weren't *entirely* lost to our sense of duty, but his forces were superior."

His gaze was steady. "He was after our souls. He set us against one another and put temptation in our way. I'll spare you the details, Majesty. I left when I realized no one else could see the nature of the danger we were facing. I tried to persuade the king to leave, but he had concerns of his own."

"Something you alone saw?" Marta frowned and tilted her head. "That seems unlikely. Temptation? One can *resist* it. I don't understand!"

He looked at her intently. "You will if you go on to Drugen's."

"*If?*" she cried. "If you are a man of honor, you will surrender at once to the guard at Zuphof. I wouldn't ask a coward to journey back with us to help."

"I wouldn't go, even under orders," he said gently. "Call me a coward—I understand. I'm your servant, and you can do whatever you like with me. My wife and I can start for Zuphof today. I married a local girl and began a new life here."

Marta studied him. There was truth in his unflinching gaze and the resolute set of his jaw. He was no liar or coward. She touched his arm and said, "On second thought, Lord Gurnemanz, please wait here for our return! The king will decide your case himself."

For a moment he was silent and then he thanked her, bowing deeply. "God keep you, Majesty!" He turned to Trimble. "And you as well, my friend!"

He put his hat on and turned the earflaps down. He and Trimble headed for the stables and after a short time returned with Toivo harnessed to the sleigh.

"You believe him, I see," Trimble said to Marta as he helped her in.

She smiled with quivering lips. "I think so."

As she tucked her belongings into their proper places, and the men worked around the sleigh to secure things, she heard Gurnemanz say in a low voice, "She won't find him alive."

Trimble whispered to him, "Pray to God that I can get her safely there and back."

Trimble boarded. Gurnemanz kissed Marta's hand and then with a grave and pitying look wished her success. She shivered. Trimble urged Toivo forward and Toivo trotted out to the street, his head up in a brisk wind.

In a moment Marta turned to Trimble. "What do you think?"

Trimble seemed to be choosing his words. "You heard him. Is he the kind of man who lies?"

"Everyone is *capable* of lying." She chewed her lip. "Perhaps it's true that when danger threatens, one learns who is really a friend."

He seemed annoyed but didn't express this. "Pardon me, mistress, but—isn't that a little simplistic, especially in this case?"

She cocked her head at his choice of words. Deeply perplexed, she hoped he was right about things and let him continue.

He ventured: "Perhaps Gurnemanz learned to draw the line with his loyalties."

She gasped. "But he swore an oath to the king. It wasn't his place to draw the line."

Trimble frowned and blinked. "Shouldn't everyone decide things of importance for themselves? Didn't *you* when you made this trip?"

She shook her head emphatically. "But what would happen if everybody did that?"

"I don't know." He sighed. "There are also lines to draw here."

She gestured with a sweep of her arm. "Everything—all order and decency—would tumble down around us."

He smiled. "If it were only up to us, yes."

She took his meaning and relaxed somewhat. "Preaching again, friend?"

He looked straight ahead and snugged his cap. "Who am *I* to preach?"

Danger

In the distance stood the last windmill, its sails at rest in the shape of a cross. Beyond it, the land went on in level, white monotony. Toivo's unchanging pace and the motion of the sleigh were becoming tiresome.

Marta put two fingers to her goose-egg and rubbed. It felt a bit smaller. "There's something about the fens!" she said. "That makes one feel they'll go on forever."

"Nothing in this life goes on that long," said Trimble.

He smiled. Under his knit cap, tied on with a yard of multicolored scarf, his eyes were filled with fun.

"Why not sing to pass the time?" he asked and then broke into song in a rich baritone.

When he had finished, she said, "You continually amaze me. What was *that?*"

"An old ballad. 'When Spring Comes to Zuphof.'"

"A little syrupy, but nice."

He laughed. "I suppose a woman of your—ahem—maturity and sophistication is above such sentiments?"

"That's right. But since there's no one to hear us, why don't you teach me?"

They sang together as they went down the road, the wind snatching the music from their mouths, the lulls making their voices ring.

"I like singing," she said. "My poor, foolish mother—discouraging the playing of music in Zuphof!"

"Never speak ill of her who brought you into the world! She's not responsible for all this—pardon the expression—royal monkey business. I'm taking liberties I never would at home, mistress."

"That's all right, Trimble. Please go on."

"You know how I felt about your father," he said. "To me, he was literally a prince among men. That said, I'm still unhappy with him. He should never have gone to Drugen's with a small contingent. Your mother has simply reacted out of unhappiness. It was raining—storming on her—so she closed the windows of the world."

"I remember her singing me to sleep."

"Ah! Did you know that your father called her his songbird?"

Marta averted her face to hide her tears.

After a moment Trimble took up the refrain. "When spriiiiingg comesss t'Zuuuuphofff—"

And she looked at him and finished. "—You'll find mee-ee-ee therrrrre!"

The sound of her own unsteady soprano surprised and charmed her, and then the wind came and stole it away.

The sun was setting at their backs. Trimble had lit the sleigh lantern. They had reached the junction of the east-west, north-south roads. Near this lay ruins of an indeterminate kind, jutting out of the snow and withered grass like huge, broken cobblestones. Stories said they were all that remained of an old giants' turnpike. Marta and Trimble would camp in their shelter, then continue east in the morning.

They had spent two days and nights on the fens and were nearing the foothills. If you stood exactly *here* and faced northwest, using your magical specs, you would see past the fens, through leagues of virgin timber, and over the storm-tossed channel to Uspenska on its isles—now part of the Duchy of Madrigal.

If you faced south with your specs, past the fens, you would see rolling dairy land and the chief cities of that region, now lost to the Duchy of Droopsk: Ittyohobonetska (City of Scholars), Blikstein (City of Churches), and humble Brughil, birthplace of Blessed Gregor, and Trimble too. Though shrinking, the kingdom was still a long trek in every direction.

Marta secured Toivo's halter rope to a sturdy bush, attached his feedbag to his bridle, and then put his blanket on him. Trimble's glance showed admiration at how well she managed. He gathered tinder and fallen branches and made a fire. He was good at this, and soon it was blazing. Marta would bed down in the sleigh, and he would keep watch and doze nearby.

He set the lantern on a low rock, where he laid out their supper: bread, smoked fish, and wine. They ate in silence and then settled near the fire.

In the warmth, their clothes began to thaw and steam. He untied his scarf and shook his cap out over the flames; she removed her hat and mask and slipped her arms out of her coat.

She sniffed her sleeve and, at last, overcame her embarrassment to ask, "Do my clothes smell, Trimble?"

His laughter rumbled. "Not yet."

She tried to suppress a laugh, but it burst out of her pursed lips.

"And how would you like some snow down your back, *butterball?*" she said, arching an eyebrow.

"Not much, *skinny*."

He wasn't fat, just ample. And she wasn't skinny anymore but nicely filled out, with an expressive face, lively eyes, and a wide smile.

"Thanks for giving up your warm bed with Tinka to come along," she said. "Being separated from her and Timka is a huge sacrifice, Trimble."

He threw more wood on the fire. "Tinka agreed that I must. She cares about what happens to you."

Marta grinned. "Generous Tinka! How did you know I was going?"

"You'd been biting your nails." Trimble chuckled. "We began to watch you. You made trips to the pantry, and stores came up missing. She found your bags under your bed. And that night, you were in bed by seven."

"Mm." Marta stared at the fire. He was remarkable, dependable. He had always been there as part of the furniture of life but surrounded by a certain sense of mystery.

"Tell me something about *you*, Trimble! About your childhood. You grew up in Brughil, I know."

"You don't want to hear about all that ancient history."

"Ancient? How old can you be—do you mind my asking? Not more than fifty!"

He began to rise from his place. "I'd better check on Toivo."

"Trimble!"

He settled back, blowing his breath out through his mustache. "Hmm, my childhood. In many ways, it was idyllic."

She leaned forward. There it was again—that unexpected turn of phrase. "Go on!"

"What more can one say?"

He picked up the knife with which he had sliced their bread and began to clean his fingernails.

Her eyebrows rose, but she said politely, "Tell me about your parents, if you don't mind. And do you have any siblings?"

"When I was nine, my father died. My mother remarried, and by that marriage, I had a little sister, Hulda. Both my mother and Hulda are gone now."

He fell to musing, the firelight flickering in his eyes.

"What was your mother like?" Marta asked.

Trimble met her gaze. "She was an angel."

Marta hugged her knees and wondered if she could ever speak about Carissima this way. *No—enough of that!* she thought. *I must think of Trimble, not my own troubles.*

"I guess you don't take after her then," she quipped.

He laughed a belly laugh. "Actually, I do. I have her blue eyes and portly stature."

"Why do you say she was an angel?"

"My stepfather was cruel." Trimble wiped the knife on his sweater vest and then slipped the knife into a pocket. "Mother never became bitter and always protected Hulda and me. What more could one want except her happiness?"

"I'm sorry!"

"One should never be sorry for those in heaven."

Marta settled her chin on her knees. "True."

In the shadows beyond the campfire, Toivo stamped.

Marta slipped back into her coat. "I'd better check on him. No, don't get up, Trimble! I want to do this."

Toivo turned his head away when she appeared. She removed his feedbag and stood by him.

"You're all right," she said.

He lowered his muzzle to her palm, and she stroked his neck.

He was a Fennish—a hardy, cold-blooded breed. Her father had brought his grandsire from the isle of Uspenska. After years together, she and Toivo understood each other, so she waited now, shivering with cold for another quarter of an hour to reassure him.

He continued to move his hooves and complain.

"Would you like to come closer to us?"

He wiggled his lips and tossed his head, so she untied his rope and led him into the circle of firelight.

Trimble looked up. "I thought you would do that."

"I told him he was safe," she said, feeling a prickle of fear on the backs of her hands. "That there haven't been wolves on the fens in over a hundred years."

"He wasn't convinced, I see."

In the stillness—on a wind that roved—a howl came. From different points of the compass, answering howls lingered.

"I wouldn't be telling Toivo lies," Trimble said, getting up. "I'll put him back in harness. If 'the impossible' should happen, we'll be able to get going quickly."

Marta hung the lantern on its hook in the sleigh and then made up her bed there. Trimble finished with Toivo, then wrapped himself in a blanket and sat with his back against the sleigh and the sword in its scabbard across his knees.

"Better say your prayers!" he said.

She doused the light and did as he had said, asking the LORD for protection and guidance and for forgiveness if the bishop was indeed right and this was folly. Then she tried to stay awake to listen for danger. There was no sound but the wind shaking the leafless shrubs and crying amidst the great, broken stones. The fire began to swim in her vision, and her heavy eyes closed.

She was jostled awake. Trimble was up beside her and driving like a madman, and the unlit lantern was swinging wide.

Toivo balked, screamed, reared.

Trimble used the lash.

Toivo bolted, and the sleigh slid sideways, righted, and then sped on.

In the darkness to their left, indistinct shapes raced out of the shadows and into the moonlight, bounding through snowdrifts and skittering over patches of ice.

Trimble elbowed Marta. "Look! *There*, the other way!"

Peering past him, she glimpsed a streak of silver, of flashing hooves and a flying mane and streaming tail. Passing through a patch of moonlight, the creature whitened. A short-looking horn pitched forward from under the forelock, goring the air, as black nostrils flared.

She gripped Trimble's arm. "I thought they were only a child's tale!"

He ignored her, flicked the lash, and shouted, "Yah, Toivo, yah!"

"We'll be safe now, won't we?" she cried.

He glanced at her but said nothing.

Frantic, she peered from side to side. Toivo's gait was now as swift as flight, the weight of the sleigh as nothing to him. He suddenly whinnied brightly, and the unicorn answered.

Marta's prayers flew along the road, past the dark trees, and through the inky shadows, searching out danger as she silently cried out to God.

Trimble suddenly yelled, "LORD, help!"

A fallen tree was blocking the road. There was barely time to rein Toivo in. Toivo jumped the tree, but the sleigh rammed it and got hung up.

Stillness circled in.

All around them, glowing eyes emerged.

Marta was squeezing Trimble's arm so tightly that he removed her hand.

"Here it comes," he whispered.

A long, low form trotted from behind the sleigh. Luminous eyes glanced their way and then winked out as a wolf moved past them toward Toivo.

A growl started throatily, then climbed in pitch.

Toivo nickered and kicked.

There was a yelp.

The sleigh shook, and the lantern wobbled.

A second and third wolf moved up from the darkness to snap at Toivo's belly. He reared and then brought his front legs down full force. The sleigh rocked, and a wolf whimpered and crawled away.

Down the road, his breath freezing into a misty halo on the air, a unicorn was stationed. He pawed the hard pack with a hoof curtained in thick fetlock, wheeled about, and then stood, staring them to stone. His short horn stabbed at the air. He snorted and pawed again.

The wolves backed off a bit.

Toivo continued to stamp and kick, and the sleigh lurched.

Marta cried, "Hush, boy!"

Trimble whispered, "*You* hush!" as he slowly and quietly removed the sword from its scabbard. In glints of moonlight, it no longer looked old, and he looked almost young.

Suddenly, he leapt from the sleigh with his sword raised and ordered over his shoulder in a tone he had never used with her, "Load the pistol!"

Shakily, she obeyed and then gripped it in both hands with a thumb on the hammer.

The wolves were moving forward again, some trotting toward the unicorn and some creeping into the shadows closer to him.

Toivo backed up, pushing against his constraints. A branch snapped, and the sleigh shuddered.

The unicorn trotted toward the wolves, halted, and tossed his mane.

The wolves pressed in.

He wheeled, kicked, and gored.

One wolf was rolled to the edge of the road while Trimble hacked away at another.

There were growls and yelps.

Toivo was blowing hard, unable to move but still trying.

"Steady, boy," Marta whispered.

Then, like shadows removing with a change of light, the wolves were gone. A carcass lay beside the road, another in it, another at Trimble's feet. He glanced at Marta, looking like a stranger as he deftly wiped his gore-spattered weapon with an old rag he used for a handkerchief.

He turned toward the unicorn.

The unicorn trotted a circle, lashing away at the darkness, giving warning nickers, like a horse unable to calm down. Then he raised his head, arched his wonderful neck, and leapt—a single grand vault worthy of any stallion of the Royal Guard.

He circled back around again to stare at them.

Trimble took a step toward him.

He reared, warning Trimble off, and then galloped down the road off into the night.

"Thank you, unicorn!" Trimble yelled. "Thank you!"

He returned to the sleigh, shaking his head and blinking his eyes as if in disbelief. Then he blew his breath out. "Woo!" He was himself again—Marta's stolid, solid retainer.

"Forgive my bossing you, mistress!" He stowed the weapon beneath the dash. "But may I boss you again? Can you lend a hand to clear the sleigh?"

She smiled, recalling his untypical ferocity in wielding a weapon. "Of course, *sir knight!*"

"*Knight?* Pih!"

He helped her out of the sleigh, and together they took Toivo out of the shafts, pulled the sleigh around the fallen tree, and got him back into harness.

"I've used a sword once or twice," said Trimble. "Nothing much to mention."

"I'm sure," Marta said, smiling to herself.

They hastened onward along the wild road bordered by ghostly trees, stopping at last to nap in a place that seemed safe, each in their corner of the sleigh.

They awoke near dawn and quickly got going into a twilit world of mists. As day broke, the mists began to fly in a wind that was rushing inland off the sea with nothing to stop it. Every limb of every tree—every branch, twig, and needle—was swiftly covered in ice so that all of it glittered, and as the wind tossed, it clicked and clattered.

Above, the drowned sun shone intermittently through clouds that were speeding across the sky.

At noon, they reached a fork in the road with a few houses near a pond—tiny Zogtromp-on-the-mere. They stretched, dined on the humblest of fare, restocked provisions, and hurried on.

The wind dropped, and the clouds totally obscured the sun. They lit the lantern, huddling side by side as freezing rain began to fall, then changed to wet snow.

Marta was close to tears. "My feet are *so* cold. I should have worn sensible boots!"

"Tuck the lap robe more tightly around them," Trimble said. "Perhaps we can find a warmer, sturdier pair in Biklava. And snowshoes for the rest of the trip. We won't be riding all the way in to Drugen's."

"You're so practical, Trimble."

"Thank you, mistress."

"And reliable."

"Hm. You wouldn't think that if you knew...all there is to know."

"What do you mean? What could *you* have on your conscience?"

"My conscience is my concern and burden. Though God forgave me, it still stings now and then."

This answer piqued her curiosity. "Your sovereign could command you to divulge its secrets. They might be of importance to her kingdom."

"I know her, and she wouldn't do that. Besides, the past is the past and is of little importance now."

She gently smiled, recalling his bravery with wolves and wanting to encourage him. "Do you know what I'm remembering?"

His eyebrows rose; he blushed as he held up a hand to keep her from saying more. "Please, mistress, don't talk about...food! I'm much too hungry to hear about cream pies and crullers, tartlets and dumplings, donuts and hash!"

Despite the cold and her weariness, she laughed.

Encounter

After a cold but uneventful night, they forged on, despite fog.

"Are we still heading east?" Marta asked.

"I think so," said Trimble. "But it would be smarter to stop till the weather clears."

He reined in and jumped down, busying himself with caring for Toivo. Marta searched through their provisions and made lunch for them on the seat beside her.

When she again looked up, a light was shining through the fog like a haloed star. The light rose and dipped and drew nearer. Mists swirled and parted. A damsel appeared, holding a lantern high, followed by a youth who was leading an old, white stallion by its mane. The stallion seemed like some worn Pegasus stepping out of the clouds. The damsel and youth were dressed with a quaint and foreign elegance.

"Hallo, friends!" cried the youth.

"Hallo!" Trimble called.

"Can you spare some bread for two hungry travelers?" the youth cried.

"Of course!" Trimble answered.

The youth let go of the stallion's mane and took the lantern from the damsel, then held her hand to help her cross the road to Marta and Trimble.

The four greeted one another as friends. The stallion walked to Toivo, and the two nuzzled and sniffed. When he suddenly turned his head to look their way, Marta spied a short, jagged horn shining with a steely gleam.

She and Trimble exclaimed over the unicorn and explained how he had saved them from wolves.

"I'm not surprised," the damsel said. "He's very brave. In carrying us away from danger, he jumped, with us astride, from a high bluff."

The youth set the lantern on one of the sleigh's runners and then helped the damsel to a seat beside Marta.

"He went missing last night," he said. "That must have been while he was helping you."

Trimble proceeded with introductions, stating the truth about Marta and himself. Wondering why he would trust the strangers, Marta glanced at him with a question in her eyes.

"It will be all right. You'll see," Trimble whispered. "I've had a little experience with such persons."

The youth, who was dressed all in gray and hunter green, swept his cloak and removed his feathered cap as he bowed to Marta. His hair was brown, his eyes gray, and his face striking.

"My name is Piers." He gestured toward the damsel. "And this is my bride, the lady Elda."

Smiling somewhat sadly, Elda inclined her head. "Your Majesty. Trimble."

Her hair was the color of a new-minted penny. Curls had escaped her bonnet of squirrel fur to tumble over the shoulders of her short cape of black, curly lamb. Her eyes were amber-colored, her skin almost too fair.

Marta inclined her head and smiled, feeling a little self-conscious about her own unkempt appearance.

"Are you folks from Madrigal?" Trimble looked from Piers to Elda. "Your accent is familiar."

"Why, yes! From Cazmarya." Piers smiled. "Have you been there?"

"Once, long ago."

Marta offered Elda curds and bread purchased at Zogtromp. Elda ate with hungry abandon; Piers smiled as he watched her and then took some too.

Trimble took a fistful of curds, popped a few into his mouth, and passed a flagon of table wine. "If you don't mind my asking, what happened that you're on the road with such a creature...and in winter?"

"We're on the run," said Piers. "Taking him to Madrigal to the queen."

Marta stopped eating. "There *is* no queen for Madrigal since the rebellion. Madrigal was part of my own domain."

Trimble whispered, "He means the queen of *Faerie,* mistress."

Marta began to laugh but realized Trimble was serious. She studied Piers; his expression was hard to read because his face lacked the supple changes that often speak more clearly than words.

"Is there such a person?" she asked but meekly. "A *fairy?*"

"Of course there is," said Elda. "And there's also our king, Lord Beauschante."

"Am I right in guessing you're on the run from Drugen?" Trimble frowned. "And that the unicorn belongs to him?"

"The unicorn belongs to no one," Piers said.

Elda sipped from the flagon, then passed it to Piers. "Drugen had captured him for his menagerie."

"How did he manage to?" said Trimble.

Piers took a long drink. "In the usual way—with the help of a young, unmarried woman. A unicorn can't resist making friends and will guard to the death such an innocent."

Trimble's tone became indignant. "Who was the young woman?"

"A Jewish maiden." Piers passed the flagon to Trimble. "Her father, a physician, had fled with her to the wilds from persecution. Drugen had her taken to a place where the unicorn sometimes appeared—a glade, where lilies and roses grow wild, at the foot of a waterfall. She was tied and left there while Drugen's hunters watched from the trees.

"The unicorn appeared, but so did a predator that had escaped its cage: a white tiger. The hunters broke from cover and roped the unicorn with a rope of ivy—the only thing that can bind one. The unicorn reared and plunged but could not get free to help the woman, and the hunters hurried him away to the castle."

Trimble's hand trembled around the neck of the flagon. "And the woman?"

"Was dragged into the trees by the tiger."

Marta cried out, and Elda turned to her and took her hand.

"Tragic," Piers said. "But from Drugen's look when he learned of this, he hadn't intended it. He had been humbling her because she refused him."

"But isn't Drugen married?" Marta said.

"That means nothing to him."

"What happened to her father?" said Trimble.

"For a day or two, he was mad with grief; then, he challenged Drugen to a duel with sabers. Of course, Drugen killed him—a man trained to heal, not to destroy."

Marta wept, and Elda, who was also crying, comforted her.

"Was the unicorn's horn damaged during his capture?" Trimble asked.

Piers crossed his arms over his chest and hung his head. His gauntlets were black, and the jeweled hilt of a dagger was visible at his belt.

He looked up again with a somber light in his eyes. "A grooms-man was exercising the unicorn in the stable yard carefully, using the rope of ivy. As he led him back to his cage, Drugen stepped between the two and examined the unicorn as if it were a mere beast of burden. Elda and I witnessed this. It made my blood boil."

"It's hard to imagine your blood boiling, Piers," Trimble said.

"I remained silent. I had to think of Elda," said Piers. "Drugen ran a hand along the unicorn's flank. The unicorn brought his head around and pushed him to the wall. As he did, he buried his horn in the stones. He had simply been warning Drugen off but was at Drugen's mercy."

Marta stopped crying to listen more carefully.

"Invoking a curse, Drugen drew his sword and severed the horn. It was clear he intended to kill the unicorn with a second cut, so I sprang to the unicorn's back, pulled Elda up behind me, and we galloped away."

Elda laughed with a lovely sound. "It was then that the unicorn leapt from the bluff."

Trimble looked in amazement at the two. "You managed to *ride* him? You're riding him *still?*"

"He permits this, yes," said Elda. "And without a rope of ivy."

"We need to be moving on." Piers gazed toward the horizon and nodded to Elda. "Drugen's men have been tracking us. How far is the next town? We need provisions."

"Even fairies need their three square meals a day, eh?" Trimble said.

Piers smiled. "Yes."

"Zogtromp is a day's ride west, but the trip could be longer in this weather. Take some of our grub, just in case." Trimble looked toward the unicorn. "Noble beast! What is *he* finding to eat?"

"He can go a long time on very little."

"May I approach this rare and wonderful creature?" Marta asked.

"Of course!" said Elda.

Marta hurried out of the sleigh but approached the unicorn slowly.

He twitched his ears.

"Be careful, Majesty!" Piers called. "You'll do well to remember what he is!"

Up close, the lenses of the unicorn's eyes looked milky. His hide was patchy, and his horn was cracked in places. Judging from the girth of the horn, it must have been a good deal longer before the fiasco with Drugen. He resettled a hoof that shone like mother-of-pearl beneath a silvery fetlock.

For a moment, Marta stood, transfixed, and then spoke to him. "The moonlight transformed you last night, old friend. Thank you for rescuing us!"

Briefly, she put her face to his and then patted his withers. Toivo nudged her shoulder as if asking to be remembered too. She stroked his neck as she kept a hand on the unicorn and drank in the sight of him with a thrill of wonder. Her hand lowered as she stared, and the unicorn lowered his muzzle to it. The sound of his mane slipping forward was like the sound of water softly spilling over the stones of a woodland brook. She pulled off a glove and put her hand beneath the strands, letting them pass through her fingers. The unicorn seemed to look through the clouded lenses of his rheumy eyes right into her soul, with a gaze as old as man in his first innocence that understood all her troubles. Again, he lowered his muzzle to her palm. His breath congealed there, and she saw within her grasp an infinitesimal star shining at the heart of a tiny galaxy.

"Look, Trimble!" she cried.

But Trimble was deep in talk with Piers and Elda.

Marta sighed. "He has missed a wonder." She stroked the unicorn's snow-white neck. "But perhaps the wonder was meant for me as a sign that all shall be well and that everything in this wide, wild world is in the LORD's hands."

She leaned for a moment against the unicorn and embraced him. To her joy, he allowed her to. She straightened and said to him, "I pray you get safely to Cazmarya and find a warm stall—if you like a stall, that is. And when summer comes, a lush meadow. I'm sure the queen of Faerie—if there actually is such a person—will treat you well."

She closed her eyes. "I pray that no one ever cages you again—"

She stopped, opened her eyes, and encountered the unicorn's veiled gaze. It seemed to be communicating something wondrous but perplexing—to be beseeching her to pray more wisely.

A change in the timbre of Trimble's snoring woke Marta from a nap in the sleigh. He was curled up beside it, the pom-pom on his cap visible from the top of his blanket.

The weather had cleared, Piers and Elda and the unicorn were gone, and there was no sign of them, except for tracks going west.

Marta stepped down from the sleigh and gently rocked Trimble's shoulder with the toe of her elegant boot. "Up, *lazybones!* The sun's out again, and we can get back on the road."

He sat up and rubbed his eyes. "I see the fairies have flown!" He rolled up his blanket and stood. "Uh-oh, who's this?"

Riders had galloped into view. They quickly covered the distance. Jumping a ditch, they encircled Marta and Trimble and glared down at them.

The rider in the tallest and biggest fur hat—it bore a crest with a wolf's head on it—snapped, "Have you seen a young couple with a somewhat peculiar-looking horse? The two stole him."

"Can't say I have," Trimble answered. "The great outdoors is a pretty big place."

The rider jumped down to examine the tracks and scowled at him.

"We're on Lord Drugen's business," he said. "If you know anything, speak up, or things could get unpleasant."

"We did see a minstrel walking his mount to stretch his legs. Said he was heading to the court at Zuphof."

The rider frowned, grasped his horse's reins, and sprang back to the saddle. "If we learn you've lied, you'll be sorry. Drugen's dungeon is no picnic."

"Probably true," Trimble whispered to Marta.

He whistled a tune as he helped her into the sleigh. Then, as if suddenly remembering, he turned to the rider and said, "We did run into some young people and a horse fitting that general description. Yesterday, it was. Heading for Brughil, they said, to sell the horse to the circus. Ta-ta! G'bye."

He flicked the lash, and Toivo took off, head high, mane bouncing.

"Poor Piers and Elda!" Marta said when she and Trimble were beyond earshot. "I hope the unicorn has some magic left."

"Magic?" Trimble shook his head and laughed. "I hope Piers and Elda are saying their prayers."

"Fairies *pray?*"

"Some do, just as some people do. More should, just as more people should."

"You seem to know a lot about this."

"A little, perhaps." He *cluck-clucked* to Toivo. "And while you visited with the unicorn, Piers and Elda told me their story."

He fell silent, frowning.

"What is it? What's wrong?"

"More bad news. Elda's mother, Imane, was sister to Drugen's wife, Schoya. Imane went to Drugen's to visit Schoya, and Piers and Elda went with her. It seems Imane confronted Drugen about his mistreatment of Schoya. Threatened him too."

Again, he fell silent.

"And?"

"And the next thing you know, Imane was dead. Her heart had simply stopped."

For a moment, Marta was struck dumb.

"Awful," Trimble said. "And mysterious."

"But in all the stories, fairies are immortal."

"Those are, as you say, *stories.*"

"Do they think Drugen murdered Imane?"

"They can't be sure. But according to Piers, such things tend to happen at Drugen's. He attracts troubles like a magnet gathers iron shavings."

Marta blinked. "So Drugen's wife is *also* a fairy?"

"Yes. And for a man like Drugen, that must be a prize to flaunt."

Marta shivered. "My small world is growing quickly. I'm not sure I can handle all of this. Fairies are real it now seems. And Drugen has married one and killed another—and brutalized a unicorn."

"Cheer up, mistress! God can handle the entire mess."

"Yes." She blinked back tears. "But what about the king? Could he have survived an encounter with such a man?"

"We don't know." Trimble glanced at her. "All we know is that you are going to have to be careful."

"Indeed!"

"You'll have to watch and pray, and I will too."

"Yes!"

"And also, you mustn't expect your due from Drugen—he won't be respectful."

"I've learned not to expect much in the way of respect from any of my subjects, Trimble. The crown has lost a lot of its luster and most of its clout."

"Your father would be sad to hear you say that."

"We must bring him home! After his poor management of the kingdom, how can I blame anyone for a lack of respect? Lots of people—Borg de Lanz, for one—could manage the kingdom better than we Happsteins have."

"The Happsteins are still a noble house."

"In need of repair." She sighed. "Why, oh, why did Father have to go on this quest?"

Trimble studied her, as if making sure she could take what he was about to say. "There's more than one answer to that question: the simple one and the not so simple one. Drugen was making trouble for some villages in the Zelhorn—Gupenstock and Nobya-tolonya. The people begged the king to intervene, and he did. But that's not the whole story. Forgive my bluntness, but the king could never stay home for long."

"What are you implying?"

"That he *needed* his quests, wizards, and dragons. They were a way of life for him."

"I've been thinking about that." She sighed. "If I could speak with him alone, I might even scold him. But why do you mention *wizards?*"

"A wizard is what Drugen *is*. A powerful sorcerer. Didn't you know?"

"I wondered if he might be but concluded that that was gossip, especially since there are no sorcerers nowadays. Don't you think that some of the stories about Drugen might simply be sensational press?"

Trimble's eyebrows rose. "You've seen enough on this trip to answer that yourself. Who knows what lives and breathes within the kingdom and beyond?"

Marta bit her lip, looking at Trimble askance. "At least there are no dragons. Of this, I'm *fairly* sure. Blessed Waromyr made sure of that when he destroyed Uxondyne's nest."

"One can always *hope*." Trimble's glance fell to Marta's mouth. "You'd better stop chewing your lips. They'll chap, and you'll be miserable."

She blushed. Sometimes he went too far with his impertinent familiarities. But thank God for him!

With a light flick of the lash, he urged Toivo uphill between leaf-less trees. They were leaving the fens at last.

"Have you met Drugen, Trimble? Visited his castle, ladled his soup, or polished his boots?"

"Long ago I met him. Loaded a gun for him at a pheasant shoot. And there have been other occasions when our paths crossed."

He fell silent, the muscles in his jaw clenching.

She put a hand on his arm, looking at him intently. "Your frank impression?"

"He's charming with the ladies. An excellent sportsman, but a poor sport. Intelligent—he can spar with the best of philosophers. He's one of a rare and peculiar breed—*the all-too-likable enemy.* Though most folks quickly outgrow their infatuation. I once heard him blaspheme—as Piers and Elda did—and have never forgotten it."

He looked at Marta squarely. "The sum of the matter is this. Beware!"

She suddenly felt exhausted and, forgetting that she'd asked his opinion, wondered why he wouldn't quit. "I'll form my own judgment of Drugen when the time comes, then deal with him."

"Of course you will, but I hope you will exercise a little humility and a lot of caution."

She looked into his smiling eyes and smiled back weakly. "Very apt advice."

His smile vanished. "In some ways, you've been too sheltered. Not only from the harsher aspects of life, but from the species of men."

She tucked the lap robe more tightly around her legs and leaned her head back. "I've observed life at court, a microcosm of the world. One can learn much from this. And I have God's Word to teach me about human nature, and human nature includes the species of men."

Trimble made no reply.

Toivo came onto a level stretch and picked up his pace.

Marta leaned forward again. "Well? What are you thinking? That Drugen will have a field day with my inexperience? I can settle business and protect my honor as well. Borg de Lanz has been my particular study of the aberrant male. Poor Betsy. I hope and pray that Ferdy is different from his father!"

As she said this, she suddenly thought of Cami. Cami and the bishop would be praying for her. She must remember to pray for little Jan!

Trimble laughed. "Borg de Lanz? Hinh!"

Trying not to cry, Marta laughed with him. "And I've learned from observing the behavior of Don Ricardo Alvarez. Now *there's* a scoundrel!"

"Compared to Drugen, he's a babe-in-arms."

"One can learn by watching Don Juans and flunkies!"

"Drugen is no flunky and no ordinary Don Juan! He is a mature and complicated man, an outlaw, and a sorcerer. He can deal with an ingénue."

Marta's face grew hot. "Trimble, that's quite enough!"

He ignored this. "Forgive me, but I'm concerned! What real experience have you had? You're a young, unmarried woman facing 'the beast.'"

She sank back again, realizing that Trimble was right. She'd had little real experience. Her only experience was with Bartolo. A long-distance romance, with short family visits at intervals, beginning when they were adolescents. She had spent the summer with his family in a villa in Sapore's rugged hills silvered by olive groves. It was a long, lovely, wonderful time full of the fun her grieving mother had seldom provided.

She had been twelve, and Bartolo fourteen. They'd spent every possible moment together, even excluding Kikki at times so that it became a joke with his family—a subject about which to gently and tactfully tease.

He had been a tease himself—a relentless one. She still remembered how he had looked: his velvet cap pushed back on his short, rough curls; his eyes filled with mischief. He wasn't handsome but commanding, even then. She had taken all she could of his teasing, then she had pushed him. He had pushed her back, so she had black-ened his eye. He had shoved her down to the stones of the terrace, forcing her to look up at him through disheveled hair. She could still see him laughing—not unkindly, but with boyish triumph—as he had held down a hand to help her up.

The storm had passed, and things ended differently. They had climbed a tree. Sitting beside her on a leafy bough, he had tried to kiss her. She hadn't allowed this but had told him with a look that she loved him.

He still wasn't handsome, but he was still commanding. There had been one pure kiss and talk about marriage. But marriage was complicated by the difference in faith, for he was a Catholic.

In the last century, there had been turmoil, wars, and persecu-tions in the wake of the Reformation. Now there existed an uncer-tain peace in which freedom of conscience, bought dearly, lived and breathed. She could not but remember all of this. She could not but hold to her reformed faith. She could never consent to bow the knee to a bloodless sacrifice on a man-made altar, when the Lord Jesus had died for their complete and perfect deliverance from sin and death.

Her world echoed with memories and reverberated with truth. There were statues of the reformers in Zuphof, plaques on the streets marking those places where men, women, and children had been burned alive. Bands of ecstatic prophets—"the dancing prophets"—roved the countryside, warning of the End of the Age. Sometimes she wondered if the end was indeed coming *now*, but the Reforma-tion *had* come, and with good reason, despite its near-lunatic fringe.

She had agonized and finally told Bartolo that marriage—how-ever much she wanted it, however beneficial it might promise to be for both countries—was impossible. It wasn't her choice but the Lord's, for he had commanded his children not to be unequally yoked.

Bartolo had affirmed that his faith was the same heartfelt trust in Christ as her own. She knew this was true, though how that could be was a mystery—the mystery of the wheat and the tares—for he also bowed to the authority of the pope, whom her people titled the Antichrist. So how could there ever be agreement between herself and Bartolo? How could Bartolo sincerely believe and adhere to the faith of the Antichrist?

Strangely, Bartolo had seemed to understand. They'd even discussed the possibility that, if they married, his nobles might rebel, and her own people, who tolerated the Catholics who lived in their midst, might be so unhappy they could become violent.

So she knew little of love and of men, except for this relationship, much of change and war, and nothing of a man like Drugen seemed to be: an outlaw and practical pagan. She had to admit that Trimble was right; her experience was sheltered and narrow. She hadn't ever even been alone, without a chaperone standing or sitting at a discreet distance, with *any* man except her father and the *butterball* seated beside her.

The *butterball* was talking to her, it seemed, and had been for a while, she realized. He was winding up what must have been another of his edifying discourses with: "...So, as I was saying, mistress, just be careful!"

She mumbled, "I'm hoping to have my father's advice on how to handle Drugen."

Trimble made no reply. He simply looked straight ahead.

Friendship

They made good time with Toivo pulling. The journey was nothing for him. As the temperature dropped, his coat simply grew thicker and shaggier. He trotted almost merrily, sometimes with his blanket buckled on.

Thank heaven for him! Thank heaven for *Trimble!* He was of greater value to the kingdom than all her counselors and knights. Those who had let the king go off, with only a small contingent of the brave, into a world full of danger.

Of course, it was hard to stop the king from doing what he wished. King Peter Josef Michael of Zuphof, scion of the ancient and noble House of Happstein, a beloved king with a reputation for being just and generous but a bit too simple and trusting about people.

For Marta, this sterling reputation had been tarnished. Doubts about him emerged to darken the heavens like bats out of a cave at nightfall. Perhaps he had *taken to* Drugen's wild sort of life; perhaps he had *decided* not to come home!

As the sleigh sped along, she murmured, "If I have to die to prove this isn't so, I will."

"I know, mistress, but it's time to stop and rest again."

Trimble squinted in the sunlight that glared off the snow. His obvious concern and her own uncertainty made her feel reckless.

"We'll stop at the next tavern," she said.

"Are you sure?"

"Never more so!"

"What will I tell your mother if some rascal carries you off?"

"I won't let that happen, and neither will you. Lend me your cap, and I'll double my disguise."

"You'll need more than my cap to really hide."

She opened a compartment beneath the dash and brought out the pistol. In daylight, the smallish flintlock shone with damascene, ebony, and horn.

"I have this." She tucked it into her sash and then resettled her coat. "And you have your sword. We can fortify for the rest of the trip with a hot meal and a glass or two. Your cap, please!"

"God bless your foolish heart!"

He gave it to her and wrapped up in his scarf. Smiling but unhappy, she removed her velvet hat and slipped it in her satchel, donned the cap, and tucked in her braids.

On they sped until Toivo, with a toss of his head, suddenly turned into a narrow lane. Down the lane, the smell of cooking mixed with the smell of an outhouse met them.

"He's got a good nose, your horsey," said Trimble.

He pulled into the yard of a shady-looking tavern. A hostler appeared to look after Toivo. Before Trimble could lend Marta a hand, she jumped from the sleigh. Her heart was racing and felt bruised and tender. Her velvet hat dropped from her satchel to the snow, but she didn't notice.

"Hurry, *butterball!*" she called.

Trimble hastened after her, buckling on his scabbard and sword.

In a moment, they were stooping under the tavern lintel, entering a low room roofed with smoke-blackened beams. Above the loud talk and laughter, music sounded—the jolly shout of a guitar and the merry voice of a fiddle played by the taverner's wife and daughter. Marta listened with Trimble as they sat at a tacky-topped table near the fire. The soup was thin but steaming. The wine was strong, and she began to feel as if she were floating instead of seated on the chair.

Trimble drank down his soup but nursed his wine, studying the other patrons with a worried look. When two strangers asked if they could join them, and Marta agreed to this, his shoulders began to climb toward his hairy ears. He glanced from one to the other, frowning as they peeled off once-fashionable coats that were now seedy looking.

Marta ordered drinks for them. What could that hurt? Wasn't that the way of the world, and wasn't she in the world and *fighting* her way through it like everyone else?

Feeling too warm, she removed the cap and mask. Trimble stared at her intently as if trying to warn her, but she looked away, simply noting that his hand had moved and come to rest on the hilt of his sword.

Soon she couldn't feel the chair at all. Trimble passed her a plate of bread and cheese, but she refused it and raised her tumbler of wine, despite his glare. When the taverner poured her more wine and it sloshed over her hand, she suddenly laughed. Her feelings were expanding like a beautiful, glowing bubble. The music stirred her. Though the strangers looked rough, that was all right! The danger seemed minimal; her strength was the important thing. In fact, she might do and dare anything, even amuse herself a bit with a small joke.

She began to tell the strangers a story about how she had killed an ogre.

They raised their eyebrows, and Trimble lowered his.

She glanced at him as she gulped down more of her drink. She would show him! *No one* was to say what she could or could not do. She had always taken care of herself! Carissima had been too sad to do this.

As the music climbed an excited scale, Marta downed the rest of her drink. "Ha! Ha! Ha! And then...I shot it!"

She opened her eyes wide, chortled, and then winked somewhat slowly at the strangers. Out of the corner of her eye, she could see Trimble barely keeping himself in check, sending her little messages with wiggles of his mustache.

To spite him, she opened her coat and revealed the pistol, patting it. "The look of surprise on that ogre's face was worth all the risks I'd taken. It was nothing then to jump to his chest and saw off his horn."

Trimble's fingers went white around his tumbler of wine.

One of the strangers chuckled, but the other slowly smiled.

When she began to laugh again, Trimble clapped a hand over hers and pinched her. It was then that the stranger seated next to her moved his hand toward the pistol.

She drew back, her face flaming. "No, you don't! This was my father, the ki—"

Trimble jumped to his feet. "Mistress, see that fellow in the corner? Isn't that the sheriff of Koblin?" His mustache was wiggling wildly. "I've been wanting to speak with him on a matter of some importance." He pulled Marta to her feet. "Nice to meet you, *gents.* Thanks for the *chat!*"

He pushed Marta ahead of him, toward the bar.

"I hope I didn't hurt you," he whispered. "Those two are the sort to take you for a ransom. What's wrong with you, mistress? We'll never come near such a place again! The whole trip has been too much for you! Sit and drink some strong tea, and put something substantial into your stomach! And put on your mask!"

The wine took firmer hold on Marta. "Trimble, ye'r won-erful," she purred. "Ye'r—my knight in shlining h'armour!"

She tripped on the leg of a stool.

He righted the stool and set her upon it. "Pih!"

"Pih!" she repeated as she donned her mask with clumsy fingers.

The taverner made them sandwiches and tea. Marta took a long, hot draught and a big bite of bread and ham. Her laughter had ended, and a fragile joy was settling in. Her conscience, with a voice a bit like the young bishop of Zuphof's, began to scold. She put a hand on the bar and, through the eyeholes of her annoying mask, studied her long, tapered fingers.

Someone spoke from the end of the bar. "Guess there's no need to say you're calling attention to yourselves?"

Marta looked up.

A youth with dark, unkempt hair was studying her with large, beautiful, slightly belligerent eyes.

"She isn't *she* to you, young man!" Trimble scowled. "She's—er—Lady Gwiniferd of Gumpsk, and I'm her servant, Algernon."

"How do you do?" The youth smiled an ironic smile. "I'm the 'sheriff of Koblin.'"

Trimble laughed till his belly shook and then swiped his mustache with a finger to suppress a smile.

Marta glared at the youth, miffed at his insolence, then looked away in embarrassment.

Trimble said to her, "Drink, eat, keep up your strength, *my lady*."

The taverner raised an eyebrow.

Marta obediently finished her sandwich.

The youth lowered his voice. "Say that you're father and daughter traveling to visit family."

Marta winced and looked at her tea.

"Where are you headed at this time of year?" he asked. "The worst weather will soon begin."

"That's our business," Trimble said.

"Drugen's?"

Trimble was silent.

The youth shrugged, then stood and slipped on his coat of shearling and hide.

"Are you interested in advice?" he asked. "Go home to Zuphof!"

He pulled on his cap and gloves and then started for the door, saying something over his shoulder.

"Ready, mistress?" Trimble tossed a few coins to the bar. "I want to hear what that fellow has to say. Bundle up. It's going to feel colder."

He hurried her out the door, crying, "*Sheriff of Koblin!*"

The youth turned and waited for them.

"It was too noisy back there," said Trimble. "*What* did you say?"

"Don't take her Majesty to Drugen's."

The youth strode out of the yard and onto the lane. Trimble hurried Marta along after him.

"Do you mind explaining?" he called. "And how do you know her?"

The youth stopped. "She resembles the king. Explaining why you shouldn't take her there would take some time. Do you have a place to sleep the night? You could stay with us at the sheepfold."

Trimble glanced at Marta, who nodded, and then he fetched Toivo and the sleigh. The youth rode Toivo as postilion, taking them farther down the lane and into wild meadows beyond.

After a short ride, he reined Toivo in at a stout gate of wicker set in a wall of rough-hewn stones. A middle-aged man in a whiskey-colored cap was leaning his arms over the gate, smiling. He opened it to the travelers.

"You've taken your time," he said to the youth, cuffing his ear in a friendly fashion. "Who have you dragged home?"

Introductions were made. The man, Glaber, bowed matter-of-factly, as if accustomed to meeting nobility dressed for the highroad. The youth introduced himself as Royal.

"We can stable your pony." Glaber helped take Toivo out of harness. "And park the sleigh beside the shed."

The sheepfold was comprised of a low, rambling house with a funny turnip-shaped chimney vent and ramshackle outbuildings and paddocks. The sheep looked stout in their winter fleeces—bundles of black, mustard, and buff-colored wool on thin, dark legs. Startled by the arrival of the horse and sleigh and strangers, the flock bolted around the paddock, and all the *bah-ing* and *bell-ing* was terrifically noisy. A svelte mountain dog managed the flock, then laid down, head up, tongue lolling.

Toivo shied at the ruckus, so Royal walked him clear of the paddock to the shed farther back.

Glaber pushed open the door of the house, kicked aside an unwashed pot, and then, with a soothing chuckle, offered Marta a hand over the crumbling doorstep.

"I suppose we ought to clean up, Majesty," he said. "But it's only we bachelors."

He tipped a stool, dumping some rags to the floor, and offered her the seat.

She whispered to Trimble, "The privy?"

"Behind the house, Majesty," Glaber said, stooping to tend a hearth fire in the middle of the dirt floor.

Blushing, Marta hurried outside. She had to set her satchel against the privy door to keep it closed. She shuddered. The privy appeared to be the haunt of spiders in better weather. When dizziness made her lean for a moment against a dirty wall, she clenched her teeth. All that she was suffering added fuel to the fire of her growing hatred of Drugen.

When she came out, she met Royal walking toward the house. Without asking, he shouldered her satchel for her. She noticed his hands then. They were rough but beautiful—a workingman's hands.

In the house, Trimble and Glaber were *jawing,* as Trimble liked to say. She perched on the stool near him. Royal hung her satchel by the door and took a seat beside Glaber.

Sighing over the warmth, she drew off her cap and mask and held her hands toward the flames. Her intoxication had faded into exhaustion and the blues.

Trimble opened his coat and smiled, showing her that he was sheltering a lamb within it. "Two days old, mistress!" His voice held a note of tender satisfaction.

Glaber lit his pipe and puffed a cloud of fragrant gray. "Its mother doesn't want it."

Marta knelt and embraced the lamb, thinking what a stern destiny that was.

"Trimble told us where you're headed, Majesty." Glaber wagged his head in disbelief. "Let Royal advise you. He knows that place and its master."

Royal shook the dark hair away from his eyes. "I'm Drugen's son, Your Majesty. His natural son."

Still holding the lamb, Marta sat back on her heels. She had met others in his situation—Ottwig de Lanz was illegitimate. She had always found it hard to pass over what was so important with mere civilities. It wasn't that she judged such persons, judged Ottwig or Royal, as *less* than others.

She looked at Royal with sympathy.

As he waited for her to say something, his gaze showed a little defiance.

Smiling, Glaber clapped him on the back.

Marta frowned slightly, not wishing to play games by pretending his statement was of no consequence.

At last, she said, "May I ask a question?"

Royal studied her. "Of course."

"Why did you warn Trimble not to take me to your father's? Is your father really the villain people say he is?"

Royal dropped his gaze. "Let's just say that no good can come from your going there."

"Listen to him, Majesty!" said Glaber. "He should know."

"I have to go. It's that simple," she said. "And either find the king or learn what happened to him."

"Send someone in your place," Royal said. "Don't go with only a single servant."

She laughed nervously. "I know it's only we two, but Trimble and I have the heart for this."

Royal turned to Trimble. "Can't you reason with her?"

"I've tried. She's in God's hands."

Marta felt the color rise to her face. "Lord Drugen is my subject. He'll have to acknowledge this and treat me as he should."

Royal gave her a wry smile.

She swallowed her pride to ask, "Do *you* know what happened to the king?"

Royal's smile became gentle. "I wish I did." He laid a log on the fire. "I met him once, when I was a child. He gave me some good advice. Told me to leave home when I was grown and make my own way in the world. Also, to come to Zuphof, for he would help me."

"I see you heeded him about leaving home."

"Actually, I was sent away to school soon after his visit. I was asking questions—too many, I guess. Later, I ran away from school; something he wouldn't have approved of."

"What kind of questions?" she asked.

"Where the king had gone in the night, for he left suddenly. Whether he and my father had fought, for everyone was whispering about that."

She bent her face to the lamb's warm fleece. "My head is splitting. Is there anything in the house to drink?"

"Your headache will soon pass," said Trimble. "Snuggle up beside the fire with the lamb."

The next day, she was ill with cramps. She lay in a small side room on a mattress stuffed with straw set on the floor. It was covered with a ram's fleece, and there was another fleece to cover with. She groaned while Trimble stooped over her looking concerned.

"How can I help?" he said.

She turned toward the wall and said over her shoulder, "Please just do what I ask without preaching! If the men have any wine or liquor, bring me some!"

"Tinka's remedy," he murmured as he hurried away.

While she rolled from side to side to ease the pain, she could hear the men talking in the next room. When rolling didn't help, she sat up, hugged her knees, and rocked.

Finally, Trimble returned with a tumbler with four fingers of schnapps.

"Thank you. You can go. I'll be fine," she told him.

As soon as he left, she guzzled the schnapps, hoping for quick relief. After the first fiery shock, the pain resumed.

In planning her journey, she had provided herself with necessities but forgotten how debilitating cramps could be. She wept and rocked, rocked and whimpered. What a fool she'd been to think herself so completely capable and strong! In wisdom, Carissima had foreseen this.

At last, the schnapps stole through her limbs, fetching away the pain and leaving a glorious, foggy comfort. She lay on her side, pulled her knees up, and pushed her hands against her belly. The fleece felt wonderfully warm.

She awoke to the sound of Trimble, Royal, and Glaber chatting as they scraped their plates. She got up, slightly bent at the middle, to make a trip to the privy, ate a slice of buttered bread, and lay down again.

The pain was subsiding and would continue to, she knew. She dozed through the small household sounds and low masculine talk. Night came on. She made another quick trip and hurried back to bed. After murmuring a prayer, she eased onto her tummy and fell asleep.

The following morning, she and Trimble bid Royal and Glaber farewell. Royal took her aside to speak alone.

"Are you well enough to go on today?" His voice was kind.

"I think so." She took a deep breath, wondering how he was going to react to what she wished to ask. "Would you come with me? At the moment I have no one but Trimble to help. From Stootna, I sent word to the Duke of Soggiorno to meet us there, but his journey will take some time."

"I can't. I'm sorry," he said. "When I go home, it will be to kill my father, and I won't go until I'm certain of achieving that object."

"*Kill* him?"

Jaw clenched, he glanced away. "For involving my mother in a life of dishonor and making her suffer cruelly."

Briefly she rested her hand on his arm. "I'm so sorry, Royal, for both her and you! But killing him isn't the answer."

"Isn't it?" His beautiful eyes searched hers. "My mother is completely under his thumb. She can't act independently and doesn't seize her opportunities to leave."

Marta lowered her gaze then looked up again. "Frankly, I've never heard anyone speak this way—and about their parents. I'm afraid for you."

"Afraid for me? Don't be! And why *shouldn't* I speak this way?" His eyes were filled with bitterness. "Because of the commandment to honor them? Yes, Majesty, even I, the son of Drugen, know the commandment. Neither of them deserves honor, though Mother deserves pity and help."

With a sigh Marta closed her eyes. "I was hoping you would be the friend I will need with such a man." She opened her eyes and found that Royal was closer.

He shook his head as if he couldn't believe his ears. "You have no idea who it is you will be dealing with!"

She humbled herself to plead: "Couldn't you go in order to help the king who was so kind to you?"

His expression softened; he hesitated then took her hand. "You need to realize that the king is probably beyond help."

Reluctantly she pulled her hand away. "I still hope."

"That is very foolish."

He looked at her keenly, as if hoping to shock her into sense, then said with sharp enunciation, "You'll find my father at his castle with his *wife*, Lady Schoya. My mother, his *mistress*, lives sequestered at his hunting lodge."

Tears stung Marta's eyes. "Again, I can only say how sorry I am!"

Royal's gaze held hers. "Learn from what I've told you, and go home! When I've done the deed, I'll get word to you."

She slowly shook her head, pitying both him and herself. "I can't go home without learning the truth."

The delicate flesh beneath his eye quivered. "And I can't go with you because the time isn't right."

Again she rested her hand on his arm, treating him as a good friend. "For your sake, I hope that time never comes."

He looked away. "So it's farewell."

She stepped back. "Yes, farewell."

He helped her into the sleigh. Glaber, his pipe in his teeth and his cap at a jaunty angle, put a hand to the cap in salute. Trimble flicked the lash, and Toivo took off, fresh for the journey.

For a moment, Royal jogged beside the sleigh, silently asking Marta to change her mind. Then he raised a hand and stood to watch her go.

"Farewell, my queen-to-be!" he cried. "Good luck, Trimble!"

Turning to watch him, Marta blinked back tears.

Revelation

They sped on past massive maples spreading their stark branches and twigs. The scent of these, and the scent of pines, was on the air.

"When Father is restored to the throne, he can help Royal," Marta said. "Perhaps with a commission in the navy."

Trimble's smile was inscrutable within his full-grown beard. "I'm sure the king would have been glad to, mistress."

The wind had changed direction and was moving out of the northeast and bearing down. It was busy reshaping drifts and scattering powder off their crests. In the stretches where there were no trees, it had blown the snow off the road and was driving a low sheet of white across it.

Marta frowned, one hand on the roof strut beside her. "Perhaps *I* can help Royal's career."

"Yes! You will be a benefactress to all your subjects."

"With God's help!"

The wind roared. The sleigh shook. Toivo put his head down but continued his steady pace. Soon Trimble was forced to rein in and jump out to clear Toivo's muzzle of icicles. He didn't dally and was soon up beside Marta again, driving with a determined look.

He rubbed his knee, then kept his hand there.

"Are you all right, Trimble?"

"I'm getting no younger. We're climbing. Wrap up tightly."

She heeded this advice and then asked, "What must it be like for Royal—and for his mother?"

Trimble scratched his beard. "Sad for both—and everyone concerned."

She took a deep breath, held it, then said, "Royal will rise above this—"

Trimble raised his eyebrows and glanced at her. "If he sets aside his desire for vengeance."

"—And reach a position of prominence." She looked at him, hoping for confirmation of this. "No one will remember his bad start."

"Woo!" He let his breath out through his mustache. "I don't mean to contradict you, but people will never completely accept him and always talk behind his back. Think of how they are with our bishop and his wife."

She frowned. "Pessimism from *you?*"

He hesitated, seeming reluctant to open this can of worms. "Realism."

Her voice shook. "I need you to be optimistic."

He looked at her sharply. "You need me to be truthful."

"Where is your *faith?*" she said—he mustn't stop being her *rock!*

He put a mittened hand to his heart. "Don't worry, it's still right here."

Swallowing her tears, forgetting propriety, she leaned for a moment against his shoulder.

Riding with Toivo was a bit like flying. As they covered the wilds her father had traversed, Marta considered his ways. Unlike Royal, he hadn't *had* to leave home yet had always found some reason to. Brave...foolhardy...thoughtless...!

Away from his portrait, she was finding it hard to picture his face. It was round, she remembered, with a fine, blond beard. But his baby face didn't mean he was weak—he was terribly strong. Could he really have been mastered by *Drugen?*

She loved how he looked in that portrait. His wide-brimmed hat, his suede breeches and jacket, his medallion glinting against his shirt of fine linen. He was holding his gloves and a riding crop. Behind him, a solid-looking Trimble stood, gripping the reins of the royal mount. The painter had flattered the king by giving him smaller feet but had caught the tall, straight stance, confident look, and raised chin. The pale, prominent, clear eyes showed only as much pride as was needed to rule.

Chin up, Marta thought. She must be chin up too! Perhaps chin up alone...forever.

Oh, Bartolo! Why, oh why, did life have to be so sadly complicated?
Wind gusted.

Snow stung her face.

Toivo went relentlessly forward.

Again Trimble had to stop to clear Toivo's muzzle. He jumped back in and on they flew—farther and farther from Zuphof, Royal, and *anyone* who might help—toward Drugen and danger. And if heaven willed, toward her father.

If the tales were true—*if*—then the king had gone on other, more successful adventures than his pursuit of Drugen. He had killed the ogre, Haukhorn, whose hide had been like armor of steel covered with ox skin. The king had tricked him into falling on a sword, the king's sword, "Brightknife," using Haukhorn's own great size and stupidity to do away with him.

Brightknife was old and so had other names as well. It had been forged long ago for Blessed Gregor. It was all that remained of him after his battle with Hexglendyia, the fiery wyrm of Spoot.

"Sharpdoom" was another name for the sword, and the thieves who had stolen the costly reliquaries from Blessed Waromyr's crypt had felt its edge. The king had recovered all of this. Could Drugen really have managed to kill a man who did such things? If indeed, he *had* done such things. *Ih!* The doubts made her dizzy! And could his famous sword, used for noble deeds, now be in the possession of a villain like Drugen?

"If it is, Drugen will pay," Marta whispered.

"Right, mistress!" said Trimble. "But it's time to seek shelter for the night."

While she had been musing, the wind had dropped, and the world had become still. Trimble reined in Toivo in the shelter of a hazel copse, the haunt of squirrels who had buried nuts there. Before Marta could object, Trimble had used his sword to kill one of the squirrels that had awoken to forage—something Trimble had accomplished almost *too* expertly. Truly, he looked incapable of much that he could do both easily and skillfully.

He dressed the squirrel out and spitted it over a fire he'd started lickety-split.

Marta remained in the sleigh. "How *could* you...for a few ounces of meat?"

Trimble looked glum. "God told us to stay strong." He glanced at her then went back to work. "To eat meat is the best way to do that."

She pursed her lips, then blurted: "It's wrong!"

He scowled. "Says who? Pardon me, but—"

"I won't pardon you!" She reddened—who did he think he was? "When we have bread and cheese to spare. Have you seen to Toivo yet? Oh, *I* shall!"

Glaring at Trimble, she jumped from the sleigh and took care of Toivo.

Trimble seemed not to notice and continued to turn the improvised spit.

Stomach grumbling, ashamed of herself, she settled beside him. "Promise me you won't slaughter Toivo!"

"How can I promise without knowing what we'll face?" His expression was kind, but he looked weary. "*You're* my concern, not him, and I mean to make it home to Tinka and Timka."

Oh! Marta thought. *How I take Trimble for granted!* She squeezed his arm and said, "Of course, of course. You'll get home to your family."

His look showed that he wasn't sure about this, and Marta remembered the bishop's warning.

The next day, they reached the Forest of Zwipplenitch. The sun was setting, blackening the trees and firing the snow and mists.

Bells boomed, startling Marta.

"I'd forgotten," Trimble said and flicked the lash on Toivo's stalwart rump. "We're near the Abbey of Blessed Waromyr. Perhaps the brothers can put us up for the night. They brew excellent mead."

He urged Toivo on. "But we have to hurry. In winter, they take the basket up at six precisely. Perhaps the king stopped there, and we shall have news of him. Old but reliable."

Toivo bore them swiftly and almost kicked in the traces, as if exulting. He glanced back at Trimble and snorted. The abbey's bells were pealing. One...two...three...

Marta smiled. "What *basket?*"

"Why, for getting up to the abbey, mistress."

They reached a cliff sprouted with stunted firs with a stable at its base. The final bell stroke rolled out onto the air. Trimble jumped out and pulled on a thick rope with a knotted end dangling from above.

The voice of a smaller, brasher bell sounded from the hilltop. A masculine voice called down, "Who's there? It's after six. Could you possibly come back tomorrow?"

"Two weary travelers, brother!" Trimble yelled. "Needing your Christian charity!"

"Stand back then! I'll send the basket down!"

Shortly, a substantial basket descended to the snow with a thump.

Marta gestured toward the stable. "Will Toivo be all right there?"

"Should be." Trimble took him out of harness. "I'll make sure he has what he needs and check on him in the morning."

"But what about wolves?"

"I'll secure the door and shutters."

She helped Trimble park the sleigh by the stable, and he helped her board the basket.

Then, hand-to-mouth, he yelled, "Pull, brother!"

While he saw to Toivo, Marta ascended, going up by starts and stops while boughs scraped the sides of the basket. When she reached the cliff top and the brother who was working the winch saw her, he almost let go of the rope.

Aware that her appearance must be somewhat wild, she said, "You have no way of knowing this, but I am your sovereign, Marta Louisa."

She held out a hand.

He took it reverently. "Of course, Your Majesty!" His look was cheerful, his face ruddy from the cold. "I recognize you from a trip to Zuphof. Watch your step getting out!"

She disembarked from the basket. The brother lowered it, and then together, they hauled Trimble onto the hilltop.

In the large refectory, a long board supported on trestles was laid with a plain but good meal. The brothers ate while listening to a lector read. Marta heard some of this while enjoying her soup and studying her surroundings.

The brothers were sneaking scraps to a dozen hounds and mutts. These lolled under the benches or begged with their muzzles on the board. A mouse was seated on the rim of a plate, for a brother had dipped a morsel of bread in cheese for her, and she was nibbling it there. In one corner, a dovecote was wintering while a sleek cat with a bell on its collar observed its nervous occupants from a nearby window ledge.

Brother Mikhail was reading from *The Chronicles of Waromyr* the passage in which Blessed Waromyr slays the dragon, Uxondyne, then destroys her clutch of eggs. Marta's appetite wilted a bit, but Trimble continued to shovel in supper.

When supper was over, *The Chronicles* were set aside, and conversation began.

Marta rubbed a hound's velvety ears as she addressed the abbot. "Sir, one of the brothers tells me that the king stopped here on his way to Lord Drugen's."

The abbot smiled—a flash of white teeth in his dark beard. "Indeed, the king did, Your Majesty. He was with us for Holy Week and Easter that year. He left after the blessing of the animals."

"You still bless the animals?" Trimble cried. "Why, I thought that tradition ended long ago."

"No, we still do this. In fact, we blessed the king's warhorse."

Trimble blinked and fell silent, and the abbot's thoughtful gaze resettled on Marta.

"I realize that it's been years," she said, "but can you tell me anything about the king? Was he well when he visited you?"

"He had been on the road for a while and lost some weight, but he was extremely hale."

Hearing this, Marta felt both joy and sadness.

Trimble leaned across her to ask, "Were all the knights still with him?"

"Yes, ten hungry stomachs and thirsty mouths. They were fond of the mead, weren't they, Brother Waclaw?"

Waclaw, a small man with dimples and a fringe of white hair, smiled and nodded.

"Did they all go on to Drugen's with the king?" Trimble asked.

"One stayed with us." The abbot turned to Marta. "The king released Segird from his oath and gave him permission to enter our order."

Segird lifted a sheepish gaze from his soup bowl.

Marta stood. "Segird?"

He hurried to her, knelt, and bowed his head.

When he looked up again, she saw a familiar, shiny scar on his cheekbone. Yes, it was Segird, just older and a little heavier and red hair softened to gold.

"If the king approved, then I do," she said.

She reached for his hands and, refusing to let him kiss her own, helped him to his feet.

"So you agree with the abbot?" she asked. "All was well with the king and his knights?"

"Yes, Majesty," Segird said. "For ten days they rested, fattened up, and prayed. They left in high spirits, singing as they rode away."

"Wonderful! You are happy here, Segird?"

"Yes, God be praised! I found peace trading my sword for a ladle. Your father regretted the loss of my cooking, he said. The lentils are my recipe. What do you think?"

"Delicious!" she said, sitting again and picking up her spoon.

Segird sat back down to his supper. "We pray for the king every day," he said.

"Is there recent news of him?"

The abbot answered, "Even the rumors have stopped. The only things of which we're certain are that he took the northern route through the Keistrel Pass and that he reached Drugen's lodge. We learned of his arrival there from a girl who left Drugen's service soon after this."

"The Keistrel? But that's far to the north!"

"The king had gotten word that Drugen was at his lodge, not his stronghold." The abbot stroked his beard. "This Easter, it will be fourteen years since the king visited with us." He looked thoughtful.

"Seven is a number of significance in holy writ and in history. Seven churches are warned or commended in the Apocalypse. Seven wild swans fed the starving Waromyr when he sojourned in Zwipplenitch before founding this holy house of God here. It will soon be twice seven years since the king left us."

Marta managed a smile. "Almost my whole life." She bit her lip. "Would you please excuse me, Abbot? I'm feeling somewhat tired."

The following morning, Marta and Trimble were granted an audience with the saintly Brother Edelbert. Strangely, Edelbert addressed Trimble before addressing her.

"So you are her Majesty's champion?" he asked.

Trimble's eyes widened. "No, *eminence!* Just the palace handyman."

Edelbert's skin was translucent, his nose mapped with veins, his eyes bleary. He had knelt for so many years, praying for the wrongs of the world, that his back and legs were bent in an S. He was seated in an invalid's chair, sustained on his bony bottom, with a plump cushion. He had no more tears to moisten his eyes, for he had shed them all. The brothers would put salve into his lower lids. He would blink, and his eyes were protected in this way. His hairs were white and few, and the stubble on his chin was sparse and silvery.

Again, he addressed Trimble. "You speak as they do in the south. Are you perhaps from Brughil, the birthplace of our kingdom's patron saint?"

Trimble inclined his head. "I was born in Brughil, yes."

Edelbert put a trembling hand on Trimble's arm. "It's a long, treacherous road to Drugen's, fraught with difficulty and testing. Have you seen the Zelhorn? Its northern flank is scored with cliffs. That is where all the trouble began—in the heart of the mountain that rears its proud head against the heavens. There, the dragons go to breed."

He patted Trimble's arm. "Only a fool or a saint would venture there, would take the queen to the lair of Drugen."

Trimble seemed uneasy. "The mistress is in charge. I'm simply along to try to keep her safe."

Marta squeezed Trimble's arm. "I couldn't have made it *even* this far, Edelbert, without Trimble's help."

She offered Edelbert her hand.

He held it in both of his. "Something in your manner reminds me of your father." He gave her a delighted smile. "I knew him when he was a lad."

"You did?"

"I taught him at the Brothers' School in Ittyohobonetska."

"How wonderful!" she cried, drawing a stool up to Edelbert's knees.

"Drugen was also my pupil. The two were school fellows." Edelbert chuckled. "What pranks they played!"

Marta glanced at Trimble as if he'd been keeping something from her. "So *that* is how Father knew Drugen."

"Their early acquaintance had nothing to do with the king's trip." Trimble seemed disturbed. "Drugen is an outlaw. Your father, his sovereign, went to arrest him."

"Oh why, oh why, didn't he send someone else to do this?" Marta cried.

"That was never Peter's way as a lad," Edelbert said. "He was brave and self-reliant. And 'the child is father to the man.'"

"And Drugen. What was he like?"

"Competitive, strong, and bright. Often in trouble, but so was your father, though they were both serious students. In fact, they competed at their studies as they did at everything."

"Forgive me," Trimble said, "but to hear them spoken of as comrades sets my teeth on edge!"

Again, Edelbert put a hand on Trimble's arm. "You were born in what year? Did you know Blessed Gregor?"

Trimble blushed. "I can't claim an acquaintance with any saint, *eminence,* particularly one who lived so long ago."

"Ah, yes! My poor brain! How could you have known him? That was three centuries ago. Gregor giving his life to save the village of Spoot from a dragon."

"I do know the house where he was born." Trimble slowly batted his lashes. "They leveled it and built a church in its place."

"That is their usual way." Edelbert turned to Marta. "It was your father, I believe, who recovered Gregor's relics—"

Trimble interrupted, "Gregor had no relics. The dragon left naught but ashes. It was the relics of your own Blessed Waromyr that the king recovered—"

Marta interrupted, "Please, Edelbert, tell me more about the king and Drugen!"

"When his father died, Drugen left the Brothers' School," Edelbert said. "The king continued two more years with us. Drugen later returned to the city to complete his education but enrolled in the College of the Knights of Marcion. That was his grandfather's decision. By then, Basilides had apostatized. He had been a Socinian, you see, who then abandoned the vestiges of the faith to pursue an interest in the occult."

Marta shook her head. "What a terrible influence upon Drugen!" Her voice sank. "And Royal too."

Edelbert patted her hand. "The king's story was quite different." He rested a hand on hers. "How important it is that influences be good!"

He thought for a moment, his eyes brightening with memory. "He was a talented musician, did you know? I kept some music he composed during his time at school."

Marta clapped her hands together. Edelbert directed her to a bookcase stuffed with scrolls and books and papers, and Trimble knelt to help her search.

"*There,* Trimble!" she cried. "What's that in your hand?"

Each held a corner of the page. Marta smiled at the childish scrawl, devouring the lyrics with her eyes. What was this? A puzzle. Another mystery to add to the others! Her father had written of the Savior's love? She couldn't remember him ever speaking in this way, though he was always reverent when attending divine service.

She slipped the music from Trimble's grasp. "May I keep this, Edelbert?"

"There may be more of Peter's. Keep whatever you find, Majesty."

She returned to the shelf, hiding her emotion, and rummaged through but found nothing more. Idly, with disappointment, she ran a finger along the book spines. Edelbert's taste in reading was certainly diverse and interesting.

Her finger stopped, and she asked over her shoulder, "You have a copy of Waromyr's *Bestiary?* May I look?"

Edelbert smiled and said, "Of course!"

Marta removed the book to a slanted desk under the window and then sat on the tall chair. Carefully, she thumbed and turned the pages. They were filled with pictures and so-called "histories" of fantastical beasts. Coming to a picture of the dragon Uxondyne, she smoothed the pages so the book lay flat.

Trimble appeared at her elbow and tapped a finger on Uxondyne's snout. "The artist got *something* right—her ferocious cunning."

"Hmm." Marta couldn't help smirking. "I don't mean to be rude, Trimble, but how would you know?"

"An honest question!" He blushed as he considered it. "I suppose I've seen so many pictures that I feel I know when I couldn't possibly."

"We all feel we know," Edelbert said, "and would recognize at once the misbegotten, monstrous, and awful."

Very quietly, Marta closed the book. Her imagination had suddenly leapt out at her like a jack-in-the-box and was filling the wilds through which they were trekking with *bogeys.* For an instant, she imagined a gigantic spider crawling over the top of a fortress wall covered with webs.

She returned the book to its shelf. "We've been speaking as if dragons exist—today—in our world."

The expression of Edelbert's poor eyes became piercing. "Many things exist *today*."

"Unicorns," Trimble offered.

"Mm," Marta agreed. "But I can't go so far as to think that dragons do."

Alone in her Spartan room, Marta scribbled in her journal:

I've declined invitations to attend Mass and divine office. Have supped again with the brothers—cabbage soup and black bread, plain but delicious.

Over supper, the lector continued to read from The Chronicles. I'm being forced, it seems, to seriously consider the existence of dragons, to stretch my mind still further. Do dragons lurk just beyond our purview, ready to swoop from the heights and bear us away to cliffs, such as Edelbert described? Did my father encounter one?

Blessed Waromyr's trophy catch, Uxondyne, was the empress of dragons, the consort of the largest creature ever birthed, Valkynde, The Chronicles name him. From Waromyr's style, I imagine a timid, grateful man who, in accomplishing this beau geste, surprised himself, as well as others.

A thought before going to bed. How grateful I am that I was taught that faith is simplicity of devotion to Jesus Christ and rest in him! Because I learned this, I'm able to see the difference in the object of people's faith. At the Abbey, in Catholicism in general, devotion is centered on our response to Christ's sacrifice—what we can do, what sacrifices we will make, how we will help others. I confess this scares me off, and I flee like a rabbit from a natural enemy. Devotion centered on what the Lord Jesus did for us invites me to come to him. Continuing with the analogy, I hop out to the rich grass and quietly feed, concealed from the enemy.

What I mean is that I see more clearly than ever the reasons for the Reformation and am happy that God wrought it, though faith is costly. Relinquishing my love for Bartolo is part of that cost.

What concerns me is whether I've taken myself out of the protection of the God who has done so much for me. Is such a thing possible? No, that can't be, even if I have indeed been very foolish.

She was standing on the hilltop near the cliff-side basket. The morning was bright and cold. The brothers had left their chores to wish her well, and Trimble was waiting below.

She was uncomfortable with this leavetaking. Would the abbot expect her to kiss his ring? At home, she could get around such things when Catholic clergy visited, but here? If she refused the gesture, would she embarrass or hurt him?

She didn't want that. She respected the brothers and knew they respected her. She had learned more about her father and had been given something of his. Segird certainly looked happy. How mysterious the providence that spared him danger at Drugen's! Somehow she felt safer knowing the abbey was here, on the brink of the wilds.

She held out her hand. The abbot looked surprised, but smiled and shook it. Relaxing she smiled in return, grateful for him. Then, stepping onto a small stool set beside the basket, she climbed in without too much loss of her royal dignity.

Soon she was gripping the sides as the basket swung out. Down she went, feeling her weight hasten her toward Trimble, who stood with his boots planted and his arms raised.

Thump! Her bones were jarred, and snow scattered.

Trimble lent her a hand, and she jumped out. Fresh snow had fallen, the air was crisp, and she felt prepared for anything. Toivo, looking even shaggier, was in harness. He tossed his mane.

She boarded the sleigh with Trimble.

"Ready, mistress?" he asked.

"Ready!"

Survival

Trimble reined in. It was now impossible to see in heavy snow that was streaming toward them.

They jumped out and got to work. They took Toivo out of harness, attached his tie weight, and threw on and buckled his blanket. They rocked and tipped the sleigh onto its side, facing away from the wind. They arranged lap robes and blankets for a snug den and then crawled in to safety.

Toivo sank to his knees close by.

Marta rested her chin on her arms and sighed, peering out occasionally to check on him. With snow piling against him, he looked monumental in the falling darkness.

Their gear had spilled out of the sleigh's cubbyholes, and the lantern was at hand. Trimble trimmed and lit it, and it did fair duty as a tiny stove. In its light, his expression was grim.

"Toivo may not survive," he said.

She burst into tears. "Pray! Please!" She couldn't stop crying and buried her face on her arms.

Trimble put a hand on her shoulder and gently patted. "I have been. Try to sleep."

It seemed as if she had slept for only a moment. She opened her eyes. Trimble was crawling out. He left their improvised curtain back. She closed her eyes against the glare of sunlight intensified by snow. The lantern had gone out, and her breath was freezing on the air. She crawled out after him into a world where shrubs were mounds of snow, and trees were tiny, white hills. Piled up behind and beside the sleigh, the snow had laid out a low, semicircular ridge of incredible proportions.

Toivo was nowhere to be seen, and Trimble was leaning against the buried sleigh. Marta attempted to stand. He grunted as he helped her and then leaned with her there.

"Where is he?" she asked.

He grimaced with a hand to his back and pointed. Nearby was a mound of snow about head-high with a dark gap toward the top.

With a cry, she began to dig. Trimble hobbled over to help. Soon Toivo's head and neck appeared arched back toward his shoulder. They quickly cleared his muzzle.

"He's breathing!" Marta cried.

Trimble winced as he bent to study him. "We need to get him up and walking," he said then slowly straightened.

They tugged on Toivo's bridle. His head came up. Snow fell away as he stood. Never before so impressed with his strength and endurance, Marta praised him. They unfastened the tie weight and drew off the stiff blanket. Gripping the halter rope, Trimble began to walk him but stopped, a hand to his back again. Marta took the rope from him and walked Toivo until he began to move with ease and tossed his head.

She hooked his feedbag on and then stood by him while he ate.

"He's magnificent," Trimble said with a twinkle in his eye. "He'll get you to Biklava, that's for sure, even without the sleigh."

"We could *try* to dig it out."

"I couldn't manage this morning." Trimble's gaze showed pain. "And our shovel won't do the trick."

"Poor Trimble!" Marta smiled in commiseration. "I'll get breakfast, and then we'll decide what to do."

"Thank you, mistress!"

His *thank you* was deeply satisfying to her, but the job wasn't easy. The water in the canteen had frozen. They had to breakfast on cold bread, and a little snow melted in a tin plate set on top of the lantern. Then Marta started digging out the sleigh. After a few shovelfuls, it became clear to her—as it had been to him—that their travel shovel wouldn't do.

They loaded Toivo with as much of the gear as they could and said good-bye to the sleigh. She put her satchel over her back and her boot in the stirrup. Gripping a pole hacked from the sleigh for a walking stick, Trimble waited, his chin sunk on his chest.

She studied him. Removing her foot from the stirrup, she handed him her satchel and reached for the pole. "Up!" she ordered.

"No, mistress. It isn't right."

"It is."

They made the trade. She gave him a boost. "We can take turns riding and walking. How far is the *fair city?*"

He chuckled as he pointed into the hazy distance. "Less than a league on the map."

"We'll stay the night and have a hot supper." She had been smiling without realizing it and now began to laugh. "It's amazing how one can just keep going! How each morning—however bad the night—one feels ready!"

Trimble rolled his shoulders and rested a hand on his knee. "That's the voice of youth!" He smiled. "I'm glad your mother can't see me ride while you walk. She wouldn't understand, and she worries about you."

Marta nodded as she trudged along. "Indeed, she worries about everything! I hope I don't become like her." As soon as she said this she felt guilty.

Trimble's tone was grave. "Never say that, mistress."

She peeked at him. "I shouldn't, Trimble, but *really*. Can you imagine Carissima tipping a sleigh and surviving by lantern glow?" She felt another pang of guilt.

He looked at the sky then down at her, his gaze boring a hole. "She's probably had a few adventures of her own."

"Pih!" She tried to laugh this off.

"And that is why she worries." He adopted his teaching tone. "Biklava is a wild place. You'll need to be careful. Don't say who you are or attract attention in any way."

"Of course not." She smothered a feeling of resentment. "Do you still have your sword?"

"I do." His gaze was steady. "How about the pistol?"

Sighing, she patted her coat at the place where it was concealed and sent up a quick prayer for forgiveness.

Tucked in bed, Marta settled her coat around her shoulders and opened her journal with shaking fingers. She had set a candle in drops of wax on an old lap desk she had found behind the dresser. She blew on her fingers and began.

We have entered the wild and weird world of Biklava, an outpost on the edge of the frontier, home-away-from-home for misfits, miscreants, and opportunists.

I've drawn my bed curtains on the rawest night in memory. My room perches on the top story of an inn of a questionable character (to say the least). My mother would be frantic. Trimble is worried, but this was the only room to be had. Ah, picturesque Biklava!

As always, he was willing to sleep in a closet as long as I was safe and comfortable. But as things are, he needs to be close. He intended to sleep sword-in-hand outside my door in the drafty corridor, but I insisted he room with me. It took a lot of doing, but at last I convinced him it would be all right. There could be no scandal where we were nobodies. We have said that he is my grandfather.

I wasn't only thinking of Trimble. The room makes me shudder. The decor is all in black and red, with faux gilding. And it feels as if someone died here. It can't have been lived in for some time, for the corners have cobwebs, and the fireplace stones are as chilly as a vault.

I sense an unhappy life lived out here. Imagination? Maybe, but it feels like the truth.

Trimble is stationed in front of the bolted door on a mattress he dragged from the trundle of my huge four-poster. He has promised that anyone who attempts to get to me will have to go through him. Bravo, Trimble! We bought a bottle of lineament for his aches and pains, and the room smells of this.

As I write, the flame of the candle flutters in a draft that rustles the bed curtains and steals down the chimney like a cat wishing to snatch the flames of a pathetic little fire that struggles to keep alight.

We have stabled Toivo for the duration at a livery outside of town and paid handsomely for this! He can't be ridden farther, for the mountains are just ahead. We must finish on foot, using snowshoes we bought here. I don't like to leave Toivo here, but I must.

Nearing Biklava, I noticed the first birds I'd seen for a while! A peregrine "stooping" (Trimble taught me the term) to take a hare. Then nearer to Biklava, crows on a snowy field—as black as ink on a white page. In town, sparrows were flitting everywhere after crumbs amidst the trash.

Biklava brings adventure, whether or not you want it. On entering town—freezing, exhausted, and famished—while stepping onto the main road, Trimble and I were almost run over by a sleigh turning the corner. The horses were high stepping, and every bell was jangling on their brightly tasseled tack. The driver cursed us before lashing his ponies on. I think he cursed—I couldn't understand, for he was speaking Zelhornish according to Trimble, who I find knows the language, as he does so many other things. We were showered with filthy slush, which amused the onlookers. Oh well!

This was humbling and, therefore, probably good for me.

As we headed down the street amidst the throng, a young man, with his hat turned down and collar turned up, bowled into me. No apology, just a look full in the face and a smile with ruddy lips and unnaturally white teeth. I wouldn't wish to encounter him in an alley! We found this room, climbed four stories of stairs as oddly jointed as a skeleton, and, from the window, I saw the same man stalk across a roof, then leap to another—like some great cat from the Orient. His eyes probably glow at night. My imagination has come to life again, it seems. Here, there are many strange persons and stranger sights to fuel it.

So we have made it this far without perishing—

She paused.

The bed curtains swayed and then were still.

A sudden thought made her search the lap desk for anything belonging to a prior tenant. With a thrill, she found a letter in a feminine hand. There were spots on it that looked like marks from tears.

My darling A., when will you come to me? I suffer without you...

Marta trembled and flipped the letter, but there was nothing more on the other side.

A polite cough sounded from the vicinity of the door. She opened the bed curtains a crack and saw Trimble looking bulkier under his blankets and still in his scarf. He blinked groggily. The odor of lineament was sharp.

"If we're going to get an early start, you'd better stop scribbling," he said.

"Oh yes, Trimble! And sorry if I kept you awake. Good night!"

He pulled the covers around his ears. "Mm-hm."

She closed the bed curtains and put her things aside, snuffed the candle, and snuggled down, enjoying the warmth of a bedwarmer near her toes.

All was total darkness.

She closed her eyes and prayed. *Who has suffered here, Lord? Please help that person!*

Resolve

The 14th of February 1622

My darling wife,

You'll be glad to learn we've reached Biklava—and with no loss of fingers or toes to frostbite. Wish you were here, for my socks need to be darned. Not really! I miss you more than words can say.

Her Majesty is her father all over again: intrepid, principled, and bull-headed. Most of the time we get along, and so far, I've managed to remain respectful. In close quarters, my charade is trying, but she doesn't suspect—thank God!

Don't look for me soon. Having crossed the Rubicon, I know she will never turn back, for it is impossible that her hope—it's now desperate—will die a natural death.

I worry how Timka is managing without me. Remind him he is to listen to you and take care of you. I worry. And I worry too that should the worst happen, he will suffer—as you will. May God keep you both! I am keeping an edge on my sword, as He wishes.

Biklava is worse than remembered.

Thank you for the vest—it's dandy!

A kiss and a roll in the hay,
G.

Trimble sealed and kissed this, then jogged to the magistrate, whom he paid through the nose to send it by courier to Zuphof as soon as the weather permitted.

Quickly, he returned to their lodgings and gathered Marta and their gear. She looked thin but fit and well suited out from the merchants at Biklava for what lay ahead. Though new lines around her smile—sad ones—troubled him.

The sun was sinking. They were slowly climbing a track through leafless hardwoods and firs laden with snow. The bitter cold and awkwardness of the snowshoes seemed all there was in the world. The snowshoes made a soughing sound. Marta's satchel felt heavier. The muscles in her legs quivered. Biklava was snowy leagues behind them, and Drugen's keep was *somewhere* up ahead.

Biklava. The image she had carried from there was the smile of a stranger they passed on the way out of town. Well-dressed and handsome, his smile thrilled her until she noticed that his teeth were filed. She had almost cried out, but Trimble had hurried her past the man.

She missed Toivo and the sense of safety he provided. She was fearful and troubled by misgivings. Drugen loomed in her thoughts as the very embodiment of evil.

Trimble was trekking behind her, his breath whistling at times when he exhaled. Hours ago, they had passed the last cottage and reached the wilds. No man's land, where the lawless carved out kingdoms for themselves, and Drugen ruled as overlord. Where creatures of legend ranged. Where her father had ventured in his simplicity and valor.

The track led up to a clearing. Trimble caught up with her, and they gazed across a forest thrown like a bearskin over low, rumpled foothills. All around them, snow was falling in silent, heavy drops.

Past the curtain of white in a deep valley lay a long lake under a thralldom of ice. On the rugged bluff above this, Drugen's castle proudly stood. Beyond the castle, the mountains began, jutting in a formidable ascent of glacier and granite toward the Zelhorn, whose summit was obscured by clouds.

"You're pushing yourself too hard," said Trimble.

"All right, let's stop for the night."

She was so cold she couldn't help him make a fire but sat on a log with her cloak pulled tightly around her, watching him gather sticks and branches, then sink to his knees and strike the flint.

The fire caught.

The twilight deepened.

Soon their small circle of warmth and light was surrounded by freezing darkness. She fought a feeling of darkness within her by reminding herself that she was called to trust in the LORD, no matter what. But was her trust presumption?

Snow continued to fall out of a sky like a void to the snapping flames.

Trimble emptied his pack of the last of their bread. "Perhaps I could use the pistol to hunt." He looked like he wasn't up to that. "A rabbit—"

"I'd rather have nothing!"

This was foolish, she knew, but the thought of the flight and death of another small creature was too much. She had heard that her father felt the same about such things. Besides, she didn't want to ask any more of Trimble tonight.

"And *you* will save the king from *Drugen*," he said.

Her own voice sounded far away. "Yes..."

"Let's turn back in the morning. We can head for the hostel we passed."

"What if Father needs us?" She stopped at Trimble's undisguised look of pity. "Why are you staring so?"

He held up both hands as if pleading with her. "I'm thinking of how to tell you that your poor father is most likely dead."

Her tears fell. "I must be certain. And if there has been foul play, bring those responsible to justice."

He shook his head. "With no one to help but *me?*"

Knowing he was probably right, she fell silent.

He sighed, broke the bread in two, and gave her the biggest half. They ate in silence. When they finished, they crawled on hands and knees to build a low wall of packed snow.

They sheltered between this and the fire.

She slept almost comfortably and dreamed.

They were flying on Toivo to Drugen's. She could see the snowy world below, like a white quilt stitched with dark trees. But as they flew, Toivo's wings began to shrink until they were as small as a sparrow's, and she and Trimble plummeted.

She sat up, a delicious smell tickling her nose. Trimble was plucking a potato out of the fire, and a few flurries were falling into a gray dawn.

"We'll probably finish the journey today," he said in a determined tone. "There's a good chance you could sleep in a bed tonight. I saved this tater."

His attitude was just what she needed. She yawned and stretched. "I dreamed about Toivo," she said sadly.

Wheels turning, he tossed the potato to her. "That's funny! I did too. He was stabled at the top of an enormous beanstalk that reached the clouds." He pointed a thumb up. "He was eating oats the size of my fist."

She began to laugh and it was hard to stop. Finally she said, "Thank you, Trimble!"

They didn't shorten the trip by crossing the lake—he didn't think it wise. They snowshoed around the lake, crossing only one small stretch of ice.

Finally, they reached the bluff. It towered above, with snow in its clefts and icicles as long as sabers drooping from some of its overhangs. They removed their snowshoes and strapped them to their backs.

"Only a little farther," she murmured.

"I'll help you," he said.

He would; she knew that. He would do anything for her. He was offering her Tinka's vest now, because here, where Drugen's castle stood, it was unimaginably cold.

She refused his offer, looked up, and shivered. Evening was just coming on, and there was light at a window in the castle wall. Harsh laughter rode out onto the air above.

Trimble tightened his scarf and tucked his mittens under an arm, laced his fingers together, and boosted her to a ledge. He put his mittens back on. They ascended, careful of handholds made with numb fingers. The wind buffeted them, but she felt his hand steadying her.

A new doubt came to crucify her. Her father had gone by way of the Keistrel Pass to Drugen's lodge—not *here*. She wouldn't find him! Nay, she wouldn't find him anywhere! He was dead, murdered by Drugen, then buried in an unmarked grave. If Drugen had done this, she would do the same to him.

"I swear it!" she cried.

"Don't talk. Climb!" Trimble ordered.

A stretch of steeper ascent brought on vertigo. As she fumbled for a hold, her mask slid over and covered one eye. She adjusted the mask, clinging one handed, while the wind grabbed at her cloak.

"Lean in!" Trimble cried. "I won't let you fall!"

She thanked God for him and found her next hold.

The gates—thick beams and forged iron—were closed for the night, and they couldn't raise anyone's attention. In the shadow of the wall, they found shelter among a stand of pines. They gathered brush, and Trimble laid a fire while she peered down through snowy boughs at the lake. She shuddered; from here, the short stretch of ice they'd crossed looked dark and thin.

"The fire's going," said Trimble. "Come closer, and don't be so sad."

In the smallish place, they huddled together. When the wind changed direction for a moment and scattered hot ash, he covered her face with a mittened hand.

They chewed the last strands of hardtack, ate some snow, then crawled beneath low branches, sat against a tree, and shared their blankets.

"Say your prayers!" he said. "We don't know what reception Drugen will give us."

"Drugen..." she murmured and then slipped into a dreamless sleep.

She awoke to sunlight, the scent of cold pines, and Trimble at the fire. He had melted snow and brewed rosemary tea from needles he'd used again and again.

He handed her their dented cup.

As she sipped, she gazed at his backpack, wondering if there were crumbs at the bottom. Surely not, for he would have given them to her! She offered him half the tea.

He said no, stood shakily, and held down his hand. "What do you say, mistress? Shall we go home? It's simple to turn around when you find you're wrong. Whether you like it or not, I can hunt. We'll make it eventually."

Her smile fell, and her teeth chattered. "No...and don't...ask again!"

He kicked snow over the fire, almost falling as he did, and shifted his pack to the other shoulder.

"All right, it's your place to say." He raised a hand in its fraying mitten and said somewhat hoarsely, "Onward! For the king's sake! For the kingdom's sake! For *yours!*"

She took his hand, and they limped toward the castle wall.

Part Two:
Her Suffering (and His)

Disequilibrium

The massive gates were closed, and no one heard Marta and Trimble shouting and calling. Even when he threw stones at a tower window, there was no response. The wall, skirted by snowdrifts slick with ice, couldn't be climbed. So they snowshoed around the wall, looking for a way in until late in the day when they found an icebound orchard and a small, forgotten door frozen ajar.

She slipped in. He squeezed through. They headed for the castle, supporting each other at times and keeping an eye on the wall walk to see if anyone was looking down.

Bearded faces under large beaver hats appeared there. In what must have been Zelhornish, a guard yelled what was probably, "Hey, you two! Stop!"

Trimble did so, putting a hand on Marta's arm.

Wanting to be sure the guards knew just who was in charge, she freed her arm and took a step away from him. "I'll speak for us," she said.

He widened his eyes and wiggled his mustache. "Of course, mistress, though you don't know a *word* of Zelhornish. If you need help, let me know."

She glared. He chuckled.

A half dozen guards, bundled in fur coats and swords drawn, lumbered down the steps from the wall and surrounded the two.

Their long beards were hung with tiny icicles, and their gaze was haughty and suspicious. Frowning, they began to argue, it seemed, over what in the world to do with the intruders.

Trimble smiled, but Marta could feel his tenseness and readiness to defend her.

The guards' glances flew from her face to her clothes. More comments were bandied. When one of the guards cocked his head toward Trimble, all of them joined in a laugh.

Marta ignored this, standing taller, and explained in courtly Zupish that she was their queen apparent and that she wished to speak with the king or Lord Drugen at once. She realized how foolish she must look. The guards talked over her smaller voice, made faces, and repeated some of what she said in a way that made it seem like gibberish.

Finally, Trimble held up a hand and said something short and sweet in Zelhornish. Abruptly the Guards hurried the two to the keep. One held his sword to Trimble's back and prodded him through the portal, nodding to Marta to follow.

Thrilled by another one of his remarkable interventions, she whispered, "What did you *say?*"

He looked down his funny nose at her. "That we've come with an important message from *Her Majesty.*"

The entranceway was circular, the shape of the old donjon around which the castle was built, with a staircase curving up into darkness. Tapestries and a good-sized hearth kept the entranceway warm. Except for the crackle of fire, all was quiet, for they were out of the wind at last. Above them, a chandelier of iron drooped on a stout chain. In the wall to their left stood lofty doors of oak.

The guard in the tallest hat struck the panels with a heavy staff, then he and the others pulled the doors around.

Now accustomed to the low-key sounds of the outdoors, Marta gasped at the roar of talk and laughter and passionate bowing of a rhapsody.

The guards led them in. A young Gypsy man and woman were dancing. Marta had never seen anything so proud and free. The musicians paused, and the Gypsies stopped and slipped into the shadows.

The hall was lit by a hundred candles, bowls of flaming oil, and a fire in the huge hearth on their right as they entered. At the hall's far end, an arched colonnade supported a gallery thick with shadows, whose stone wall was pierced by high slender windows that were darkening with the fading of day. The side walls were draped in tapestries that lay partly in darkness, partly in flickering light.

Trimble coughed to get Marta's attention, and her gaze followed his. In the tapestry nearest to them, demons were tumbling out of a lurid sky to a dim, forested world enclosing a tiny, walled city. One of them had a compass, with its needle pointed south, in place of an eye; another had a louvered door, attached by a single hinge, in place of a wing.

Trimble slowly let out his breath.

Marta blinked and looked all around and above.

The windows were now dark—day had swiftly withdrawn. The rafters quivered in the changing mix of light and shadows, and gargoyles leaned overhead. Something moved among them, and an eye looked downward. Higher still, all was pitch dark as if the hall was open to a starless night. Below, at the center of an elegantly-laid table, Lord Drugen sat on a high-backed chair covered with a sable throw adorned with the heads of minks, his bejeweled hands resting on chair arms carved as ravening wolves.

He turned his gaze to Marta.

Marta's heart failed her in confusion. She hadn't expected him to be so striking-looking. Everything—the hall, his Lady, his courtiers—was like the extravagant setting for a gorgeous jewel.

She glanced at Trimble, who was gawking.

The guards pushed them forward.

Trimble uttered a yelp, and Marta tripped and fell on the hearth tiles. For a moment, jade squares emblazoned with golden serpents held her gaze, then Trimble gave her a hand, and they walked forward.

Drugen stood, and Marta's glance fell to his scabbard. On the sword hilt, in quiet splendor, a dark garnet shone in the setting of a silver cross. Yes! It was Blessed Gregor's weapon—her father's!

Drugen approached and, as he did, something stirred beside the hearth. Chains clinked as a large brown bear raised its head.

Marta looked in amazement from the bear to Drugen, taking in everything about him in a glance: his handsome clothes, dark beard with its strands of silver, sardonic mouth, straight nose, eyes like Royal's but with a spellbinding and seductive look.

He said something in Zelhornish to his courtiers. They smiled, and his Lady leaned forward in her chair.

Marta endured her scrutiny to study her. Her lovely eyes and perfectly oval face showed in a strangely inhuman transparency her deep unhappiness. Her odd smile seemed stamped there. Her copper-colored hair, gathered away from a forehead that was too high, tumbled over her shoulders down her back. Her exquisite gown was the style of an earlier age.

She met Marta's gaze with a look of sympathy. Drugen, who was now so close that Marta could smell his cologne, bowed to Marta. Self-conscious, she raised a hand to her borrowed cap. It fell off and her long braids, which hadn't been washed in weeks, unfurled.

Trimble stooped to pick up the cap while she struggled for composure as the hall filled with low laughter. The laughter sounded freakish, as if animals, as well as people, had expressed amusement.

"You must be Peter's daughter," Drugen said in a heavy but pleasant voice. "Yes, there is a resemblance. Please forgive the rough treatment of my guards; we men of the Zelhorn have our rough edges."

She felt acutely the weight of her sodden clothes and awfulness of her hair but raised her chin. "I forgive them." She removed a glove to extend her hand. "Yes, I am the king's daughter, Marta Louisa, queen apparent of all Zuphof."

"All Zuphof?" Drugen's mouth twitched as he bent over her trembling hand and then looked up at her.

Surprised by a feeling of fascination, she turned her face away.

He straightened. "Your father was once my guest."

She turned back to him with the cry, "Where *is* the king?"

Drugen glanced at his courtiers. "Dust to dust, as you Christians like to put it." A frown wrinkled his brow. "I'm sorry to give you such news, but I would have thought it had reached you long ago."

She rested a hand on Trimble's arm. "Recently I learned something that made me question his death. I came to find him or learn what happ—"

She covered her mouth with her hand. Trimble offered her his handkerchief. She clutched it while her tears fell.

When she grew calmer, she said to Drugen, "How did this happen, sir?"

Drugen's eyes narrowed as he appraised her. "We fought, and he was killed."

She swayed on her feet, and Trimble took her arm to steady her.

Drugen looked at him as if he was someone he knew and despised.

"I didn't want to fight," he said. "Fighting was completely pointless."

He turned his head to say something to his courtiers. With a hand to her throat, Marta stared at him. His courtiers chuckled. When he turned back to her and took her hand, she was startled by the warmth of his touch and snatched her hand away.

"I was merely saying that you will want to freshen up before dining." His gaze was like thin ice over fathomless depths. "Then please rejoin us—Majesty."

"Thank you, but I'll dine with my servant, Trimble, in the kitchen."

Laughter escaped Drugen's nostrils; seemingly without respect or shame, he looked her up and down.

One courtier said loudly in Marta's native Zupish, "Is that the woman's servant or her *paramour?*"

Trimble moved his hand to the hilt of his sword and cried, "How dare *any* of you malign the queen!"

Blushing furiously, Marta squeezed Trimble's arm to check him, then said to Drugen as calmly as she could, "I've come for one reason only. I'm not here to join your party. When I have dined, we shall speak."

She turned to go but stepped on the hem of her skirt.

More laughter assaulted her. She nearly collapsed against Trimble, but he tightened his grip on her arm, and they headed for the doors. Beside them, something caught her eye. Her father's guitar was leaning in a chair. Under the sheen of its many sandings and finishings, the Happstein heraldic was pricked with points of firelight.

A guard accompanied them to the kitchen. It was a grand place with several hearths and ornate stoves, a master cook, a master baker, cook's and baker's assistants, and a troop of servant girls and pages. When Marta and Trimble appeared with the guard, they all stared for a moment, then went back to work.

The guard spoke with the cook, who shouted an order, then the guard stationed himself in a chair with his musket at hand.

Marta and Trimble laid their coats over a noodle-drying rack that stood near the smallest hearth, settled on a bench before this, pulled off their boots, and set them on the hearthstone, not far from a basin of slaughtered pheasants.

Trimble leaned his scabbard with its old sword in a corner.

The guard glanced at it.

The clatter of utensils, shouts and talk, and the kitchen's very busyness, gave Marta a chance to cry on Trimble's shoulder. Shortly, she straightened and wiped her eyes.

A servant girl brought the three bread and soup, then hurried away.

Marta lifted her bowl to study the pudding-like soup. Its odor was mild, but its color was a red so dark it was almost black.

"I can't, and won't, eat blood soup!" she said.

"You can and *must*," Trimble said.

She set her bowl on the bench and broke off a piece of bread.

"Do as I do." He sopped the soup with bread. "I understand how you feel, mistress, but—it's this or nothing."

She nibbled her bread while tears spilled down her chapped cheeks. So it was true. Her father had died, and Drugen had his sword, a weapon used to protect and save. Another of its names was "Defending Angel."

"He mustn't keep a sword that bears that name," she said.

"You're right!" Trimble's eyes were rimmed with red. "But there's nothing we can do about it now but wait for your friend, the prince."

Her chin quivered, and her hand, with its bit of bread, dropped to her lap.

Trimble set his bowl down. "It's easy to see how things happened to the king."

She stared. "What do you mean?"

"Dare I speak, implying that I understand him and how he would act in such a situation?"

"You were his friend, Trimble!"

"And I'm yours. I would die to keep you safe."

A cook's assistant had appeared to pluck the pheasants, and the guard, although busy with his supper, was still close by, so Marta and Trimble turned around on the bench with their backs to both.

Trimble whispered, "The king began his journey intending to arrest Drugen. Along the way, his intention may have changed. He may have decided to reason with his old school chum."

He sighed. "Edelbert's memory of their friendship is something he likes to speak of. Did he speak with the king about it? Did this soften the king's resolve?"

He fell silent.

Marta blew her nose, then said, "Please go on!"

"I can see how easily their friendship was renewed." Trimble scratched his unkempt beard. "The king tended to believe the best about everyone. It would have been easy for Drugen to string him along. Then somehow, at Drugen's instigation, they fought, and the king was killed. Drugen would have dealt with the knights already, you see, dulling their wits and corrupting their loyalties with leisure and pleasure, perhaps even killing one or two."

Marta's eyes widened. "You learned all that in the few moments that passed between us?"

"And more." Trimble dropped his gaze. "I learned what he intends to do with you. He means to corrupt then kill you."

She blushed. "I would *never*—"

He looked at her again. "Of course you wouldn't, but everyone has their weaknesses, and sometimes these aren't apparent until it's too late."

For a moment, she hung her head, then looked up and whispered fiercely, "We must avenge Father!" She glanced at the guard then studied Trimble's splotchy face. "Bartolo may not make it here. What can *we* do?"

"Not a thing. Here you're—forgive me!—'a nobody.' And there's only we two. It's going to be hard enough simply staying alive. And remember, mistress, vengeance isn't the province of mere mortals."

Very gently, he tapped her soup bowl with his spoon.

Magic

The kitchen emptied as servants climbed the backstairs to their quarters. The last to leave was the master cook, who climbed slowly, holding his small dog under an arm.

No one had offered Marta a room, so she was camping in the kitchen with Trimble. Through a crack in the door to the hall, she watched Drugen and his courtiers passing the time in revelry. At the moment, he was baiting the bear, gripping its chain and teasing with jabs from the sword.

She began to chew her fingernails.

Parked on the bench, Trimble was cleaning his boots. "Perhaps you shouldn't watch. You may not like what you see."

The bearbaiting stopped, the musicians played, and everyone danced. Marta watched with her arms crossed over her wrinkled bodice.

"Drugen's wife is lovely," she said.

"Schoya?" Trimble polished briskly. "Fairies are. But don't be envious. Think of the brute she must live with."

He looked up. "Do you remember hearing of a count from the Eastern Marches, Vlad Ostreich? He took a fairy as his wife, Bellefleur. Bellefleur was Schoya's mother, and the mother of Elda's mother too."

Marta rested her head against the door jamb and followed the dancers' moves. Drugen seemed like the dark side of the moon, Schoya like its sad, luminous face.

"Mistress, did you know I've met Bellefleur?" Trimble went on. "And that she put a spell on me?"

Marta turned to him and raised an eyebrow. "What sort of *spell?*"

His shoulders shook with laughter. "She changed me into a porker and took me to hunt for truffles."

She didn't want to encourage more of his clowning but had to smile. "You ought to be ashamed telling such a story!"

Belly still jiggling a bit, he looked at her. "I made you smile."

"You're incorrigible!" She mused. "All I know about fairies is what I've learned from tales and from the little Piers and Elda told us."

"They're beautiful but terrifying," said Trimble. "Because, you see, 'the sons of God went in to the daughters of men.'"

Her eyebrows shot up. "You don't mean...?"

Frowning seriously, he nodded. "I *think* so. It's only a theory, but one that has merit. But really, I did meet Bellefleur, and she did try to hex me."

She shook her head at his persistent nonsense. "Trimble!"

He seemed serious. "I'd spoken with her about Jesus."

Marta gaped then smiled.

He went on polishing.

She held her hands out palms up. "So, what happened?"

He smiled. "The hex didn't work—and do you know why? Because you can't curse what God has blessed. Remember that, mistress!" He polished, looking up and grinning. "Bellefleur got so angry she nearly blew her cork."

Marta cocked her head. "*And?*"

He chuckled. "I prayed, and she flew away."

Marta laughed, then turned away to watch the dancers. "Their wings must be magnificent!"

Trimble came to her side, and they watched together.

"They can be sheer," he said. "Or feathered like swans' wings. Most of the time they don't let you see them. Then all at once, they open them wide to frighten us humans. Some of us have literally been scared to death."

When Schoya and the courtiers retired for the night, Drugen stalked off.

"Now is the time to confront him!" Marta turned to Trimble with an eager look.

He set down his rag and dusted his hands on the thighs of his britches. She could see the wheels turning as he decided if she was right.

He tilted his head back to study her face. "There are circles under your eyes. Maybe you should wait till you've rested."

She pursed her lips and shook her head. "I'm going. Are you coming with me?"

He quickly rose from the bench. "I'm not about to let you go alone." He removed his jacket from the back of a chair, threw it on, and joined her at the door. "Look, the chamberlain's locking up for the night! He could take us to his master."

The chamberlain led them along a passageway flanked by portraits of members of Drugen's peculiar family. Oily eyes scrutinized Marta. Trimble followed a few steps behind her. The smell of the outdoors was still clinging to him.

The chamberlain announced them, then ushered them into what had been the chapel. At a folded icon screen set upon trestles, Drugen was seated to play chess. A second chair, on which a wine bottle and goblet stood, was pulled up to his knee.

The chapel was on an outer wall, and braziers fought to keep it warm as wind rattled the panes of tall windows. The vault, inlaid with tesserae, twinkled in the light of flaming tapers set in a candelabrum that was a dragon with several heads. The altar was hidden by a scarlet cloth, and dice and cards were scattered there. Behind and above the altar, a leather dartboard hung.

Marta shivered with cold and foreboding. She had never witnessed deliberate sacrilege before. She was grateful for Trimble's presence; this, and her scraps of stubborn courage, held her there. She raised her chin, the only gesture she could make. She considered signing the cross upon herself to let Drugen know how she felt but didn't. Only the Lord, and Trimble, would know.

When she had entered, Drugen had half stood and inclined his head. He was back at his game but had left her standing. She tapped a toe and looked around for a chair.

Trimble, who was stationed behind her, whispering prayers and snippets from the Psalms, suddenly uttered a low cry of outrage but recovered himself to find her a chair.

He placed it by the icon screen.

She thanked him and sat.

The waiting continued. She could feel Drugen making his point by taking his time. When her glance lit on his weapon leaning near him, she stared at this reminder of loss.

He moved a pawn...a knight...

Her frustration increased. By the time he looked up, she was flustered and spoke first about the sword.

"Sir," she said, sounding stilted even to herself, "that weapon belongs to the Royal House of Happstein. You will return it at once!"

"The weapon is now mine," he said. "I won it in a fair fight with your *illustrious* father."

She bit her lip. "I've heard that you and he liked to compete."

He smiled. "*You* have been speaking with Edelbert."

She calmed herself. "This particular competition...was it fair?"

"We both began it with open eyes."

"What you consider fair and what *is* fair may be very different."

Still smiling, he wrinkled his brow. "Is this the polite approach you usually take?"

"Are you the one to teach me manners?"

For a moment, as he slipped to a knee before her, he seemed to remember his place, but then he looked straight into her eyes.

"Excuse my forwardness, Majesty," he said, his voice subdued and intimate. "As I told you, we from the Zelhorn—"

She lowered her gaze. "Please sit down."

He balanced on the edge of the chair, a move that brought him closer. She felt a mixture of horror and interest.

"About the sword," he said. "To return it would imply that I'm at fault. I won't do that. I'm sorry. I'm especially sorry about your father."

Marta began to tremble. "He was your sovereign. I am his successor. You will submit!"

Drugen stood and looked down at her. "He is dead. He didn't rule while alive. Should I allow him to rule from the grave? And you. You have no authority here. Your perceptions and expectations are those of a child."

As she rose to her feet, she felt the pistol hidden in her pocket. "You will obey!"

He folded his arms. "I will obey only my own best interests."

"How horrible!" She was now shaking uncontrollably. "At least be kind enough to explain what happened!"

Again, his gaze seemed like ice over deeps. "Yes, it was my sword stroke. Indeed! A man has the right to defend himself. But it was his own foolish inclination to fight that destroyed him."

Marta cried, "How dare you speak of him in that way! As if you are his superior in station and character! You're the mud under his shoes!"

Strangely, as Drugen stared at her she felt the stirring of desire.

He slowly smiled as if pleased to see her descend to his level.

She dropped her gaze and slipped her hand into the pocket where her pistol was, thinking, *Father is destroyed and so am I! What have I to lose?*

Behind her, Trimble stumbled over something. It fell over with a *bang*. In a moment his hand closed over the hand in her pocket.

She turned, rudely pushed past him, and ran down the passage-way. Reaching the kitchen, she fell to her knees on the hearthstone and sobbed her heart out with shame and grief. How she hated Dru-gen! *Hated* him! That he could evoke both hatred and desire was too much! Right now and forever, she must give all of her feelings to the Lord!

Soon her weeping subsided. "God help me to *keep* hating him," she whispered, now fully aware of the danger to her soul.

Stooping beside her, Trimble put a hand on her shoulder. "That isn't the best of prayers, mistress, yet the Lord will hear you. Perhaps you've prayed more wisely than those who pray with less passion."

She remained where she was, quietly crying. He made her a bed of blankets and rolled up a sweater for her pillow. She stood and removed the pistol from her pocket, set it beside the sweater, and lay down. He searched the mantel for a pipe, drew a chair toward the fire, sat, and smoked. The smell of pipe smoke was soothing, and she stopped crying and turned her face toward the fire. He leaned to throw the edge of a blanket over her shoulder then resettled in his chair.

Soon she heard pages rustling as they turned. He read to her from John's gospel, beginning at the place where the Lord admon-ishes, "'Let not your heart be troubled...'"

He read through this passage and the Lord's passion and then fell silent as he relit his pipe.

Even here, in the stronghold of the worst of enemies, God's Word brought peace. The fire seemed brighter, her makeshift bed felt more comfortable, and Trimble's presence and the aroma of his tobacco was greatly consoling.

"Please forgive me for shoving you," she said.

"I do, mistress."

"It must have been terrible for Father."

"I'm sure it was. But for now, put all of that out of your mind! Say good night to your Maker, and get some rest!"

She awoke in the wee hours. The kitchen was dark except for the glow of embers, and Trimble's feet in their unwashed socks were resting on a stool close by. On the hearthstone, a mouse was nibbling crumbs, its eyes and whiskers faintly glimmering. She prayed for the tiny creature, for here in Drugen's stronghold there were sure to be traps and cats and heavy boots.

Trimble had shaken her awake. The kitchen was bustling with preparations for breakfast, and a servant girl was bending over her with a message from Drugen: a room was being made ready.

The villain! Marta sat up and smoothed her hair. Why didn't he see to this last night?

As she rose to her feet, Trimble drew her aside. "My sword is gone." He pointed to the empty corner.

A chill went through her.

"I heard someone joke," he said. "That it was so dull it couldn't be used to chop off the head of a chicken." He glanced from side to side to see if anyone was listening. "On a hunch, I went to the window and saw the tip buried in a chopping block. We're about to be separated. Watch your step."

She nodded, feeling a pang at parting from him, and followed the servant girl upstairs to a heavy door tucked in a stony corner of the old donjon tower.

The door resisted on hinges that needed oiling. What a gloomy room! What a monster of an old bed with plumes crowning the dusty canopy! Its mattress looked lumpy but would be wonderful after sleeping outdoors for so long.

The servant girls bustled about doing their best. They changed the linens, laid a fire, and swept a bit. Then they filled her a copper bath from steaming kettles.

Marta stepped behind a screen and donned a dressing gown placed there for her. When she returned, she stepped into the hot water, slipped the gown off, and sank down, leaning her head back on a rolled towel. Tears of joy filled her eyes.

One of the girls opened the doors of a curious-looking armoire and gestured to its contents. Marta understood that she could dress in whatever she found there. With a smile and more gesturing, the girl made her understand that she was also offering to help her dress.

Marta was amused. She had forgotten about such pampering. But she would need help to manage a heavy gown and would be grateful for help with her hair, so she nodded, then held a finger up to show she wanted a little time.

The servant girls left. She had only her thoughts for company and was glad. She washed her hair, dunked to rinse it, and then wept.

Her father was dead. After all she had endured, it had *always* been so! He wouldn't be going home with her to Zuphof, explaining what had happened in his ingenuous way, and making her laugh with his own infectious laughter. Drugen had explained it all in a few blunt words.

She cried until she couldn't cry any more and felt a little better.

Soon, a doubt intruded on her solitude. It was a cruel stranger who spoke with a voice that made awful sense. Perhaps her father had been unworthy of her love and respect—and of Carissima's trust. If hope could deceive, love could...

She sat up, sloshing water over the rim of the tub. No, love *couldn't* deceive! She must believe in her father's integrity and the Lord's absolute goodness—in common sense and the plain light of day. She wouldn't look for lies everywhere, or she would become cynical as Carissima had warned, and perhaps even lose her mind.

She reached for the towel on the chair by the tub, wrapped it around her, and stepped out.

The only thing that had changed was that now she knew for certain that her father was dead. He hadn't changed—the lovable *child!* And the LORD was the same yesterday, today, and forever!

And she? She mustn't change in her determination to discover what happened and seek justice. It was clear that her father's death had been wrongful and that Drugen was to blame, but how and why had it happened?

She tucked the end of the towel under her arm and stepped to the armoire. Its knobs were carved as the heads of vixens, and she gripped these with a feeling of distaste as she opened the doors.

The armoire was curiously deep and filled with numerous drawers that seemed to open at a touch to disclose treasures: silk scarves, jeweled combs, and soft gloves. As her touch lingered on a delicate lace collar, she again thought of Carissima. She stood for a time, her gaze filled with all of this, and her nostrils tingling from the scent of sachet. Then she sensed a trap. Shivering in the damp towel, she quickly made her choices and closed the doors.

Blessing each article, she laid it upon the bed, frowning, wanting yet not wanting the lovely things. She had to dress in something. Didn't she have the right to dress according to her station? So why was her conscience troubled?

Kikki and Betsy would approve her choices—simple but gorgeous—her style, and the fashion too: a gown of burgundy velvet with full sleeves and an ivory ruff, with a skirt that would just cover slippers of burgundy satin. She smiled at a matching cap fringed with seed pearls.

Gently, her conscience complained in a voice like Cami's, but she silenced it by saying, "It isn't a sin to dress nicely."

She donned the undergarments, then rang for the servant girl. Dust puffed out of the ancient bell pull.

The girl helped her to dress and do her hair. In the dressing-table mirror, Marta observed their faces together. The simply-dressed girl looked more content than she did in her finery.

With a sincere "thank you," Marta dismissed her. After all Marta had been through, she saw courtesy as more than mere civility. It was a gift understood in any language.

She put on the cap. The clustered pearls set off her eyes. Immediately, her heart accused her. For whom was she dressing?

She slipped to her knees—her wide skirts around her—and closed her eyes. "LORD, please help—" she began, and then opened her eyes.

Perhaps the things from the armoire were enchanted! She could feel the faint touch of the pearls at her brow and ears as something almost magical. She shook her head and felt them toss.

Again, she closed her eyes. "LORD Jesus, please forgive my inadequate prayer! Be with me, I pray, and grant wisdom..."

As she lowered her head over her hands, she felt the movement of the pearls. Distracted, the pistol suddenly came to mind. She grabbed her satchel, which was leaning against a bedside table, and rummaged through it past her New Testament to the bottom. The weapon, along with the shot and powder, was there. This was Trimble's doing, for she had lost track of it.

There was a note tied to it with twine:

I hope you won't need this, mistress, but if you do, aim for the heart.

G.

PS: It's cleaned and loaded.

G? That was an odd mistake! Or perhaps his given name began with that letter. She must remember to ask him.

She concealed the weapon within her wide sash—she was now thin enough to do this—and checked her reflection. She didn't linger before the mirror for there were tales of mirrors that had driven people mad. Perhaps Schoya or Bellefleur had peered into it and kissed her own image!

Beyond the door, two of Drugen's footmen were waiting to accompany her to the hall. Tall fellows, dressed in livery of gray and red. Though she wanted to hurry, she forced herself to descend the stairs with them at a normal pace.

Trimble was seated beside the hearth outside the hall. He was dressed in the same gray and red—the fit was snug—and was munching his way through a plate of onion tarts while attempting to make small-talk with some guards.

Marta smiled—he looked at ease in his finery—then blushed when he looked up and saw her. What would he infer from what he might call her gorgeous getup? He had seen her dressed nicely numberless times, so why was she bothered? Her conscience was like a cat that refused to be put in its traveling crate.

Trimble stood and set his plate on the chair. She went to him, and they put their heads together for a private chat.

"I had a bath at a barrel, and they gave me clean duds." He tugged at his jacket. "I have free run of the place. They're not afraid of someone, even the so-called 'champion of the queen,' who looks like I do."

Marta studied his shaved chin and trimmed mustache. "You *are* my champion." She lowered her voice. "And a greater threat than they know. You look nice all freshly scrubbed."

The corners of his mustache lifted; he stood back and took in her dress and cap. "Don't have more than one drink." His gaze was kind. "You'll need your wits."

She began to confide that she was carrying the pistol but stopped, smiled weakly, and headed with the servants into the hall.

Villainy

As Marta walked with practiced grace, but with her heart in her throat, to a seat beside Schoya, everyone stood except Drugen. She inclined her head to show she noted their homage. They would soon be laughing at her again, she knew, but they would be forced to remember this moment of truth.

She let out her breath, unfolded her napkin, and listened carefully to the conversations around her—hoping to catch a sense of what was being said and learn Zelhornish quickly.

To her right sat a gentleman who introduced himself in fluent Zupish as Merl la Corneille, Schoya's uncle. He was quite tall and, having to look up when speaking to him, she noticed that the long hairs in his nose hadn't been clipped.

To her left sat Schoya. Beside Schoya, Drugen was brooding. Beside Drugen sat his knights, Baron Ghenter and Lord Falconier—vigorous middle-aged men who roared with laughter at his chance remarks. They were already drinking heavily.

Candles flickered everywhere in a bewildering bedazzlement, on the table and mantelpiece, harpsichord, and even the floor. At the points of the compass, tripods cradled lamps of translucent alabaster, wicks ablaze in perfumed oil whose scent was drug-like. On one wall hung Drugen's long banner of wolfish-gray with its blood-red crest, on the rest the strangely disconcerting tapestries that provided another reminder of danger.

Shortly, servants appeared with steaming platters and tureens. Marta's heart leapt with anticipation, but then she remembered to be cautious. She could easily be poisoned, so she ate only what was offered from a common dish while nursing one cup of wine.

After supper, Falconier and Ghenter gave a drunken display of swordsmanship. Ghenter tripped over a chair leg and landed in the lap of a lady who feigned alarm. He growled and pretended to bite her neck. Marta had seen this kind of thing before—at home, sad to say—whenever Carissima was away and the courtiers drank too much and forgot themselves. However, Ghenter's act seemed a little too realistic.

Drugen asked Schoya for a song and accompanied her on the harpsichord. Her voice settled on the luxuriant opening chord like a lark on a bough while he played for her masterfully, passionately. When the song ended, Schoya returned to her place at the table, but he remained at the harpsichord and summoned a page, who hastened away then back with a guitar.

It was the king's! Marta glimpsed the checker-work back of rosewood and bone. She started to object but didn't carry through with this, waiting for a better time to open the battle.

As Drugen cradled the instrument and began to sing, he sought her gaze. She was startled and, despite everything, fascinated. Then she felt Schoya tense in the chair beside hers and, realizing what was happening, broke eye contact with Drugen. God forgive her—Gurnemanz was right! Drugen had an extraordinary power over others.

He finished the last sweeping chord.

The courtiers praised him.

Marta folded her hands on the table and promised the LORD that Drugen would never sing for her again. Before that would happen, she would smash her father's guitar.

The courtiers were chatting again, and Marta blinked as she studied them. Something seemed to be happening to her vision. They resembled animals—weasels and rats, apes and crows, and a long-necked crane—under some enchantment that enabled them to sit up and talk over wine after dinner. No! It *wasn't* her vision. She had heard stories about "changelings" and realized that *that* was what she was seeing. She shivered, squeezed her eyes shut, and then opened them again.

Drugen was just handing the king's guitar back to the page and studying Marta as he did.

"How did you like a song of the Zelhorn?" he asked.

She replied that the melody was beautiful but then went on to speak from the heart. "However, beautiful things put us under an obligation. They demand that we handle them carefully." She tried not to look at Drugen in any way that he or anyone else could mis-construe. "The king didn't play as well as you, but his style was pure."

Drugen smiled. "Was it?" He frowned slightly. "How old were you when he left home?"

"Old enough to know him well," she answered.

"What a pity, his taste for adventure. In many ways, he was remarkable."

Her heart raced with all she wanted to say, but she calmed herself. "His chief weakness was that he wasn't a good judge of character."

Drugen's eyes glittered as he took her measure. "Touché."

Falconier said something to him in Zelhornish; a discussion began between them that was entered into eagerly by Ghenter and Merl la Corneille.

Schoya glanced at them, as if making sure she wouldn't be over-heard, then said to Marta in lilting Zupish, "Majesty, please don't imagine you can match wits with my husband."

Her faint, somewhat odd smile was kind. She sipped from her goblet, and the hand that held it was small and adorned with rings. "Those who attempt to do this live only at his pleasure."

"Are you referring to the king, Lady Schoya?"

"To him and to others."

"Did you know the king?"

"Yes." Schoya sipped again and set her goblet down. "Long ago he ventured to my parents' home in the Eastern Marches. When he came to seek my husband, I did not see him. That happened... elsewhere."

Marta smiled. "I'm very grateful for your counsel."

Schoya looked at her pointedly. "I hope you will be led by it."

Marta raised her chin and said with confidence, "God shall lead me."

Schoya nodded; tears glistened in her eyes. "You are fortunate then," she said.

Marta leaned toward her, wanting to reassure her. "You too may be as 'fortunate.'"

Schoya shook her head. "Not I! I am one of those with whom God is angry forever."

Feeling sympathy, Marta put a hand on Schoya's shoulder. As she did, she felt the tiny protuberance that wasn't there on humans. Not wanting to reveal her surprise and thus embarrass Schoya, she kept her hand there.

"The Lord isn't angry forever with anyone but the unrepentant, Schoya," she said. "He loves and has made a way for you and your people."

"You speak of the cross," Schoya said in a sorrowful tone.

Marta smiled gently. "Yes."

Schoya's expression showed fear and pain. "It is not for such as us, the Vile."

Shocked by her choice of such a strong word, Marta stated her case in no uncertain terms. "But, Schoya, we are *all* vile in our sins. We must *all* call upon Jesus to be saved."

When Marta spoke the Name, many things happened. The atmosphere in the hall changed as if freshened by a breeze; Schoya looked at her with wonder, hope, and love; and the candles and the hearth fire and the flames, swimming on oil, shone more brightly but with a softer radiance.

Drugen, who was all but forgotten, said in a harsh, excited tone, "If you're going to discuss philosophy, I must join you!"

He returned to the table, snapped his fingers for a chair to be placed opposite Marta, and called for more wine. He sat smiling with a bitter look, a foot crossed on a knee and a thumb in the pocket of his silk vest.

Schoya said, "Please don't do what you mean to, Alexander. Leave this *innocent* alone."

He sneered. "But, my darling, she has spoken and must be answered."

Eyes shining, Schoya said, "*I* shall answer her."

He sat forward, glaring at her, and banged his fist on the table. "And *I* shall!"

She lowered her gaze and sat very still.

"No one speaks of God here except as a theoretical construct," he said. "As a straw man to knock down or burn or a doll to push pins in!"

Schoya looked at him. The air shimmered all around her. A glow fell upon Marta's gown, the table and its settings, and Ghenter's tipped goblet.

Schoya said, "If you don't stop right now, Alexander, I shall go."

Drugen opened his mouth, gaped at her, then slowly smiled.

She stood.

His face flushed with anger as he rose, leaned on the table toward her, and mouthed the words, "Go then!"

Her wings bloomed, sheer and glorious.

He laughed, but his laughter was short. "My beautiful, beautiful *butterfly!* Someday I'll pin you to a wall like a specimen or clip those hideous things!"

"Someday you will be sorry!" Schoya's lips quivered; her wings drooped then faded. "Imane shall be avenged!"

"So sad about *her*."

"—and Ariel shall—and Reba!"

At the mention of Reba, Drugen's countenance fell.

The courtiers had been laughing. Merl la Corneille was laughing so hard that he was holding his sides.

"Alexander! Alexander!" he cried. "If my niece continues to be obstinate, I'll peck her eyes out for you!"

Drugen lifted his lip in a sneer of pleasure.

With a tremor, Marta turned to Merl. His eyes were a bird of prey's; his nose, a beak. She gasped and put a hand out toward Schoya, but Schoya was gone.

Then, from the shadowy colonnade at the end of the hall, raucous cries arose—falsetto and basso. "*Hail!* Hail!"

Marta turned toward the sound, the knuckle of her index finger between her front teeth.

Drugen cried, "Better yet!" He picked up then dropped his chair to face the other way. He sat, slouching elegantly. His profile, usually handsome, was convulsed with anger and shame he was attempting to conceal.

A troop of actors exploded into view. A dwarf in a gilt crown was trying to stay in the saddle of a papier-mâché horse worn by two more of them. When the horse neighed then snickered, the courtiers howled and hooted.

The actor wearing the horse's head and forelegs knelt before Drugen, lowering the head so the dwarf rolled out of the saddle and onto his feet.

He straightened his crown.

A lordly-looking personage appeared, the folds of his cloak settling around his dark boots.

The dwarf drew his wooden sword and cried, "Submit to my authority or else!"

The lordly one unsheathed a sword of steel and said, "Never! For here I am lord in my own right!"

The dwarf and lord parried thrusts.

"Fie!"

"*Fiddlesticks!*"

The dwarf's crown was knocked off, and it rolled away. His sword was flicked from his grasp into the shadows, and he scurried after it with the lord in pursuit.

Drugen was chuckling but still discomposed; he raised his goblet to his lips.

Marta watched him, wishing that there was poison in his cup. Startled and guilty, she covered her mouth with a hand and silently prayed. Flight was the only thing left to her, but as she stood, her chair scraped noisily.

Everyone turned to her.

Ghenter stared, wolfishly.

Drugen looked around in his chair and said, "Of all the arts, I like drama best, Marta. It's the most *realistic*. Don't you think?"

Marta slipped her hand into her sash. A picture of Trimble scolding her flashed through her mind, but she dismissed this warning and drew the pistol. While she was shakily taking aim and trying to squeeze the trigger, Drugen reached her, forced her aim toward a bare corner, and then mashed her fingers against the grip until she relinquished her hold.

"That was foolish," he said with a look of triumphant hatred.

He summoned the guards and gave instructions. She and Trimble were under house arrest.

Suffering

The guards marched Marta upstairs. Below in the entryway, Trimble was shouting her name and arguing with someone. Punches were thrown, and a chair screeched and toppled. There was the sound of his "*Oof!*" and "*Uh!*"

The guards banged open the door to her room and shoved her inside. She glared at the last one to leave.

He glanced over his shoulder then whispered, "Forgive us, Majesty! You have friends and won't be forgotten."

He closed the door. She heard him barking orders, and then a key rattled in the lock. There was a sound of guards settling in chairs.

She went to the window and peered through a crack between the shutters. Others were coming out into the ward, lifting torches to light their way to the wall. Two of the strongest had Trimble in tow.

She rested her feverish cheek against the cold shutter. What had she done, and how would she mend it? She imagined Trimble saying she had only herself to blame—she had *let* Drugen provoke her—and now they were both in a kettle of fish.

She chewed a fingernail. Thank heaven she hadn't killed Drugen! She would now have murder on her conscience, and the truth might be beyond her reach.

Shivering, she went to a chair by the fireplace. The fire was dying, and no logs were laid by. As there was little chance that anyone would see to her needs tonight, she lay down in her dress and pulled the covers up. She prayed for forgiveness then turned onto her side. Tears slid over the bridge of her nose as she suddenly wished for Keyah.

Another dawn. I've thrown the shutters wide to watch a heavy, silent snowfall. I've neither seen nor heard anything more of Trimble. He must still be in the guardroom in the wall. Is he busy persuading his captors to release him and fight with him for me, or has he been silenced like the rest of the wintry world?

My door is locked from the outside, and my meals and a few logs for the fire are regularly brought to me. No one hints of what is to happen. So I, Marta Louisa Happstein, Queen apparent of Zuphof, am writing with my own hand to declare that, if I should die, Lord Alexander Montanus Drugen is responsible. Deal with him severely, for he also killed the King.

I must stop. Someone's turning the key...

Drugen was removing his court to his hunting lodge deeper in the wilds. The entourage of men on horseback and ladies in sleighs displayed both pomp and swagger.

Marta and Trimble were making the trip with the wagons and rearguard; she was riding an old stallion, which was lame and slow, and Trimble was trudging beside her. Just ahead, a cart carrying the bear in a painted cage bumped in and out of the ruts of the lane. The bear was headed for Drugen's menagerie.

Marta and Trimble were dressed in borrowed garb—she in a moth-eaten coat of dark, curly lamb and a too-large cap of the same make. Her grandmother, Queen Wilominna, had had such a coat, and Marta had snuggled her cheek against it on winter rides. Wilominna was now in heaven with the king. Could those in heaven see their loved ones in trouble in the world below? Trimble was wearing the canvas coat of a servant who had recently died. It was dragging as he walked Marta's mount along a lane between white-robed spruces. The wind scattered stinging drops from their boughs, and she tucked her chin into her collar.

Her mount had been hamstrung long ago. He halted frequently, lowering his huge, dark head. His coat was winter-thick, and the gloved fingers of Marta's manacled hands were entwined in his rough mane.

The company advanced slowly, and the courtiers broke up the trip by riding down the line, circling the wagons, and then galloping ahead. Ghenter and Falconier were amusing themselves by getting too close to Trimble. They finally managed to knock him down.

He got up somewhat stiffly and brushed himself off. "Isn't there a saying, mistress—'noblesse oblige'? But not everyone who calls himself noble really is."

Ghenter and Falconier wheeled their mounts with another kick of snow his way, then rode back up the line.

"We should be careful," Marta said. "There's no use provoking them further."

Trimble blew out his breath through his frosty mustache. "True, but it's tempting to tell them off."

The company was skirting a dense woods, the edge of the Forest of Zohemia, which hugged the lower slopes of the Little Kapstein. They entered the woods, and Marta and Trimble followed along a narrow track. The air was so crisp that she could hear Drugen hailing someone ahead.

They arrived at a broad clearing where Gypsies were encamped. Bright wagons, whose roofs were covered with thick quilts of snow, encircled a bonfire. The men of the camp approached Drugen and bowed deeply.

"It seems we're going to stop, mistress," said Trimble. "I'll help you down."

"I don't wish to get down! I want to get wherever we're going quickly."

"Drugen's master, for now." Trimble began to smile, winced, and blotted his cracked lips with a sleeve. "Here, take my hand!"

She took it reluctantly and slipped like a stone to his arms.

"*Oof!*" he exclaimed.

She tottered on her numb legs, straightened, and together, they hobbled to a group seated on logs set around the fire.

The ladies had been invited by the Gypsy women to get out of the cold in the wagons. Marta sighed. They would probably be given tea, perhaps cake. She squeezed onto the end of a log with Trimble and watched a Gypsy dish up a thick stew. Its aroma was mouth-watering.

Cups or bowls were passed to everyone except them.

Falconier tossed some bread to Trimble. "For the *dogs!*"

Trimble passed it to Marta and said so as to be overheard, "Don't let their rudeness bother you, Majesty! There are many ways to take an insult depending upon who insults you. When a devil does, take it as a compliment."

Falconier moved a hand to the hilt of his dagger.

Ghenter's lips parted over teeth that looked dangerous.

Trimble offered Marta a cup of the stew passed on the sly with a glance of fellow feeling by one of the Gypsies. She ate a little, leaving the rest for him. She was becoming terribly uncomfortable. Fighting tears, she scanned the clearing.

"*There's* what you're looking for," Trimble whispered as he pointed to a lean-to. "It looks like they've dug a trench."

He helped her cross the uneven ground, then waited at a distance.

Within the small disgusting space, faint with misery and hunger, she thought for the first time that death was certain. Her strength was fading, her faith faltering. She felt very small and totally insignificant—a snowflake dropping to a raging blaze.

Through the canvas, Trimble said, "Hurry! Drugen must want to get going. He's sending someone to fetch you. Get out here, and keep what's left of your dignity!"

She came out to a wind that buffeted.

Trimble offered her his arm.

"You've been a true friend," she said.

"Pih! You speak as though life were over. You'll feel better when we get where we're going."

As they approached the fire, some ladies were exiting a wagon. One was showing her palm to a friend while speaking excitedly. Laughter rode the air like the ring of sleigh bells.

Marta quickened her pace, her heart bumping a little. They'd had their fortunes read!

A young Gypsy woman, in a bright dress and a fur vest cinched at the waist, was with them. She turned as Marta approached and looked at her with eyes that were startlingly blue. Her glossy, black hair was banded around the forehead with a bright paisley scarf, and she was wearing a gold ring in one of her nostrils.

Marta halted, wrestling with her conscience, and then hastened forward.

Trimble caught up and said in a low voice, "You wouldn't be so foolish as to seek this woman's counsel? Of what use would it be? Her head is filled with nothing but mischief and nonsense!"

Ignoring him as she stared at the Gypsy, Marta was startled by Drugen's voice close to her ear. His breath was warm and smelled of spiced meat.

"If you want her counsel, I'll pay," he whispered.

His compelling voice was impossible to ignore. She turned to him. His gaze sought mastery of her. She looked away, thinking, *Perhaps I can use him as he uses others.* He pressed a ring into her hand. She closed her fingers around it and hurried to the Gypsy. The Gypsy glanced at Marta's manacles, then looked to Drugen. Whatever she saw in his glance freed her to take Marta's hand.

The ladies of Drugen's court stepped back to watch in silence.

Trimble huffed.

The Gypsy rubbed a thumb over Marta's palm, then looked at her with pity. She began to say something in Zelhornish. Drugen corrected her, and she went on in Zupish.

Her very blue eyes met Marta's. "Love is coming to you."

Feeling Drugen's gaze, Marta pulled her hand away. "Love is always coming in a Gypsy prophecy."

The Gypsy studied her with eyes that seemed knowing and friendly.

"You insult me, but no matter." She again took Marta's hand. "I will read for you, nonetheless. I see *this,* Majesty. There is no need to look for love, for it is looking for you."

Trimble turned on the Gypsy, scolding her in Zelhornish, then in Zupish. "If I had a whip, I'd use it! Your oracles are nothing but lies dressed in the rags of old sayings!"

The Gypsy stared at him with a look that wished to kill.

He turned to Marta. "Pay her, mistress, and get back on your horse!"

Marta dropped the ring to the Gypsy's palm. As it glinted there for a moment, she saw that it was a man's ring inscribed with characters like those carved over the doorway of Zuphof's synagogue.

Without looking at the ring, the Gypsy slipped it into the purse at her belt. "Love will come when it is least expected, perhaps disguised as hatred."

Marta stepped back and laughed with quivering lips. "Now I *know* that you lie. Do you think you can frighten or thrill me as you can these simpletons? Or are you perhaps in league with someone?"

The ladies stared and whispered. How lovely they seemed with their fresh faces framed by the lush fur of their hooded cloaks—but how wicked they were! They were like cats mewing and hissing around a bird that had dropped to the ground.

Trembling with fury and fright, Marta turned to Drugen and cried, "I know whose ring that was! Ariel's!"

Drugen's eyes darkened under his tall hat of astrakhan.

Trimble grabbed Marta's arm and hurried her toward her horse, then boosted her unceremoniously to the saddle.

Still trembling, she looked down at him. "Sometimes you go too far, Trimble! You must know your place!"

Immediately, she regretted her words.

He looked at her calmly. His face was streaked with tears that had frozen. "You say I must know my place. Sometimes that means checking your folly. Your tongue can have a keen edge, and they're not the sort to forgive."

Her chin began to wobble; she blinked.

"Didn't you see the mark on that woman's hand?" he demanded.

"I saw something...a star, perhaps—"

"She's been tattooed with an inverted cross. And you placed your hand in hers."

"I didn't see...I didn't know...God forgive me!"

Jaw clenching, he looked away. "The others are heading out. If you want to stay alive, watch what you say."

He led her horse instead of walking beside her.

At the end of the long day on the winter trail, the company was riding in silence. She and Trimble were plodding behind the wagon of provisions. He was once again beside her. She was famished, and the wagon was sure to be loaded with every delicacy: venison, smoked pickerel, caviar, liqueurs, and pastries. At the lodge, a hot supper and drinks would be awaiting Drugen and his hangers-on, while she and Trimble supped on what? A coddled egg would do for her, for she was almost too tired to eat. But would their needs even be met? To keep from being disappointed, she imagined being offered nothing at all.

As they climbed a rise, the pines gave way to birches. Through the fluttering, tattered bark of their trunks, the horizon blazed with fiery clouds that pillared a dark dome of blue and purple on which a single star shone. The star seemed to draw them on, in through gates on which lanterns glowed, and up a curving drive to the sprawling lodge and its longed-for comforts. For the others, this would mean servants and baths. For Marta and Trimble, this would mean at least getting out of the cold.

He helped her to dismount, and then they stood and waited for what was to happen to them.

He patted the neck of the old stallion. "This is your father's horse. Do you remember Nostratu?"

She shook her head and put a hand on the horse's dark, darkly-speckled withers. "Can that really be?"

"The brothers blessed him. That could have added to his years."

"How lovely that it was he who carried me! But Trimble, how did Father and the knights get up to the castle on horseback?"

"Remember what the abbot told you? The king and his men were heading for the Keistrel Pass."

"Ah, yes, I was forgetting."

"It's the only way into the mountains on horseback and would have been clear in spring. The abbot's statement sheds light on the events. It must have been *here* that the king confronted Drugen."

"That also agrees with something Schoya said."

Marta gazed about her. The ground beneath her feet, the evening star, and the lodge, all took on another aspect. She could almost feel that her father had been there.

"The Keistrel would have been blanketed with violets," said Trimble, "as the king rode confidently and joyfully up to the place of his death."

"Oh, Trimble, you have made me see him! How lovely to think of him as confident and joyful!"

"That was his way."

"So Drugen crippled Father's horse." Tears stung her eyes as she stroked Nostratu's mane. "He probably thinks such a mount suits me."

"No, his rule of thumb is simple expediency. Such a horse can't be ridden away. Nostratu has probably carried many a prisoner along this road."

Marta put her arms around the horse's great neck and whispered, "Blessed beast, you have served Father and me well! Eat your fill, and take your rest!"

Ignominy

Drugen was greeted at the door by his mistress, Isabay. She was holding a little girl.

Marta turned to Trimble and whispered, "This upsets me more than words can say."

"Don't let *him* see that it does."

The courtiers were falling over themselves to be the first to greet Isabay.

"Don't they have any sense of loyalty to Schoya?" Marta asked.

"Schoya is leagues away, and as you've probably noted, they live for the moment."

Drugen took his little girl in his arms and stepped through the doorway. The sight touched and yet troubled Marta for everyone's sake.

Shortly, she and Trimble were swept off to the stables, where the smithy cut their manacles. Trimble remained there to live and work. She was escorted to the lodge, where she was given a guarded freedom and a small room.

The rooms at the lodge were named for faraway places or jewels—anything romantic. *Perhaps Isabay named them,* Marta thought.

Marta's room in a turret was "The Room of Stars." She hurried across the small, frayed rug to the window. It was too narrow for escape. She went to the bed in the alcove and sat. The mattress was thin, and the alcove was hung with curtains that would be inadequate with only a tiny fireplace. Yet, somehow the room made her feel welcome. Had her father stayed here? Looking up, she found that the conical ceiling was painted with the mural of a night sky—blue-violet with luminous gray clouds and golden stars. The vision was soothing, and she tugged off her boots and lay down.

A genteel rap sounded on the low door recessed in an archway. A matron entered with a tray. She smiled kindly, and Marta sat up and smiled in return.

The matron asked her to be seated at a small table and set the tray there. As Marta nestled into the chair, the matron lifted the cover from the dish. Fragrant steam arose. How good the Lord was! He had given her exactly what she was hungry for: a coddled egg, buttered toast, and hot chocolate.

The matron curtsied and then said in very good Zupish, "My Lady Isabay welcomes you and hopes you will be comfortable, Majesty."

"Please thank her for me!" Marta tilted her head at the matron's command of Zupish and respectful demeanor. "Are you from the coast, matron? Your Zupish is excellent."

"I was raised in Blikstein."

The two embraced.

When Marta resettled and reached for the pot of hot chocolate, her hands shook, so the matron poured for her. As she did so, she kept glancing at Marta as if wishing to speak and finally said, "You have many friends here, Majesty."

Marta smiled. For one utterly happy moment, she felt that everything was going to be all right.

The matron went to the door, stepped into the hallway, then turned back with a hand on the knob and nodded.

Marta raised a trembling hand and turned to her supper. She bowed her head with the purest gratitude she had ever known and then took a fork full of tender-white, sparingly-salted, and dripping with scrumptious yolk with a bit of the buttery toast. She chewed slowly and sipped the hot, sweet drink, gazing at times at the ceiling of stars.

She exercised her limited freedom by exploring the lodge, peering at paintings, and examining knickknacks, observing the others as they gossiped or diverted themselves with cards or charades. She now understood a little Zelhornish and could speak a few phrases.

She would stray from room to room and come back to the others, sit on the edge of a chair, open and close a book, walk to a window to look at the snowy trees—wondering what in the world to do and speculating about what had happened here. The facts were few, like the dim outlines of furniture in a darkened chamber. Her restlessness prodding her, she would jump up and walk away again, glancing back at the others with contempt or pity.

The lodge seemed to be more of a home than the castle because of the child, Veronique. The rooms were in a state of comfortable disorder, with open books, toys thrown about, and cups with the dregs of chocolate on tables and window ledges. Waiting to be mended, Veronique's nightgown lay draped over a chair arm, and on the flags of the hearth in the back parlor, two pairs of slippers, showing the faint contours of feet, stood side by side. The paneled walls glowed with candlelight and echoed with the child's laughter. The fringed carpets showed a pleasing wear and tear. Isabay's taste was evident everywhere: in miniature portraits, jewel-encrusted enamel eggs, boxes painted with mounted knights and flying firebirds, and a blue plume placed beside a music box of gleaming cherrywood.

The lodge made Marta feel as if she was walking in the woods. Its beams, paneling, and woodwork seemed to run with sap, and the air was redolent of the firs that bordered the garden. When she climbed the stairs, the banister carved with nuts and leaves felt lovely beneath her hand. The spindles were carved with loping wolves that seemed to run along with her whenever she ran the stairs—she still did this occasionally, even here. "The Room of Bloodstones"—filled with long guns, bows, hunting horns, and trophies—seemed carved from the heart of an old, old forest.

Wherever she found herself, whatever the room or view, she would always think, *My father stood here and noticed this.*

One day, as she investigated, she met Isabay and Veronique, who were seated at a window seat on the broad landing. Isabay was holding the child so she could breathe on the panes and draw in the mist. At the sound of Marta's step, the two turned to her. Isabay smiled. Her smile was like Royal's, and she had the same dark hair, which she wore in a braid, entwined with ribbon, forward over her shoulder.

Isabay stood, inclined her head, and then bade Veronique curtsy to the queen. Veronique wouldn't comply, and Marta and Isabay shared a moment of laughter. Then, bidding Marta good day and taking Veronique's hand, Isabay slipped into a room and shut the door.

The click of its latch was gentle, as gentle as Isabay—gentle and graceful, and a bit like Carissima. Marta frowned at a surmise. Could her father have been drawn to Isabay? Had he *loved* her? Was this the reason why he stayed so long? If so, he could have made Drugen angry enough to kill him.

Shattered by the thought, and struggling against it, she sank to the window seat, where she was confronted with Veronique's tracings: a cat's head and two overlapping, lopsided hearts. The awful surmise lingered, growing into a feeling of certainty.

Lord, no, please!

When her heart at last grew quieter, her gaze focused past Veronique's tracings to a figure in the stable yard. It was Trimble! How wonderful to see him! He was exercising a horse and working up a sweat, it seemed; for his cap was pulled up off his ears, and his cheeks were rosy.

Suddenly, the horse shied, and Trimble held fast to the rope. At the same time, a sound reached Marta—a deep cry that had shattered the peace of the rustic scene; the bellow of a beast which she couldn't identify.

One evening, Marta was asked to join Drugen and his courtiers, who were performing a play that one of them had written. The off-color innuendos and awful snobbery were as plain as the nose on Trimble's face. How had her father endured such people? What had he found to keep him here?

Fretting, she asked for wine. So far, she'd succeeded in remaining vigilant, but tonight, she felt that it would be the greatest relief to simply get drunk and do something stupid, despite the warnings of conscience and commonsense—despite Trimble's warnings.

As the servant poured, Marta smiled as if to say to those around her, *I, your Queen—a Christian—am really just "one of you."* Though she knew that could never be so.

She quaffed the wine and held the goblet up again.

An actor with a hand to his heart was spouting something grandiose when Marta hiccupped, then began to giggle.

The actor paused in his lines.

Drugen turned to Marta. "What is so amusing?"

She covered her grin with her hand. "Oh, nothing."

He glanced at her drink, then winked at Falconier, who winked at him.

The awful play dragged on. Soon Marta began to snicker then chortled. The players stopped and stared at her.

Drugen turned around in his chair. "Perhaps *you* would like to entertain us?"

Her eyebrows rose, and she blushed.

"Dance for us, why don't you?" he said, getting to his feet. "The play can wait."

"Yes!" cried Falconier.

"Your father liked to dance," Drugen said. "In fact, he danced with Isabay. Did you know that? You dance, and I'll play, as I did for them."

Marta rose, swaying and clutching the back of her chair.

He held out his hand.

"Never!" she said. "For you killed him and have made yourself my everlasting enemy."

"Your father didn't consider me an enemy. Nor did he think of Isabay in that way. Ask her, why don't you?"

Isabay cried out and stood, knocking over her goblet of wine.

Drugen stepped toward Marta, gripped her wrist, and then pulled her toward him. She resisted. Holding her fast, he drew her to the fireplace and forced her face downward toward the leaping flames.

Isabay appeared and held his arm. "No, Alexander! I pray you, *no!* Just *forget!* You know she's been drinking!"

Marta straightened and, with a hand on the mantelpiece to steady herself, stepped back.

Drugen shoved Isabay aside with a look of fury, slipping off her shawl as he did. Then, keeping hold of the ends, he threw it around Marta, drawing her close and forcing her to look at him.

For a moment she did. She looked into his eyes, but only for a moment, for she was already dizzy and becoming dizzier. She found herself gazing into an abyss of madness.

"Dance!" he commanded.

She shuddered. The courtiers were whispering and murmuring—no one was laughing now—and the sound was like dead leaves twisting on withered branches in a wind that was unholy. Glancing around, she glimpsed faces possessed by malevolent sprites, faces changed into those of animals.

Sobered, frightened, yet sensing the LORD's nearness, she saw with her inner eyes a vision: drops of blood falling to a cup of golden wine. Had this something to do with her father? She herself had forfeited control in drinking. Had he done the same?

Then the wine she had consumed began to race in her veins. It overcame all insight and expanded her senses with an awareness of Drugen alone. She squeezed her eyes shut, but not before she had glimpsed something else hidden from ordinary perception: his childhood injuries and losses—the still bleeding wounds of the villain.

He seemed to sense that she had seen into him and released his hold.

Touched with pity, and weakened and disoriented, she raised her hands to dance.

His face changed. Contempt glowed in his eyes. He tossed the shawl to her.

She reddened to the roots of her hair and, while Ghenter roared with spite—his spittle was flying—she fled the room then raced the stairs.

With a bang that echoed, she slammed the door to The Room of Stars, leaned back against it with her fingers twisted in her hair, then slid to the floor, sobbing.

After a few moments, she crawled to the bed, searched, and found her New Testament beneath the bolster, and then she began to read with dimmed vision, with the moon to light the page.

The LORD Jesus was teaching in his hometown of Nazareth, in his own synagogue, when his neighbors became enraged with him, crowded around him, and pushed him toward the brink of a hill to cast him down. Suddenly, he passed through them and escaped.

Marta laid her forehead on the page. She wept. How many tears were in the bottle he was keeping in remembrance of her suffering? And she had betrayed him.

Sometimes Marta was allowed to get a little exercise outdoors. In a wood of imported lindens grown to a hundred feet, their snow-laden branches hung with oriental birdhouses, she discovered a cottage with closed shutters, crowned by a copper weather vane, a crowing rooster covered in ice. The cottage was never mentioned or visited, except by servants running out with meals and clean linens. Through a crack between shutters, Marta watched, unable to tear herself away, as a feeble-minded young man played the clavier with incredible skill. His nurse stood by him listening, watching with a tender but sad expression. The young man's face, hair, and build were reminiscent of Drugen's.

"Come away from the window before you break your heart," said Trimble.

Hands to knees, he rose from a seat on a barrel by the stable doors. She crossed through the lindens to him.

"It's best not to let Drugen catch you there," he said.

"Who is the young man?"

"His younger brother, Albert. He's hidden away. Another blight on the family tree, Drugen thinks. Heaven knows that is far from the truth!"

"I thought he might be Drugen's son by Schoya," she said.

"Drugen has given Schoya no children. They say he told her that she is his prize and his source of power, but he doesn't wish to bring more of her degenerate race into the world."

"And poor Schoya?"

"Mourned for a while, but is glad now, they say."

With growing curiosity, Marta asked, "And the rest of Drugen's family?"

Trimble folded his arms. "He was raised in a kind of *madhouse*. He's descended from a long line of madmen and geniuses. Both of his parents abandoned him. His mother left and his father shot himself. Do you remember Edelbert speaking of his grandfather, Basilides? It was Basilides who raised Drugen, and apparently Drugen was also his star pupil."

Trimble put his hands into his pockets. "Basilides was an alchemist. He tinkered with the natural world. Some say he even made a creature that was humanlike. The experiment ended in disaster when the monster turned on him."

Marta pulled her coat more tightly around her. "One almost feels sorry for Drugen!"

"Almost," Trimble said. "As a youth, Basilides had studied for the priesthood. Later he denied Christ. It was he who enrolled Drugen in the College of the Knights of Marcion, an order infamous for its occult rituals."

"I know we're all responsible for our actions," she said. "And yet, all of this must have affected Drugen. Basilides will have to answer to God. How awful his judgment will be!"

Trimble nodded. "It's *very* sad."

"And who is Isabay?"

His face lit up. "Isabay? What a sweetie! She's the only child of Gaspar, Count of Beaubois. She was fifteen when Drugen seduced her. They say she nearly died bringing Royal into the world."

The wind gusted, and Marta shivered. "Poor Royal!" She studied Trimble, wondering what else he had heard. "The servants certainly talk a lot! Have they told you how I embarrassed myself when I drank too much?"

"That's not the way the story is told. Everyone says how brave you were. And when you fled the room? Brava! You made Drugen look like a fool."

"*I'm* the fool. And he and the others are watching every foolish step I take."

"Poor souls. They're under his spell." Trimble frowned. "He's powerful. He has some power over you, mistress. Have you learned what that is?"

"I hate him, Trimble, but I can't help pitying him." She frowned as she rested a hand on Trimble's arm. "About that awful evening. Drugen said that the king danced with Isabay, but he implied more. What do you think happened?"

"The devil plays with our hopes and fears—a game of cat and mouse. *That* is what I believe about what Drugen implied. Keep your wits, and don't play the game. God will show you all he wants you to know, in his own time."

He took her hand. "You're no longer a pie-eyed child. You must comfort yourself for the loss of a sense of your father as...perfect. I don't mean to be disrespectful, but it's time to accept the truth that everyone falls."

"Father was no scoundrel!"

"Heaven forbid! But he had his weaknesses." Trimble looked sad. "As we all do."

Her tears began to fall. "That's very true."

He squeezed her hand. "It's a good thing Drugen put me where I hear the talk. Do you know what I learned? On his way here, the king killed a dragon."

She dashed her tears away. "How did he accomplish this wonder?"

"I wish I could say. But from what I can gather, Drugen was none too pleased."

"A man who slays a dragon is a certain kind of man."

Trimble nodded as he patted Marta's hand. "Have you been thinking of a way to escape?"

"I've been trying to learn what happened," she said. "And we're here for the duration. Winter's longer in the mountains. It would be nothing short of a miracle if the heir apparent of Sapore arrived with his troops before spring."

"With God's help, we could leave tomorrow. Alone." Trimble tightened his grip on her hand. "I feel I must say something. You've accepted your father's death, but there is more work to do. Lay aside your desire to know everything. And this business about pitying!

That's a one-way chat with the devil. End it, and we can leave in two shakes."

She pulled her hand away. "Drugen isn't the devil."

"He is the devil's man, and you had better stay clear of him as much as lies within your power."

She dropped her gaze, then again met his. "Yes, friend."

He gazed at her kindly. "God keep you, mistress! Let me know when you're ready. The LORD will help us get away."

Later, back in her room, she scrawled in her journal:

I've come to the place where my father spent his final days. Will I die here too? It is a place of frost and firelight, wind and snow, blunt speech and tormenting mystery. A slender pavilion of pleasure in the wilds. All is beautiful but fragile—an ornament of glass hung on a bough to dazzle the beholder. Any gust may make it plunge and shatter. With a covetous finger, the others lift this bauble to admire it—a world of pleasure they think will be endless.

I now understand the plight of Gurnemanz—poor man! But things are better for me, for I have Trimble, an ally who helps me see and sees with me. I'm unhappy with Father, but if he indeed betrayed Carissima, there must be more to the story. Trimble is right, however. We should try to escape at once. And yet perhaps just a little longer and I may know all.

Alchemy

Aside from their conversation in the stable yard, Marta saw little of Trimble and was grateful when he joined her and the courtiers for an outing to Drugen's menagerie. The two fell behind to speak alone. The weather was bitter cold, and the flagstone path was slick. Trimble took her arm, asked how she was faring, and explained life at the stables.

They rounded a bend and reached the conservatory. It was a five-sided structure, with large windows and a glass dome, and was painted lichen green with trim of deep red. They stepped inside, into a wonderful warmth, for there was a substantial stove with brass reflectors. The courtiers were already loosening their coats.

Drugen was providing introductory remarks about the exhibits. As he strolled past Marta and Trimble, he leaned toward Marta to say, "I think you and your friend will be interested in all there is to see."

Trimble raised an eyebrow.

Marta held firmly to Trimble's arm, steeling herself against the unpleasant things that were sure to come.

They toured the ground floor. The dome, swept after snow-falls, magnified the sunlight and forced exotic plants to burgeon and bloom. On the floor directly beneath the dome, a fountain plashed into a marble basin in which were lilies and hybrid carp of orange and white, and white and indigo. Hummingbirds flitted amongst the blossoms, and the place echoed with the warbles of songbirds. A heady scent of growing things perfumed the air.

Flanked by dwarf ornamental trees, a large cage stood beside a wall of glass. Sunlight shone upon its sullen tenants. Two large birds of a worn and dirty blue perched, facing each other, close together on a branch bolted inside the cage. Their crests lay flat against their heads, and the tips of their long, curling tail feathers brushed the droppings that littered the cage floor.

The birds remained utterly still, not even opening their eyes when Marta leaned to look at them. Some glory, which couldn't be caged, had departed from them.

"They have so little room!" she said.

"Do you know what you're looking at?" Trimble asked. "They're firebirds."

She was speechless as she studied them, her tears welling up. She blinked these away and stared. Her gaze had been captured by a jewel-like chameleon that appeared for a moment on a branch above the cage, then faded like a dream.

Drugen whistled, an unnerving sound that called her back to the world around her and its troubles. The company gathered to him and followed him up an echoing, spiral staircase of ornate ironwork.

"Watch your step!" he called.

An unusual scent, as evocative as the smell of kindled incense, wafted down.

Ghenter took the steps two at a time. Falconier drew one of the ladies along by the hand. As he looked at her, his expression was hungry. Reluctantly, Marta followed with Trimble, who sniffed the air and wrinkled his nose.

At the top, everyone gathered on a platform that divided the curved space below the dome. Before them, behind thick bars of bronze on a shelf of porphyry, lay a huge aerie constructed from hemlock boughs and sprays of mistletoe. An odd mixture of smells hinted at some alien presence.

Trimble whispered to Marta, "I think we should wait below."

Drugen turned to him. "She isn't leaving just yet, but you can go."

Trimble removed his cap, bowed, and backed away, glancing at Marta to seek her permission.

"It will be all right," she said but knew it wouldn't.

He started down the staircase, his steps ringing. There was a noise as if he had tripped in his haste.

Marta called to him anxiously, "Trimble, are you all right?"

His voice was strong as he answered, "If *you* are, mistress!"

The men of Drugen's court pressed forward to see the specimen identified on a plaque on the wall as "draconis cappadociae." The ladies huddled together, laughing nervously. Marta edged toward the staircase. Drugen stepped behind her and pushed her against the bars, stationing himself so that his shoulder pinned hers.

Upon the hemlock and mistletoe, partly camouflaged there, two large eggs with reticulated, pliant-looking shells were nestled. Remembering Edelbert's remarks, Marta murmured, "They must be from the Zelhorn..." Her glance flew above and all around, then she asked, "Where is their mother?"

"She warmed them with her breath, then departed," Drugen answered.

"And their father?"

Drugen glanced at the others, gathering their gaze for a joke. "I suppose that one could say *I* am their father now."

The courtiers began to laugh but stopped.

Drugen released Marta.

She reached for the railing of the staircase, saying, "It is foolish to keep such creatures for show."

Another cage facing that with the dragon eggs now came within her line of vision. Something like large leather sacks hung from high beams. One of the sacks expanded, and a bat stretched and revealed

jointed wings, fox ears, and a long snout. The bat yawned, showing its teeth. Its feet clutched and clutched as it repositioned on the
beam. Other sacks expanded and shifted, other wings drooped, other
faces appeared. Some of the bats jostled each other, and there was a
squabble. Wings unfolded, clacking, and teeth were bared.

Marta ran down, around and around the echoing staircase, hurrying to where Trimble stood, the fingers of one of his hands fiddling
absently with the latch on the firebirds' cage.

Drugen called down to her, "Who says I keep them for *show?*"

Marta nearly walked up Trimble's heels as she followed him out
the door.

"We'll try to see as little as possible, mistress," Trimble said as he led
her past the outdoor exhibits. They were keeping out of the way of
the courtiers, who had left the conservatory, pushed past them, and
then walked on ahead.

The courtiers paused and gathered at a railing overlooking a pit.
The sides were daubed with mud like those of a wasp hole. *Something*
was down there. Trimble moved so that he was standing in front of
Marta, peered down, and then led her forward.

"You can't see anything," he said. "But read the sign."

A foot-square plaque was attached to the stout railing. Inside the
railing, and overarching the pit, was a heavily-secured canopy of iron
bars. Around the pit, pintsized shrubs, dusted with snow and splattered with filth, struggled for life.

There was a stench. A sound of scraping arose from the depths.
The plaque glinted in the lowering sun.

ogre: This specimen is the result of careful
experimentation across many decades. Bred from
two very distinct species (the Great Bongo, mon-
arch of primates, and the White Rhino), its blood

*was mingled with other rare elements. The result
is a near replication of the orcus, a beast indig-
enous to the wilds of Zohemia.*

Basilides Drugen, Count of Mortomyr, 1585 c.e.

Marta tightened her grip on Trimble. "I think I've heard it sometimes at night."

"Let's go!"

The others were leaving, breaking away in small groups, while
expressing their disappointment that the ogre hadn't shown itself.
Trimble and Marta turned to go, but a sound recalled their attention.
He turned to look, and she peered past his shoulder.

Digits, then hands, then a horn as narrow as a needle at the tip,
then a head that was disproportionately small, then huge shoulders
appeared as the ogre climbed with something dangling from its
teeth—the carcass of a bat.

Trimble bolted, whisking Marta away. They ran, got turned
around in the maze of paths with the setting sun glinting off the
flagstones, then stopped for a moment to catch their breath, staring
at each other wide-eyed as they gripped each other's forearms.

After a moment, he slowly shook his head. "I've actually heard it
said that Basilides was a genius who was misunderstood by smaller
minds." He shook his head again.

Their breathing grew calmer. He took her hand and hurried her.
Around a corner, they found themselves standing before a smaller
cage of iron sunk into the rocky ledges of the hillside. The air smelled
of musk. The bear. When it saw them, it moaned. It had always sad-
dened Marta and was the last thing she wanted to see at the moment.
It rocked on all fours and swayed its great, pathetic head.

Trimble took a step toward the bars to study it. It swept a paw
toward him, turned away, and lumbered back.

"I have sort of a fellow feeling for it," he said. "I too am cooped
up."

"How it must hate that!" As Marta observed it, she was stunned by another surmise. "There are *stories,* Trimble! Of hags who turn people into swans...or toads..."

"Or bears?" He faced her. "I understand that to be an allegory of how the envious injure others with their malice."

"Yes, but in a world where sorcerers and dragons and ogres exist, such a thing could happen, couldn't it?"

She stared at the bear. On closer view, she noticed that it had been roughly used and remembered with a pang how Drugen had teased it.

Trimble bent to look into her face, confronting her with his baby blues. "You're not thinking...?"

"It *might* be."

There was a sound of boots crunching the snow, and Drugen stepped through a gap in the hedge of hollies.

"Perhaps you're right," he said, smiling as the bear began to pace and blow. "And this is someone under an enchantment, a hapless knight or foolish king."

Marta clenched her fists.

Drugen folded his arms and laughed.

Some others were approaching. Two of his courtesans, their faces flushed and their eyes bright, slipped through the break in the hedge and ran to him.

He draped his arms around them then waved a hand toward the bear. "Behold, my beauties, a prince under an *evil* spell!"

He smiled, and the women giggled.

"Who can it be, sir?" Snow White cried.

"Release him at once!" Rose Red commanded.

Drugen threw back his head and laughed. "Perhaps I will. Some-day. Have you seen the griffins yet?"

Rose Red almost purred, "We were hoping that *you* would show them to us."

Snow White sounded truly afraid. "You can stand between us and the danger."

"Stand between you and the danger?" Drugen smiled with one side of his mouth. "And why should I do *that?*"

The three laughed, turned away, and stepped through the hedge, which was darkening in the fading light.

Marta watched them go, then breathed more freely.

The bear had halted behind a patch of wild scratchings in the snow. Marta cocked her head in hope of deciphering these but found they revealed only that the bear was miserable.

Again, they hastened on and passed a high enclosure in which a small, white stag was feeding from a manger. It raised its head with a rack sheathed in velvet as white as ermine, then walked away, flicking its tail. Marta and Trimble commiserated over the creature's confinement and then ran on in the direction of the sun that seemed to be hastening to set.

At a corral with a dome of brazen bars, they paused. At first, the area seemed empty of all but shrubs and rocks and a few scattered bones. Then the griffins loomed, lying at length on their tawny haunches with their tails stretched behind. Their hides were resplendent with the sun's shooting beams.

Marta drew back.

The ice beneath her boots crackled.

The griffins cocked their heads at the sound. Great eyes, fierce glasses, pierced her and Trimble with sidelong looks. The outsized beaks and talons looked incredibly cruel. The tips of their tails twitched. One griffin stood and stretched both legs and wings.

"Monsters!" Trimble exclaimed. "If I had my sword I'd—!"

"What, *butterball?*"

"Send them back to the hell they came from."

The two raced on, helping each other over the slick places and hearing the ogre scream.

Safe in her room, Marta returned to her journal.

Today I learned what lies beneath the surface glitter and glamour the others covet so much. Trimble and I went along with them to Drugen's menagerie, and together, we passed the time looking at his monsters. Drugen isn't ashamed to appear as either a monster or a monster maker.

Gently, The Room of Stars led her into its calm. She paused, then wrote:

I hate but still pity him. His early life must have been a house of mirrors! He keeps a bear and has been trying to make me believe it is Father, probably to unloosen the hinges of my mind. Like the ninny I've proved to be for so much of the time, I was the one to suggest this fantasy. Then he toyed with the suggestion to rub my nose in it.

No. Father's death, though difficult to accept, is certain. What troubles me is the possibility that he was unfaithful. But aren't we all in some way? Isn't that why Jesus came to die?

Peace settled within her while the tender gleam from the ceiling of stars brooded all about her.

I must stay sober to watch and pray. And trust that, as the Lord has told us, there is nothing he cannot cover with his love. Love covers a multitude of sins. So then may it cover Father's! I wonder if, all along, Carissima has been so wise and loving as to do this. Mother, I forgive you! I hope I live to tell you so!

Her fragile hope fluttered like a fledgling. She set down these words:

I know that my mother and Tinka, the bishop and Cami, and all those at home who know the Lord Jesus as their Savior are praying. Victory will come. When it does and Drugen is finally vanquished, I pray that Trimble and I can free the stag and firebirds and bear. But who will put the monsters to the sword? Will it be Bartolo?

Infamy

She wanted to be sure that the evening's amusements were over, that she wouldn't be summoned. Everything had been quiet for a while, and she had heard Isabay come up the stairs to go to bed, but she needed to be certain.

She was standing with a hand on the newel post, peering over the staircase railing, poised to return to her room if she heard anything at all. She hadn't seen Trimble for several days.

A guard appeared at the bottom of the stairs. He started up them, noticed her, and said, "The master is asking for you, miss."

She requested a moment to fetch her shawl and returned to her room. She stood there almost breathless, as if upon the brink of some terrible change, and then looked at the ceiling of stars. It was dark, except for a faint glimmer of gold.

She prayed, tucked her Psalter in one pocket, a comb and handkerchief in another, then left the room, perhaps forever, and went down the stairs.

The guard led her by the arm to The Room of Bloodstones. Drugen was stationed at the fireplace, gripping an andiron as he stared into the flames. On the mantelpiece, a dark liquid shone in a crystal goblet. Over the mantel, pistols were mounted, their wood and metal gleaming in the firelight. Several of the courtiers were standing or sitting in the shadows. Marta approached Drugen, but not too closely.

He said, "You're soon to be crowned, I hear."

He glanced at someone, Ghenter, though all that could be seen was his heavy hand holding a drink and his white teeth.

"In May," she murmured.

"Ah, the merry month!" With the andiron, Drugen stabbed at the burning logs. "I'd like to celebrate with you." He held her gaze. "We *all* would, though it was Falconier's idea."

Beads of sweat stood out on the flesh over Marta's upper lip. Her hands grew clammy. "I don't see the point and must decline the invitation."

The edges of Drugen's mouth flicked downward. "This isn't an invitation."

"I must still say no. Thank you."

Falconier stepped into the light.

Snow White's face appeared from out of the shadows, like the face of the drowned rising to the surface of a dark pool.

The shadow that was Ghenter arose from his shadowy chair.

Marta didn't intend to, but her hand moved toward the pocket in which she had put her Psalter.

Drugen saw this. "What do you have?"

She didn't answer.

He snapped his fingers, then pointed. "Give it!"

Slowly, she brought out the Psalter and lifted it toward her lips, but before she could kiss the cross on its cover, Drugen snatched it. He rifled through its pages, shook them out, and then cast it into the fire.

She screamed and crouched by the fireplace, reaching for the fireplace shovel to rescue it.

With his boot, Drugen pushed her away.

Flames licked at the slender volume, then began to devour it.

"Please!" She knelt as she implored. "*Please...*"

"Please?" The line of Drugen's lips was thin. "Tell me why I should please *you*, Marta, when we are everlasting enemies?"

He jabbed the Psalter deep and flipped the cover open.

One after the other, the pages curled and blackened. She hung her head and closed her eyes, weeping as she remembered the bishop's warning, and begging the LORD to impress upon him and Cami, Carissima, and others her desperate need.

Beyond the fragile refuge of her lowered eyelids, the others began to move around. Someone grabbed her arm and raised her to her feet. She looked. It was Ghenter. Though something about his face had changed, it was he!

He continued to alter before her very eyes, and she cried out, "LORD Jesus, save me!"

Ghenter's great paw came down backhanded across her mouth, and she tasted blood.

The men threw on their coats and took her from the lodge with only her shawl, which quickly fell away. Turning her head, she saw a few of the ladies watch from the doorway. One of them stooped for the shawl and rolled it up.

She was marched into the night. The moon, serene and tender, was looking away at the sun that couldn't be seen.

Ghenter's laughter erupted.

Falconier uttered words Marta tried her best not to understand.

Merl la Corneille threw his head back and screamed as if from the heights.

From its pit, the ogre roared.

A sleigh without horses awaited her. The men threw a horse blanket around her, shoved a crown of prickly holly onto her head, and set her on the seat. Falconier blew a staccato blast—interrupted by chuckles—on a hunting horn, and Ghenter gripped the shafts of the sleigh and took off with it in tow, chuffing like a beast of burden as he pulled. When he turned to mock Marta, she saw a bestial countenance and deadly fangs. She sank back into a corner with her hands over her open mouth.

"Wait! Wait!" Falconier cried, looping the belt of the horn over a shoulder, then pulling a flask from his pocket.

He uncorked the flask. It was passed from hand to hand through the crowd, spilling some of its contents. Someone tipped her head back while someone poured the liquor down. She knew about this drink, for she had smelled it on the breath of a corrupt servant at home. It was *adder's tongue*. She tried to push the flask from her. She kept as much of the liquor in her mouth as she could, then spat it out. They made her swallow more. She choked. As the men jostled, the sleigh tipped, then fell back onto its runners.

Merl climbed aboard, putting an arm around her. She turned her face aside and prayed that she wouldn't be violated. His face drew nearer.

Suddenly, Drugen pushed through the crowd and cried, "Enough!"

Merl jumped down from the sleigh.

Marta let her breath out in relief, but Drugen reached into the sleigh and dragged her out, then shoved her along the path toward the stables. The wraithlike branches of bare trees spun overhead. She tripped and fell, and her hands were cut on the icy gravel.

Drugen yanked her up and drove her on. The other men were keeping back—thank God! Her heart filled with gratitude and then courage. Perhaps she could try to...She slipped from Drugen's grasp and ran a few steps.

A hand like cold steel clamped around the nape of her neck. He hissed in her ear, "How far do you think you'd get? In this cold? In a world of winged furies?" He licked his lips. "And what would become of *Trimble?*" He said this name with the utmost hatred.

Marta quickly moved a hand toward the sword in Drugen's scabbard.

He wrenched her arm behind her back. Pain shot through her arm to her shoulder.

"Don't think...you're any match...for me!" he said and tightened his grip. "Not even your father was...the hero...the white knight...the *saint!* I killed him not far from here, you know, over Isabay!"

All Marta could think was that Trimble was at the stables and that she was going to him—that somehow she would make it to him and safety. She kept up, though at times she felt like a puppet jerked this way and that.

They reached the stable door.

Drugen pounded on it.

Trimble opened it, and Drugen pushed her toward him.

"I haven't decided the fate of your *queen*," he said, took a breath, went on. "For now, she can room with you and the other beasts."

As if by some deeper and unknown enchantment, Trimble loomed tall and stepped in front of Marta.

"If you've harmed a hair of her head, I'll—!" he said in a voice that menaced.

Drugen glared. "You'll do *what*, fool? *Pray?*"

"My faith, as simple as it is, is a match for your darkest sorceries!"

Drugen studied him, then turned and walked back along the path toward the lodge. A long shadow passed near him, and he drew his sword and hurried.

Trimble kicked the door closed and then bolted it. "The very *devil!*"

Marta fell against him, murmuring into his shirt, "Please don't, Trimble. You're frightening me!"

He put his arms around her. "Mistress, forgive me." He held her. "Hush! Hush. I'll keep you safe, if I have to give my life."

As she vomited into a bucket, Trimble held her hair back. Someone brought a towel and basin of water. Clumsy hands used the moistened towel to wash her lips and cool her feverish forehead.

As she sank against a bale of straw, a sprig of holly tumbled from her hair.

She closed her eyes.

Voices whispered.

It was Trimble saying, "She's fallen asleep at last. Leave her here for now."

Someone else offered, "Cover her with this."

A third voice chimed in: "Put this pillow under her head."

Trimble placed the pillow. Someone laid a coat over her. She tried to open her eyes. Faces appeared, then faded.

Camaraderie

Someone was gently shaking her, tenderly calling her out of dreamless sleep.

Trimble.

From behind him, another face under a shabby hat, and with a ragged silver beard, studied her with a concerned look.

Someone else, hidden from view, said, "Thank God that Peter didn't live to see this day!"

Marta sat up, smoothing her disheveled hair. Who was speaking of her father so familiarly yet with such genuine affection?

The stranger in the shabby hat smiled. If only he would step aside so she could see the one who had spoken!

She managed a polite, "And who is this, Trimble?"

Trimble rested a hand on the stranger's shoulder. "Mistress, allow me to introduce Gaspar, Count of Beaubois. Isabay's father."

Marta reached out a hand to Gaspar in surprise and sympathy.

With an expression of great sadness, he raised it to his lips. "Majesty, if only we were meeting under happy circumstances."

She smiled. "Meeting a friend is a happiness in itself."

Trimble squeezed Gaspar's shoulder.

The two men stood aside, and the other man came into view. He was rough clad, wearing a felt cap from which unkempt, salt-and-pepper hair fell to his broad shoulders. His eyes were badly scarred, and he appeared to be blind.

Trimble said, "Mistress, I believe there's no need for an introduction."

Puzzled, she shook her head. "No, Trimble, I think you must be mistaken."

Then the man stood up. The years fell away. She was a little girl again, and a knight was leading her on his charger in a courtyard where scarlet and gold leaves were skipping over the cobblestones. A lock of his thick, straight, brown hair blew across his eyes. His eyes were warm brown, his smile warm and real. Sir Thomas of Fredersberg!

He stepped toward her, his hands raised to find his way, then knelt and lifted his blind gaze.

"Thomas?" she murmured, as if dreaming.

He removed the cap from his mussed hair, his gaze flicking from side to side, then coming to rest. "Yes, Majesty."

She began to weep, took his hand, and chafed it. "Praise God!" Tentatively, she touched his cheekbone below the eye. "But what happened to you?"

He lowered his head, jaw clenching, then raised it again. "An and-iron heated in the flames."

"There's no need to say more. I know who did this. I'm so sorry!"

He kissed her hand, then made his way back to his place near the woodstove.

A deep sigh escaped her. How good the LORD was! Above, on a rope, shirts and socks were drying. All around, bales of straw and odd pieces of junk furniture were arranged into a snug living space. In a wink, she had been transported back to the world of ordinary things, inhabited by ordinary people, safe people—some who even loved her. In the midst of tribulation, she had been given the gift of friendship.

Trimble quietly led her past the men, lifted a coat from a nail by the door, and gave it to her. She threw this around her, then walked out with him into Drugen's domain transformed. Every trace of the mischief of the night before was erased by a fresh fall of snow.

Trimble pointed out the privy, then climbed to the far side of a drift. She went inside the cramped, smelly place but didn't weep or complain. Her joy and hope had been renewed. When Trimble began to sing to ensure her sense of privacy, she even laughed.

Returning with him to the stables, she settled by the stove with the men. They breakfasted companionably, and the only egg was offered to her. After their meal, Thomas brought out a dog-eared copy of John Calvay's translation of the New Testament and held it out toward the place where Trimble was seated.

Trimble turned the pages, found what he wanted, then began to read. "'Behold, I give you the authority to trample on serpents and scorpions, and over all the power of the enemy, and nothing shall by any means hurt you. Nevertheless do not rejoice in this, that the spirits are subject to you, but rather rejoice because your names are written in heaven...'"

After sleeping the day away, she awoke to the sound of wind in the rafters and the aroma of stew. Atop the stove sat a blackened pot simmering with tidbits of rabbit, a rich broth, and chunks of carrot that hadn't been properly scraped.

Trimble dished up a heaping bowlful for her. She overcame her fastidiousness with gratitude. She sipped some broth and then asked Thomas, "Do you remember walking me on your horse in the castle courtyard? It was a sunshiny day in autumn."

He carefully lifted his bowl with both hands, in gloves with the fingers cut away, and blew on the stew to cool it.

"I do, Majesty, perhaps better than you." His tone was warm.

Marta smiled, remembering a joy that would always be hers no matter what happened. "My parents were watching," she said. "Father had his arm around Mother." Her smile widened.

Thomas gestured with his spoon. "She was going to have a child."

Marta started. "Yes, the child they lost. I'd almost forgotten."

"The prince," Thomas said.

She bit her lip and nodded, then took a deep breath. "So, my brave knight—friend of the king! What can you tell us about your gracious master? Was he well? Was he happy on that fatal trip?"

Thomas smiled as if seeing him. "He was. Though for him, it was always the merry month of May."

He took a spoonful of stew, chewed, swallowed, and scraped up more. "The king was singing as we rode along. Then too we had tracked and slain a dragon and he was drunk with joy. Its horns were slung from his saddle as we came up to Drugen's."

"He came here merrily, then—in friendship not war?"

"I wouldn't say friendship." Thomas's expression grew stern. "But in hope of persuading the friend of his youth. But he had planned, if Drugen wouldn't be persuaded, to take him into custody."

Afraid of the answer, Marta hesitated before asking, "What happened to the other knights?"

Thomas's pained expression showed that the memory cut deeply. "Most were killed. A few deserted." He fell silent.

Marta was angry. "And you were left behind *alone?*"

Without any rancor in his tone, he answered, "I was a liability. Don't be too hard on the others. But I wasn't alone, Majesty. The king was still alive then."

She brushed a tear away. "What were his plans, his aims?"

"In the end, just to make it out alive." Thomas tipped his bowl to drink the broth. "And he would have—and would have taken me with him—but he had put off escaping. He had his reasons, but the day came when it was too late for him to do anything but die with honor."

"Did he die with honor?"

Thomas felt for the bricks beneath the stove, then set his bowl down. "I wasn't present, Majesty. We'd been separated. All I know is that he fought Drugen and was mortally wounded."

Marta had forgotten her bowl of stew, and it began to tip.

Trimble steadied her hands around it, saying, "Eat."

Obediently, she took a little more.

Thomas went on. "Those who knew all the facts were afraid to speak. Still, something was in the air. For whenever the king was mentioned, in a whisper, it was with respect and awe."

Marta slowly smiled. "Thank you, Thomas, for your service to him!" She turned to Gaspar. "And you, Count, did you witness anything?"

"I wasn't here at the time," said Gaspar. "However, I know what happened. Isabay told me." His gray eyes, earnest and empathetic, held Marta's. "Your knight is being careful of your feelings, but I'll tell you the truth. Shall I?"

He studied her.

She nodded.

He said, "From the moment the king arrived, he showed concern for my daughter and her child. He found an opportunity to speak with her alone, counseled her to leave Drugen, and offered his help. That was when his knights were still with him. He must have felt able to fulfill such a promise. If she had gone with him then, when they first spoke, both might have escaped. But she took too long to consider his offer."

Gaspar set his bowl down. "And Drugen had been watching them. He could see that Isabay admired the king, and he sensed the king's concern for her. He forced Isabay to reveal what had passed between them and then, in a perverse kind of jealousy, encouraged their relationship with his subtle arts—toying with the two while planning his revenge."

Gaspar paused.

Marta sat trembling.

Trimble took away her bowl. "Perhaps that's enough, Count."

Marta turned to Trimble. "But it isn't, my friend. I need to know."

Gaspar said, "Then you will forgive my candor, Majesty, when I tell you that the king and Isabay became lovers."

Marta looked down at her hands lying open and empty in her lap. "I was afraid this was so."

"However, the king repented—"

She looked up, heart pounding.

"—and ended the relationship. Isabay was stricken, and Drugen was angrier than ever. How he mocked the king's repentance!"

"If, as you say, it was the king who ended the relationship, why did he fight Drugen over Isabay? That is what Drugen told me."

Gaspar seemed to make an effort to smile. "The king fought him to secure her freedom."

Marta sank back, overwhelmed but grateful. The pieces of the puzzle fell into place with a holy symmetry. She started to smile, then stopped.

"The king's death, Gaspar. Was it quick?"

"He lingered, Majesty." Gaspar took her hand. "But Drugen's aunt, Dame Anna, she who looks after his brother, attended the king. She's an excellent nurse and a godly woman."

Tears coursed down Marta's cheeks. "Where is he buried?"

"In the grove of lindens. In winter, the grave is hidden, snowed under. But in better weather, it's easy to find, for it is marked with a cross. Isabay saw to this, and somehow Drugen has never dared to remove it or desecrate it as he has so many other things. He seems almost afraid."

Marta rested her forehead on her arms upon her knees, weeping with grief and joy. The king's dear face had become, once again, very clear to her.

Trimble put his arm around her.

She looked at him. "Why didn't you tell me, Trimble?"

Gaspar kept firm hold of her hand. "He too is learning the whole story for the first time."

Marta put her other hand in Trimble's and squeezed his.

"Peter is with the Lord," said Thomas. "The death with honor you asked about, Majesty? None of us witnessed it, but we are all certain that that is the way it was."

Her tears streamed. She couldn't stop them, for they came from a well deep inside. After a little while, she wiped her face, blew her nose, smiled tremulously. She felt such sympathy for these men, all of whom had suffered unjustly with few complaints.

"How long have *you* been here, Count?" she asked. "And why are you, Isabay's father, quartering in the stables?"

"Five years ago, Isabay wrote, asking me to bring her home." Gaspar shook his head. "When I arrived, she had changed her mind, for she was going to have another child."

"Veronique! She's a darling little girl!"

Gaspar smiled. "She's the image of her mother at that age." His smile fell. "Isabay was little more than a child herself when Drugen, as a guest in my home, seduced and carried her away.

"You ask why I'm playing the hostler, Majesty? Because I couldn't hold my tongue. My frankness landed me here. And Drugen enjoys humbling me."

She thought, *How concerned he must be for those he loves!* She leaned toward him. "There's no way to leave?"

He shook his head with a firmness that showed he wouldn't change his mind, no matter what the cost. "I won't leave without Isabay and Veronique, and Isabay must be the one to decide to go. While I await her change of heart, I try to play the guardian angel."

"May I ask what happened to your own men?"

Anger flared up in his eyes but died away. "They fled when my champion, Guyon, was killed in single combat with Falconier."

"How awful!" She squeezed Gaspar's hand.

"Yes, their treachery rankles." Gaspar looked thoroughly weary. "But my chief heartache is that my wife died in my absence. Isabay was our only child, a girl who loved whoever seemed to love her. That is her weakness, and it has been a crueler master than Drugen himself."

Marta lowered her gaze.

Gaspar said, "Please pray for her and Veronique."

She looked up. "Of course. Of course I'll pray!"

He rested his elbows on his knees, locking his fingers and rubbing a thumb over the thumb of his other hand.

"I pray earnestly for Drugen's wife," he said quietly.

"Poor butterfly," said Trimble.

The wind picked up, rattled the doors, and threw them wide. Freezing wind and flurries rushed in upon them.

Trimble and Gaspar put their shoulders to the doors to close them and slid the bar across.

Shivering, Marta knelt by the stove to warm her hands. "It's really growling out there!"

Trimble said, "Hopefully it's winter's dying breath."

She had braved the weather to run to the privy and, hurrying back, had settled with the men, all of them bundled in coats and blankets near the stove.

Gaspar approached, holding out what looked like a slender, hand-written manuscript. The writing scrawled over pages bound at the top corner by twine passed through slits, probably made with a knife, and then knotted.

"This is for you, from Isabay," he said.

Marta held the pages close. "Thank you, and please thank Isabay!"

"There were other papers the king left, including letters under the Royal Seal for the Queen Mother and you, dictated on his deathbed to Dame Anna. Drugen burned those. After the king's death, Isabay found a portion of a manuscript hidden in his room."

Marta trembled with fury.

"Don't allow Drugen to trouble your peace," Gaspar said. "Read!"

She quieted her spirit and nodded slowly. He went back to his chair, and she sat for a time, simply holding the pages to her.

Trimble got up to bring a lantern closer.

"Thank you, friend," she murmured.

"Don't read too long, *skinny*. You'll hurt your eyes."

She smiled gently, and he returned to his place by the stove to discuss the weather with Thomas and Gaspar.

Leaning, she let the light from the lantern fall onto the pages. There was no title page, but on each page in the upper right were the words "Parzival Tempted by Peter Happstein." At the bottom of each, a tiny page number was scribbled in pencil. The text on the last page broke off in midsentence.

How strange it was to see her father's name written in such plain fashion! Again, she held the pages to her. Here was something of his— his words, his hand, perhaps his story. The words began as though continuing from a previous page.

—of his holy venture, we find Parzival detained by the Necromancer's maidservant, the Sprite of the wood. The setting: a hill rising out of a dense woods through which a torrent races and facing a cliff on which the Necromancer's castle stands:

PARZIVAL SPEAKS:

" While trekking the vale below,

I came upon a wild apple tree

felled by lightning. Without fruit,

it was twice dead. It seemed like

a portrait of my own soul..."

THE SPRITE ANSWERS:

" Knight, you are simply tired

203

and can go no farther.
Delay your quest
to rest a while with me!"

PARZIVAL:

"Tempt me not, Sprite!
For I go to gain the cup of wood
hallowed by the touch of Christ,
and the lance that spilled his blood
and holy is because of this!
Then shall I rest in deeds well done,
my quest attained
for the weal of the world."

FROM HER SEAT IN THE GRASS, THE SPRITE SMILES SADLY,
SLIPPING HER FINGERS INTO HIS.

"Beware, my lord!
Such unalloyed goodness
will drive you mad!
Choose rather this leafy bower
and its blooms! Come!
Here, be soothed of
your too-high and troublesome quest and
thoughts which punish you to risk all
for the unreachable!"

PARZIVAL HANGS HIS HEAD. HIS SWORD TRAILS IN THE GRASS.

HIS SHIELD SHINES BUT DULLY.

"Pity me, Sprite! I'm only a man!
Alas! Already the vision fades..."

HE RAISES HIS HEAD.

"But perhaps, as I persevere,
It shall return..."

HE GAZES DOWN AT HER.

"But your small hand in mine
brings such blessing of human warmth
that I am tempted to lay aside my shield and sword
and forget everything in your embrace."

THE SPRITE:

"Yes, forget everything...everything....!"

PARZIVAL SHAKES HIS HEAD AS HE PEERS INTO THE DISTANCE.

"Nay, Sprite, for the mist dispels!
Beyond those heaven-blasted trees
on yonder cliff, I see
the keep of the Sorcerer—
foul thief of cup and lance."

HE LOOKS HEAVENWARD.

("Lord, assist me in my task!")

Maria Tatham

HE SWEEPS HIS GAZE, LISTENING.

"Hark! From some chapel,
hidden in the vale below,
comes the tolling of sacred carillons.
And there—on that nearer prominence—
a messenger from heaven stands,
his boots in the blackened bracken.
Sword drawn, wings raised,
he summons me. Lead, O captain!
my courage rekindles!"

THE SPRITE LACES HER FINGERS MORE TIGHTLY IN HIS.

"I hear naught of sounds most holy.
Though there, on that low hill,
someone seems to beckon...
Ah! A shadow passes over
his countenance and wings.
They darken! I fear he is
an angel from a crueler region,
whose sword shall mean loss!
Stay until he wheels for hell!
You are too simple for
such terrible things!"

PARZIVAL:

"Nay, Sprite, I go!
For in this grip of flesh and blood,
I hold a sword with a cross in its hilt.

It shall cleave a demon or salute an angel!"

THE SPRITE MEANS TO HOLD HIM, BUT PARZIVAL GOES.

"Adieu, Sprite, whoever you are,
disguised as beauty beyond compare!
By heaven's will, none may stay
Heaven's fool!"

THE SPRITE CRIES:

"Wait, knight! I will go with you!
Too long have I had this monster
for my master! I go to gouge his eyes
with these two little thumbs!"

PARZIVAL CRIES AS HE FLIES FROM HER:

"I am not...upon...hell's quest!"

THE SPRITE FOLLOWS, CRYING:

"I am well-rebuked, knight!
But shall...go with you...
for the good!"

Marta lowered the manuscript to her lap. She glanced around. The world seemed dull and blank after her sudden, swift journey into her father's noble-hearted thoughts.

Trimble coughed.

She looked at him and the others. They must have been watching her, for they looked elsewhere, as if embarrassed.

"It's all right," she said. "Everything is really and truly all right."

She closed the shutter of the lantern, lay down, and covered up, while the men talked on.

Perhaps many are praying for me and Trimble, she thought. She sensed their prayers holding her up so that she felt, now for a moment, as if her feet would never touch the ground again.

Lord *Jesus, thank you for the bishop's prayers—and for Cami's! Wise, funny Cami! Thank you for Mother's, Kikki's, Betsy's—Bartolo's! Help each one! Thank you for Tinka's! I know she prays, so she must be praying now. Remember the time I found her on her knees in tears? When she arose in haste, she looked serene.*

Thank you, Lord, *for all their prayers! Help them—and young Timka! Help little Jan, who always seems to be sick! Help those others, particularly Ester, for whom I don't want to pray. Help me obey you, for you command us to pray for our enemies. I must pray for Drugen then too. To pray for him seems a mighty task that only you could undertake. But I can do this much—pray that it shall no longer lie within his power to harm others.*

She'd been fast asleep before Trimble opened the squeaky stove door to feed the fire. Watching, she saw him glance at her and smile. As he stood again, he grunted, and his knee cracked. She snuggled deep into her blanket, savoring the sense of security she felt because he and the other men were near.

Soon, she slept and dreamed.

She was journeying to visit Carissima's aunt, whom she had never known in waking life but whom she knew and loved in the dream. She was traveling by open carriage with a single servant. She could see his ample back where he sat perched in front of her on the driver's bench. They were riding through low, wooded hills. The beautiful trees were aglow with every poignant shade of autumn. At each bend of the road, fresh vistas met her, filling her with joy and a nameless longing, both for that place and for something or someone. Everything was haunted by this joy.

She was pulled from the dream by someone ordering, "Wake her now!"

It was Drugen's cruel but mellifluous voice.

Strong hands raised her to her feet and maintained their irksome grip. By lantern glow, she saw Drugen's guards looking ashamed, and Drugen, cloaked in furs, with his hat tilted over eyes alive with spite.

Trimble was on his hands and knees, blood flowing from a gash at his hairline, and Gaspar lay facedown with the boot of a guard on his back.

Thomas rose onto one knee and stared. "Have you no fear of God, Drugen? She is your queen!"

"Of what use are titles to the blind and dispossessed?" Drugen said, then turned on his heel and went out.

The guards pulled Marta along behind him. She snatched the coat from its nail and pushed her arms into the sleeves.

In the yard, dogsleds waited. At Drugen's approach, teams of wolves lifted their long muzzles from basins filled with something dark and thick.

Gesturing toward Trimble, Drugen commanded the guards, "Keep hold of that one. Never underestimate him!"

They hurried Trimble so that he stumbled and groaned. A guard struck him with the flat of his sword.

Frantic, Marta pulled away from the guard walking beside her, glaring so fiercely that he let her lag behind to wait for Trimble. Weeping, she put her arm around Trimble's shoulders. He put a shaky arm around her waist and leaned on her for support.

"Are you all right?" she whispered.

He grimaced, then studied her face. "If you are, yes!"

The two were pushed to one sled, Gaspar and Thomas to the other. She boarded behind Trimble, and Drugen raised a whip.

The other driver—those were Ghenter's broad shoulders— turned to await the signal from Drugen. By the light of the moon, she saw the werewolf's beetled brow and prominent jaw. Crying out, she shoved her face against Trimble's shoulder.

Drugen lashed his team. They took off through the shadowy lindens, went past the darkened conservatory, then through a gap in the hedge. In the open, he whipped them again and jumped onto the runners.

The stride of the wolves lengthened on open ground and slowed to plunge through trees. Even there, Drugen flailed them. Snow stung Marta's face, and again, she hid it against Trimble.

When she next looked up, the teams were racing single file on a path beside a lake that looked gray and ominous.

They began to climb.

Drugen lashed in a sort of frenzy.

The wolves came onto a rise, poured over it, and then raced down a long decline toward a place where the ground seemed to end.

He cracked the whip, and the team leapt out into nothingness. The sled seemed to fly, then dropped, skidded, and raced on. Before them lay dim open reaches rolling away toward mountains mottled with trails of ghostly white.

The werewolf pulled his sled alongside Drugen's then swept ahead.

Drugen urged his team on with shouts and cracks of the whip. They were nearly flying now over vast reaches of snow dotted with dark copses that seemed to crouch and cling.

The werewolf shifted his weight and brought his sled across Drugen's path.

Marta opened her mouth in a soundless cry.

They entered a village. The pace slackened a little. They drove past moonlit walls like papier-mâché and windows like eyeholes in a mask. At a bridge of stone, the path bottlenecked. The werewolf cut Drugen off and took the lead, and the teams climbed on a track between trees whose branches lashed them.

At last, they dropped over a ridge to a glen—a great, quiet bowl of snow studded with the vague, distorted shapes of boulders and surmounted by falls that had frozen. An ice-covered pool stood in the midst, and over and above loomed the immense Zelhorn.

Drugen reined in his team, leaning for a moment to catch his breath, then grasped the collar of Marta's coat, along with a fistful of her hair.

She screamed and put her hands over his, trying to pry his fingers loose. He struck her, then dragged her from the sled and shoved her forward. Objecting and frantic, Trimble hurried to catch up.

Drugen unsheathed the sword and faced him. "Take the lead now or she dies!"

Trimble trudged ahead, fell down, and got up.

Drugen pushed Marta along the line of wolves, who snapped at her coat.

"Drugen! Drugen!" she cried. "How did you come to *this?*"

He pushed her. "Don't...be childish. *Move!*"

With his lash, the werewolf was prodding Gaspar and Thomas up some ledges toward the mouth of a cave. Thomas stumbled, and Gaspar steadied him. Trimble followed them, turning often to look at Marta.

She kept moving. Behind her, Drugen was still breathing raggedly.

Finally, he said, "Here, you will at last learn all you need to know!"

Darkness

"Mistress, you need to be prepared for the worst. We may die here—a death that will test your faith."

"I know that, Trimble."

Stretching her chain to its limit, she crawled to the mouth of the cave and looked out past the icy-lipped ledge. There was little to see but a severe sky of cobalt and a wilderness of white overhung by the fantastic, eerie shapes of frozen waterfalls.

"Perhaps we'll be forgotten or simply left to die," she said. "But live to escape in spring."

"No, Majesty," said Gaspar. "Drugen means to finish us soon."

The coals in the only brazier were burning low. Marta crawled back to her place and tightened her coat around her.

Fighting tears, she looked from man to man. "Gaspar! Thomas! Forgive me for bringing Drugen's wrath down on you! And Trimble, I'm so sorry for involving you in my folly!" She began to cry and held her head. "So sorry about Tinka and Timka!"

"Hush," said Trimble. "It isn't your folly but that *villain's!*"

Thomas's eyes flicked from side to side as if he were trying his best to see her. "There's nothing to forgive."

Gaspar's smile was kind. "*Nothing.*"

Her tears let up. She wiped her eyes and nose with the back of her hand.

The setting sun illumined the ledge. Trimble stared at this, the edges of his mustache drooping, then squeezed a hand into his pocket and brought out a pistol.

"In all the monkey business, I forgot this," he said.

Thomas raised his hanging head. "What, friend?"

"Her Majesty's weapon. A guard slipped it to me as we loaded onto the sleds. The work of angels, don't you think?"

Thomas smiled. "They do seem to have a soft spot for people like us."

Marta sniffed back her tears. Her skirt was damp with urine, and she was held fast by chains, but she felt above her troubles and free. Freed by the LORD, she was truly free.

"I'd forgotten about angels," she said. "Do you think they can help us vanquish a sorcerer with only a pistol?"

No one answered; all were staring at the small, seemingly useless object.

The werewolf—a shadow against moonlight in the mouth of the cave—entered, carrying something in his arms. He went past the place where Marta lay rigid with terror, stooped, and deposited his burden, then kicked it with a heavy foot. He looked toward her with eyes like burning coals and threatened with a hand pointing five clawed fingers, then went past her and out of the cave again, for an instant eclipsing the moonlight.

She sat up.

Thomas leaned up on his arm and said, "Ghenter's been here, hasn't he? And he's brought someone. I heard and felt it."

From the place on the stone floor where Ghenter had set down his burden came the sound of a woman groaning.

Gaspar's eyes gleamed in the moonlight. "Poor creature," he said. "Who can it be?"

Trimble sat up. "Can you reach her, mistress?"

Marta crawled to the end of her chains and stretched out a hand to the shadowy form. "Not quite!"

The woman moaned, her teeth chattering. Marta shivered as she looked toward her.

Trimble balled up his blanket and tossed it to Marta, saying, "Gently, gently, throw this over her!"

"Turn!" Marta whispered as she watched in the early morning light. "Turn so that I may see your face before you go from here, perhaps forever!"

The woman lay still. Blood had stained her gown at the shoulders and ribs.

"Lady!" Trimble called. "You've got friends. Why not wake up and talk to us?"

The woman stirred, then cried out as she shifted position. Her long, copper-colored hair tumbled to her waist, hiding the stains as she eased herself up and leaned against the wall.

She turned her face toward them. Her tongue moistened her lips. Her voice was hoarse as she whispered, "Trimble...Majesty..."

Together the two cried, "Schoya!"

"Did he cut you as he threatened?" Marta asked, feeling both curiosity and dread.

Schoya shook her head and said in a stronger voice, "He had Falconier beat me and Ghenter to finish the job. My wings were already gone, you see, and he was furious."

"Your wings are *gone?*" Trimble wrinkled his brows, then his brows suddenly shot upward. Slowly he smiled until his face was beaming. "That means one thing only."

"You know of this?" Schoya asked, her eyes shining.

He nodded. "I've *seen* it, dear lady."

215

Marta turned to him in disbelief. "You *have?*"

His eyes were filled with wonder. "Many years ago in Alvanay. I never thought I'd see it again." He laughed softly.

Schoya laughed with him. "The other fairies always insisted the stories were lies."

"What stories?" Marta asked, feeling a little left out. "What is it that has happened?"

Schoya's hair, tangled with filth and bits of straw, framed a radiant smile. "Christ has found me and remade me into a wingless creature no longer vile—his child."

"Ah!" Smiling, Marta leaned toward her. "I'm so glad, Schoya! I've been praying that you would come to Christ."

"I was listening when you spoke to me." Schoya looked at her hands which were resting in her lap, then looked up at them again. "I trusted Jesus, just as you said, despite what I was. And he heard me—how good he is!"

"Yes, how good!" Marta sighed with happiness. "But tell us, how did Drugen know of your change?"

"As soon as it happened, I journeyed to tell him." Schoya's features showed an inner stillness. "But before I could explain, he said he had guessed my news because his power had diminished. I told him I relinquished all claims to him. He thought for a little, then said my life was worth nothing to him now that I had lost my magic. So he said he agreed with me, the marriage was over."

Trimble looked grave. "May God forgive him!"

Marta's tears welled up. "Schoya, I'm so sorry!"

"There's no need to be, Marta, for the LORD has set me free." Schoya lowered her head. "Though I am still somewhat afraid of what is to come." She looked up with an expression of sympathy and smile of friendship. "We shall help one another now."

Marta gestured to her small company in chains. "What can *we* do against such a man?"

Schoya's expression was maternal. She looked as if she was a mother who must teach and guide a child to higher thoughts. "I do not mean that we shall fight Alexander, but that we shall strengthen one another so our faith does not fail."

Marta squeezed her eyes shut, refusing the possibility that there might be no human vengeance. Opening her eyes she cried, "But he must be stopped, *punished!*"

Schoya was weeping tears of compassion for her. "Marta, remember!" Her voice sank and her mouth quivered. "Retribution will come, even if we do not live to see it."

For a long moment Marta and Schoya looked at one another. Both of them had been injured by Drugen. Each understood the pain resulting from his selfishness and folly. Marta smiled at Schoya then turned her gaze to the entrance of the cave. Beyond it was the radiant blue of the heavens...Heaven! Heaven was her home and her father's, and now it was Schoya's too. Though Drugen had the power to harm and even kill them, he could do no more than that. Their souls were safe with God.

Convicted of refusing to give up the need for personal vengeance, she confessed this to the LORD. After a little while of soaking in the beauty beyond her narrow prison, she turned to Schoya and held out a hand that couldn't reach her. "You are right, friend! We must pity and pray for Drugen."

All was darkness. The moon was hiding its face. Lantern aloft, Ghenter entered in human form and opened a pouch at his belt. With a hand that was human, he drew from it something like glittering dust that he threw onto the coals burning in the brazier. Then he studied the prisoners, but his eyes weren't as keen now, and he didn't notice Marta watching.

He set the lantern down. Its lurid glow lit the floor. The cave began to fill with the scent that had descended the iron staircase at the menagerie. Sparks began to play among the coals. Trimble suddenly snorted in his sleep. The others were breathing as if they too were sleeping soundly. Marta's eyes grew heavy, and she dreamed.

A majestic being, whose dusky wings shadowed his face, stood at the summit of the Zelhorn with his calves deep in snow. He raised a fist against the heavens and threw his other hand downward with the fingers splayed. Out of the mountain, phantoms of the night slithered and flitted.

Marta tried to scream but couldn't. She was still chained within the cave, but in her dream, the chains covered her mouth as well.

Ghenter was suddenly there in the cave of her dream. He stepped to Schoya, lifted her, and carried her out onto the ledge, raised her above his head, then cast her to the glen below. He turned back for the lantern, then fled, taking its glow with him.

Marta struggled in her sleep, and finally, the chains on her mouth broke, and she was able to cry out to Jesus. Dreamless sleep enfolded her.

The prisoners spent the day praying and talking. Schoya was gone, but they couldn't be certain what had happened to her because Marta may only have been dreaming that part.

"*Now,*" said Gaspar. "Now Drugen will come for us."

Thomas asked in a thoughtful tone, "Do you think he could be the man of sin?"

Trimble turned up his collar and leaned back against the wall. His knee was bent and the hand that rested on it was wrapped in a blood-stained rag. He said, "Over the years, I've seen *many* sons of the devil come and go."

Once again Marta was astonished by his wealth of experience. "Really?"

"Yes, and Drugen's scope is far too limited. God's Word explains that the rule of the beast will be universal."

Frowning, Thomas pondered this. He raised a finger and said, "Perhaps Drugen is about to reveal himself and take power."

Marta considered this. She wasn't a scholar, but it didn't square with what she had learned. "Isn't the pope the Antichrist?" she asked. "This was the view of the Reformers."

Gaspar's temper flared. "You forget, Majesty, that *I'm* a Catholic. The pope *cannot* be Antichrist." He leaned forward and caught the gaze of everyone in turn. His manner was forceful, but a tear glittered in the corner of his eye. "Not only is the pope Christ's vicar on earth, but he doesn't meet the ultimate test."

Marta wished she hadn't spoken. "What do you mean, friend?"

Gaspar looked shaken; fear and hope warred in his gaze. "*The* Antichrist, like all antichrists—and Drugen is one—denies the Father and the Son. Denies that Christ has come in the flesh. The pope *proclaims* that Christ has come in the flesh, so it's plainly impossible."

Marta was surprised that his argument, which she had never heard, was reasonable. "You may be right!" She thought a little longer. "I've never considered this. Though—" She stopped, not wishing to hurt him or shake that part of his faith that was genuine.

"Though *what?*" Gaspar's brows lowered with grief and anger.

"Nothing," she murmured. But she had been remembering a pamphlet she had seen in which the pope and the LORD Jesus were compared in side by side pictures. In the first, the pope was seated to receive homage, kisses on the feet from his disciples. In the second, Jesus was on his knees to wash the feet of his apostles.

"What?" Gaspar repeated less urgently.

"My dear Gaspar, let's not speak of this. It serves no purpose." Marta felt compassion for his dilemma. "I know you love the LORD, and that many of the Church of Rome love him."

Gaspar laid his head on his arms and wept bitterly.

The sun sank, leaving the cave in darkness. The moon arose, lending it a little light. The coals in the brazier burned out. The prisoners wrapped up more tightly. Silence hung over them.

Suddenly music resounded in the glen, pipes and drums and tambourines mingled with shouts and laughter. In the dimness the prisoners peered at one another, each face shadowed with alarm. Trimble sat forward, listening closely. Marta heard shuffling steps, labored breathing and snarls as the werewolf climbed to them.

He loomed in the entrance and stood there, his nightmare shape horrible, his face obscured except for a glint of fangs. Suddenly she understood that this night would be different. He wouldn't throw them a bit of bread or give them a sip from a bucket, or throw coals on the inadequate fire. Savagely, he wrenched their chains from the wall rings, then, with his whip, prodded them out of the cave and down the ledges. He used the whip a lot on poor, slow Thomas. Gaspar came to Thomas's side to support him, while Trimble hobbled along helping Marta.

Frozen waterfalls hung suspended around them. Frozen rivulets lay across their path, making it treacherous. The werewolf stopped to stare at the moon, which was full and huge and red along its edge. Then he hurried them down to where a bonfire blazed and Drugen and his courtiers were gathered.

Sleighs were parked around the bonfire, and pavilions stood between them. Knights' chargers and the horses that had pulled the sleighs stood beneath heavy blankets. A picnic was laid, and a samovar was heating. On ledges overlooking the glen, smaller fires were burning, and torches flared and smoked. Piles of brushwood and tinder lay all around. A Gypsy man and woman were dancing, as were some of the courtiers. Others were embracing, eating, drinking. Some drunkenly skated the pool in their boots.

Trimble held Marta's hand, keeping her close. The werewolf led the prisoners to Drugen, who sat in state on a campstool upholstered in mink with his courtesans Rose Red and Snow White at either hand. On a low table near him, the king's sword—Blessed Gregor's holy weapon—lay in its tooled scabbard.

Drugen raised a stein with a dragon's head carved in the handle, drank, studied the prisoners, and then shouted to his courtiers, "Our guests have arrived. Come and greet them!"

At first, the courtiers went on with their games but at last paused to bow and scrape or raise a goblet higher. There was laughter, cat-calls. Rose Red smiled languidly. The werewolf guffawed through shining fangs and hopped around on one heavy foot then the other, lashing at the air and snowy ground with his whip of snakeskin. Snow White's face looked as pale as ice; her eyes were fawn-like and afraid.

"Enough!" Drugen shouted. "Enough for now."

He drew Rose Red close, put his head back and laughed, then stared at Marta shamelessly.

Trimble stepped in front of her to shield her from Drugen's view. Marta silently thanked God for him.

Trimble's voice rumbled. "I've had my fill of your nonsense! Where's Lady Schoya? What have you *done* with her?"

Marta peered past his shoulder.

"Schoya?" Drugen's lips twitched. "Is 'sleeping the sleep of the just.'" His expression grew solemn, his eyes wild. "And *who* shall awaken her?" Then he suddenly laughed again, showing teeth stained with wine.

Trimble straightened his stance. "Vengeance won't tarry!"

Marta's admiration for Trimble knew no bounds. She rested a hand on his shoulder to encourage him, for he might really be as afraid as she was.

The werewolf pushed between Trimble and Drugen, bringing his face close to Trimble's and trying to stare him down. The fur along his neck and spine was standing on end. He was so close that Marta could smell his appalling breath. It smelled as if he had just devoured carrion.

Trimble's gaze remained rock steady. The werewolf's was fierce, but at last it wavered and turned aside.

Marta sighed and leaned against Trimble's shoulder.

Drugen noticed this and leered at them. He invited the prisoners to take a seat on a carpet laid with a feast.

Gaspar didn't move. "Where is my darling child? My Isabay?" he asked.

"Safe at home, for now." With a dagger, Drugen stabbed a slice of raw filet of beef and brought it to his lips. "She must have some reward for giving me a son, though he isn't all I could wish for. Safe, until she displeases me again."

Gaspar sank to the edge of the carpet where the other prisoners were crowded. "Thank God she's still among the living!"

Music filled the night. The dancers whirled. Rose Red rested her head on Drugen's knee and smiled at the prisoners with pointed teeth. The werewolf leaned against a barrel, flicking the whip out and drawing it back slowly so that the end wriggled.

"Eat!" Drugen cried, then crammed his mouth with caviar and bread. "Eat! There's no poison." He passed his tongue over his teeth. "Soon enough, soon enough we shall all be entertained."

As the musicians paused to set the pace for the next tune, a roar rumbled across the distances.

The horses neighed and stamped. Drugen raised an eyebrow, chuckling to himself, and set his teeth into an apple. Juice wet his beard, and he wiped it with the back of a gloved hand. Rose Red rose to her knees, put her arms around him, and laid her head on his shoulder. Her raven locks draped Drugen's arm in its costly coat.

Staring at the two with obvious disgust, Gaspar blurted, "Whatever you mean to do to us? Get on with it!"

Drugen stood, his face bright with firelight. "Of course, *father-in-law!*" He gestured to the werewolf, then commanded, "Go get the surprise!"

The werewolf gamboled toward a sledge used for transport.

Goblet in hand, Falconier trudged after him.

"Don't use the horses, fools!" Drugen called. "They'll be unmanageable!" He gestured to some guards slouched against a sleigh. "*You*, up! Get the horses into a cave and tether them there!"

Ghenter and Falconier got between the shafts of the sledge and began to drag it out of the glen. They got only a few feet before halting.

"You others, help!" Drugen ordered. "Meljahkanz, you're the strongest!"

Marta, who had been noticing Snow White's reactions, saw that she was silently appealing to her with eyes full of terror. She gently smiled to acknowledge and reassure her but did not know how she could possibly help.

While Drugen was busy shouting more orders, Marta and the other prisoners spoke.

Gaspar leaned in to whisper, "What can we do?"

"Little," Trimble said, stroking his beard with a hand wrapped in rag.

Earnest, Marta looked from man to man. "We must be careful of what we say. I'll try my *best* to be careful."

Trimble smiled at his prize student. "Tact is always a good plan, mistress, but *now*, if you have anything to say to that *rascal*, say it!"

"The pistol," Gaspar said, eyes glittering. "I'm a good shot."

Thomas shook his head. "It's not for murder but defense."

Trimble said to Gaspar, "And it would be as tricky passing it, my friend, as pulling it to shoot."

Thomas punched a fist against the palm of his other hand. "It isn't time for Her Majesty to die! How can we three protect her, such as we are? We must pray."

At once the prisoners bowed their heads. Marta silently interceded for Snow White, something, she knew, she should have done long ago.

Drugen returned to his campstool, noticed them, and said, "You *fools*, it's no use praying here."

The prisoners, who had just traveled to heaven and back again, looked at him as if he had suddenly dropped from the moon.

"It's as good a place to pray as any," Trimble said in a calm tone.

Drugen drew Rose Red close. "But will heaven hear *you?*"

Trimble's gaze was piercing. "We shall find out, you and I!"

Marta stared at Trimble as if he were the hero of some saga of old.

Drugen's face, as he studied him, was a mask of contempt. "Does your *queen* know why I question heaven's response?" He drew Rose Red closer. "Does she know who you are and what you've done?"

Trimble glanced at Marta, and she saw that he was surprised and shaken by what Drugen had said. He hesitated, his eyes studying some inner script. At last he said in a low voice, "She hasn't *needed* to know."

Drugen laughed. "That's pure self-interest, *saint*."

Shaking her head in confusion, Marta gripped Trimble's arm and said, "What are you talking about? Tell me at once!"

Trimble covered her hand with his. He seemed to be expecting something from her. It seemed that he wanted to risk *everything* if she would only be there for him.

Drugen's tone was self-satisfied as he interjected, "You're about to find out about your *saint*, Marta. About the friend who is a little too good to be true."

Gaspar gaped at them.

"*Saint?*" Thomas murmured, the dawning of some realization lighting up his face.

Marta pleaded, "Trimble, what is Drugen saying?"

Trimble lowered his head, seemed to consider, and at last looked at Drugen. "You're right," he said. "I was *glad* she didn't know. But it wasn't only for my own sake. When the king left, never to return, her confidence and trust were shaken. I thought that if I could be faithful and true to her as her 'Trimble,' she would be helped to trust and someday love. And in this way, I could make some small amends for the past."

He turned to Marta, took a deep breath, and then expelled it. "Majesty, please allow me to explain! You see, I am Baron Gregor of Brughil."

ℒigℏt

"What do you mean?" Marta frowned slightly. "That 'Trimble' is your nickname, but your given name is 'Gregor' and you were named for the saint?"

He looked at her with a look that said he hoped she could forgive. "Nay, my queen! What I mean is that I am he who *died* defending the village of Spoot from the fiery wyrm, Hexglendyia. But as you can see, I'm still kicking."

Her eyes widened, and her jaw dropped.

He slowly batted his lashes. "Everyone thinks I went out in a blaze of glory, sacrificing myself for others." He shook his head as if amazed. "Churches were built in my honor. A cathedral was named for me.

"The truth is that, after a brief face-off with Hexglendyia, I *ran,* leaving Spoot to fend for itself. I went back later, but it was burned to the ground. Still, folks canonized me—the blessed *babies*—for they had found my shield and sword amongst the rubble.

"I had been commissioned to slay her—consecrated to this task, with all the pomp and hoopla—but she turned out to be a nasty bit of work. The following summer, it took five of the best to bring her down."

He shook his head as if to say, *Can you believe this?* "To finish my tale of cowardice, I never disabused anyone of their notions. The only ones privy to the truth were your father, my wife, and Drugen."

Gaspar looked stunned. "But this means, that when I was praying to Blessed Gregor, I was actually—"

Trimble nodded. "—Praying to *me*. Sorry, friend."

Marta slipped her hand into his. He had relaxed somewhat and they were sitting almost comfortably there. He went on, sounding relieved to be unburdening his heart.

"I kept on the move and used different names," he said. "Centuries passed. Then the king made one of his trips to Uspenska. I was working at an inn where he made a stop. He smelled liquor on me, rebuked me for drunkenness, and asked why I felt I needed the stuff."

Marta lowered her eyes. "Did the king feel strongly about abstaining from liquor?"

"Yes," Trimble said, squeezing her hand to reassure her. "I told him who I was, and confided that after centuries I still had no peace. You see, so many had died because of me. He heard this *coward* out, even when I whined that I had no place to call home, and that everyone I'd known and loved were dust and ashes. He urged me to trust in the Savior, and took me into his own service as valet. When he returned to Zuphof, he took me with him."

Marta could barely contain her joy. "How generous of him!"

Trimble nodded, blinking. "That was the king. Because of him, three centuries of misery ended in one day."

Marta shook her head in wonder. "Three centuries?"

Trimble gave her a wry smile. "Yes, for you see, I benefited from my brief encounter with Hexglendyia in longevity. Or perhaps it was just that I was 'too sad to die,' as the old saying goes."

Marta squeezed his rough, cold fingers. All that was inexplicable and unique about him fell quietly into place. Awe and gratitude and pity filled her heart.

Thomas patted Trimble's shoulder.

Gaspar, who had been staring in amazement, said, "All is forgiven, Gregor."

"A picturesque tale," Drugen said, his eyes narrowing as if he envied them. "But too sentimental for my tastes. And I promise you, the ending won't be happy."

Trimble's gaze grew stern. "Your great-great-great-granddaddy had something to do with rousing Hexglendyia against Spoot, didn't he? It was his way of settling a dispute over a boundary stone." Trimble's gaze was open and free from apology or pride. "God has forgiven me. He will hear me."

Drugen smothered a look of uncertainty. "But will he answer the way you *want?* Will he save your *queen?* That citadel of maidenly virtue and tower of strength!" His look hardened into smugness. "And even if she survives, will she ever be happy again? How could she be, when her father was an adulterer and you—her second father—are nothing but a base coward?"

Marta's temper flared. Trimble seemed to sense this, for he gripped her hand more firmly. She watched his face as he answered Drugen.

"The queen now understands that *everyone* falls," he said. "But that what matters is whether one gets up and finishes the race."

His expression changed to one of appeal as he adopted his teaching tone. "Come, Drugen! You can stop all this in a snap." He tried but failed to snap his cold fingers. "Fold up the tents of wickedness and go home! For the sake of those you love—those who will suffer most from your crimes."

"*You* preaching to *me?*" Drugen laughed Trimble to scorn. "And about *love?*" He laughed again with a bitter look. "I love only my hatred. It grows every day—an enormous Zelhorn rearing against the heavens."

Trimble studied him, then said in a guileless fashion, "How you must have hated the king, our noble and meek master."

Drugen's face convulsed. "It was the greatest of *pleasures* to simply stand back and watch the fool destroy himself."

Marta cried, "Monster!"

Gaspar reached for her arm and squeezed it, whispering, "Be still, Majesty!"

How she loved faithful Gaspar! Gently she pulled away and said to him in a normal tone, "I can't be still! It's time to speak."

She turned to Drugen. She still felt pity but understood that her feelings shouldn't rule her. He was looking at her as if through the eyeholes in the mask of his sophistication. The eyes that stared out showed hatred and a little fear.

"To simply stand back and watch someone destroy himself is to help him do this," she said. "That is what you've done, *destroyed* a man—a man better than you." She looked down at Trimble's hand clasping her own. "But you will never destroy his legacy of courage and love."

Drugen held out his goblet for Rose Red to refill, quaffed the contents, and ran a finger along the rim. His thoughts were almost visible, as his eyes followed his finger.

Marta sat very still, understanding that he would retaliate.

He smiled as if in pity, almost paternally. "Are you really so sure, Marta, that *that* was his legacy?"

She bit her lip and clung to Trimble's hand.

"*I'm* sure," Thomas interjected. "The king was a true child of God—fallen but faithful. A hero with clay feet, but a hero, no less."

"Your observations count for little." Drugen sneered. "You were blind to all that was happening—sulking in a corner over your own *petty* problems."

Thomas's voice had a keen edge. "You'd be surprised how much the blind can see."

Gaspar interposed. "I too am sure of the king's legacy, Alexander. And I offer as evidence two strong proofs: the character of the woman now speaking with you—his daughter—and the word of Isabay."

"You're always interfering, *Count*," said Drugen, glaring. "You've often interfered between Isabay and me."

"The Lady Isabay isn't your wife." Gaspar's gaze, filled with a light that was solemn, and his grim mouth speaking truth, were framed by the wisps of his dirty hair. "You and she have no union sacred to God and man on which another may be said to intrude. You have no claim to her loyalties—none. Though she has a claim to yours."

Drugen's grasp tightened around the goblet. "She will be loyal or die."

Gaspar sounded utterly certain. "It would be better for her to die."

The two locked gazes.

Marta put a hand over Gaspar's. "God will help Isabay. Don't lose heart!"

With renewed courage, she turned to Drugen. "You ask if I'm sure of the king's legacy? Yes! Others have told me of his failure and repentance, and that the reason he fought was to set Isabay free from slavery to you. You lied when you implied that it was because he wanted her! I would have known much of this sooner if you hadn't destroyed his letters. How *could* you?"

Drugen seemed rattled. "I couldn't keep them or give them to you, could I—when they testified against me?"

Marta moved past her pity to finish her God-given task. There was a possibility that she could help Drugen. "Yes, Lord Drugen, as always deceit and treachery were necessary to you. You've chosen the wrong path, but it isn't too late."

He put a second hand around his goblet to control a tremor.

"But all you accomplished in this way worked for my good," she said, a smile flickering. "For, you see, we Christians are *commanded* to walk by faith—something I've balked at—and you have been the strange and awful instrument God used to teach me about this."

231

She took a deep breath. "I know the truth—and rejoice in it—and trust those who revealed it, including the king, my father. For, yes, Drugen, you failed to find and destroy a crucial paper of his that gave me some of his story in his own words."

Drugen's forced smile faltered.

Marta briefly closed her eyes, summoning her strength. "And now the truth is mine forever. It can never be snatched away and burned."

He seemed to recover his composure, set his goblet down at the side of his campstool, then gazed at her intently, as if trying on her those powers that had proved so fatal to others.

"Faith is a mere delusion," he crooned. "And there is *nothing* which one may call 'the truth.'"

She refused to meet his gaze and instead considered her response. Should she meet him on philosophical grounds? But how could *she* attempt such a thing? Even the best argument of the best rhetorician could be countered by the unscrupulously skillful. Words, like swords, were often crossed in such a way that the innocent were edged into a corner.

Finally, she answered softly, "All I know is that no one can change the truth, however much she wants to, and that everyone—even a queen—must bow to it in the end."

Around her, flames crackled, degenerates leered, and monsters lurked, but she forged on as if with her father's courage.

"I'm sorry for you, Alexander," she said. "You believe you are so much better than others but are no different. You too are but a mist that appears for a moment and then is gone. The world will forget you, just as it forgets us. May the Lord Jesus deal with you in mercy!"

Drugen looked thunderstruck and stood hastily, took a few steps with his back to them, and then, in a hoarse voice, yelled, "*You over there!*" A few of the guards who were speaking aside turned to him. "Lay the field with fire!"

He turned back and, without looking at the prisoners, grabbed the scabbard and sword, buckled them on, and then strode away, barking orders. The guards went to work, moving brushwood and tinder into place, then rolling and opening barrels. They built an enclosure by piling the wood between boulders and then drenched the wood with oil from the barrels.

Rose Red ran to Drugen's side, put an arm around his waist, and spoke into his ear. He took her hand and drew her up toward the fire-lit ledges, where cushions and throws were in place. The courtiers climbed behind the two.

Marta had been staring after Drugen, her whole being tightly strung. Now she began to weep with relief. She had managed to confront him. Trimble put an arm around her and the other men leaned closer.

Thomas's eyes were wet. "God bless you, Majesty!"

Gaspar looked proud of her and deeply moved. "You're a brave young woman!"

At times, while the men consoled her, they stole glances at Drugen and his minions to see what they were up to.

At last, with a tender smile Trimble said, "It's time."

Suddenly Marta was terrified.

Thomas raised his blind eyes to heaven. "God help us to be strong!"

Snow White came to them then, shyly, slipping in beside Marta, who studied the young woman's pale face that had so often seemed drugged but which now was alive with fear. With a shaky hand she took Snow White's hand, and together, they looked up at the courtiers settling in the fire-lit gloom. They had filled the ledges from which they gazed down to the enclosure. Wine was passed from hand to hand, laughter erupted, and occasionally they peered, as if in expectation, into the darkness beyond the glen.

Drugen stepped to the brink of the ledge, his gaze ignited by firelight, opened his arms, and then began to chant in the baleful language used for the casting of spells. His voice grew stronger, masterful.

Marta shuddered with nausea. Snow White cried, "Jesus, help me!" and hid her face against Marta's shoulder.

Trimble cried, "Mistress! Everyone! Do as I do!"

He closed his eyes and covered his ears with his hands. The five, ears covered, huddled together, and the chanting seemed to come from afar. After a moment, Marta opened her eyes and saw lightning at play along the horizon, illumining the mountaintops. An out of season storm was approaching.

Thomas began to pray.

Marta uncovered her ears, exulting.

Snow White turned and looked at Thomas, then bowed her head.

Thomas's voice was filled with quiet power. "Out of the depths have I cried unto thee, Oh, LORD!"

Trimble responded with a sturdy, "Oh, LORD, hear my voice!"

"Amen, Jesus," Gaspar said quietly.

For a moment Marta's fear was removed. She felt nothing but Jesus' love.

A guard yelled, "*Now!*" and used the LORD's name in vain.

How little he knows about him! Marta thought.

Using torches, guards fired the brushwood at various points. Flames raced along as if eager, united, and shot into the night with a roar.

Another noise reached them, a tumult—shouts, the cracks of a whip, and the voice of a tiger.

War

The werewolf, Falconier, and guards appeared from out of the darkness, towing the sledge on which they had secured a steel cage. They seemed drunk with danger and were laughing, falling down, standing to laugh, and falling again. One of them dropped a torch to the snow and retrieved it. At every jolt of the cage, the white tiger trapped there lashed out or gnawed the bars.

Another creature came into view, bent-backed, horned, goat-legged, with the torso of an old, wizened man. He was gripping a pole with a stiletto lashed to the end, with which he sometimes jabbed the tiger.

"Altamente! Altamente!" Drugen grinned as if the satyr's appearance had brightened his mood. "News travels fast!"

"The night is filled with it!" cried Altamente.

He came on crookedly, shaking off a frosty hoof, then gestured the others forward with a lean and shaggy arm. Clutching prods and hooks, pikes and swords, with heavy ropes, they dragged the cage off the sledge and drew it over the uneven ground through the opening in the enclosure. Crouched, ears flattened, the tiger bided his time.

Some of the men settled the cage in place. With blows that rang, others began to drive a tall stake into the snowy ground.

Drugen shouted to a guard standing idle, "You over there! Get the *queen* and her men and that fool who has joined them!"

The guard hesitated.

Swiftly, Drugen pulled a flintlock and shot him.

Other guards answered Drugen's call and fetched the prisoners. Snow White clung to Marta's hand. Marta turned her head as they were hurried along and saw Trimble struck to the ground. Up again, he placed a hand over the pocket where the pistol was. As she paused with Snow White to watch, Ghenter cracked his whip, and Snow White's cheek trickled with blood.

The four were brought within the circle of fire and rock. A guard shoved Thomas forward. With a hook, Falconier prodded Gaspar, and the werewolf collared Trimble.

A second stake was pounded into the ground. The guards tied Marta and Snow White to one, Thomas and Gaspar to the other. Trimble, his coat open and dragging in the snow, was left free. One of his eyes was swollen shut, and he blinked in the light of the raging fires.

Drugen, who was overseeing all of this from his ledge, unsheathed the sword, spat on it, and then tossed it toward Trimble.

The sword landed at Trimble's feet with the point toward him.

A quarrel broke out about who would do the dangerous job of unlatching the cage.

Twisting her hands to try to get free of her restraints, Marta stared distraught as the rabble came to blows not far from her.

"Steady, Mistress!" Trimble called. "Maybe they'll kill one another!"

Altamente broke up the brawl, using his fists like hammers and kicking with his slew-hoofs. Sullen and resentful, the rabble subsided like a sea that seems calm but is dangerous.

Altamente forced his makeshift lance on Falconier, then he and the others moved back. Eyes wide, looking completely sober now, Falconier hefted the weapon, while with his free hand he used a hook to undo the latch. Then, as if on a signal, he and Altamente and the rest stampeded out of the enclosure, covered the opening with firewood, and doused this with oil.

The fresh firewood ignited.

Flames shot heavenward.

A man shrieked.

Snow White yanked hard against her restraints.

Though terrified, Marta found Snow White's hand and held it firmly. "Trust in the LORD and try to keep calm," she said to her.

Drugen watched everything with a satisfied look.

"LORD, save us!" Trimble cried.

Then, with his good eye, he studied the layout of the field of battle. Fires and boulders fenced them in. Behind him, the prisoners were secured to stakes. Before him, at the far end of the enclosure, the cage stood. He stooped, grasped the sword, and straightened.

The tiger, who had been sitting and panting, stood and laid a paw on the door, which opened. With a roar, its breath freezing on the air, the tiger sprang out.

Cheers went up.

Snow White screamed.

Marta turned her head away from the sound and sank a little in her restraints, her prayers creeping toward heaven. She heard Gaspar and Thomas encourage each other. Then Thomas yelled, "God save you, my queen! God save us all!"

Trimble swayed, put a hand to his injured face, and steadied himself.

Over the Zelhorn's shoulder, the moon sank blood red, and the werewolf, who had climbed to Drugen, changed before their eyes into the rough drunkard, Ghenter, with the degraded and unhappy face. He grabbed a flagon from someone, put his head back, and guzzled.

Above, lightning flickered closer as the out-of-season storm was driven toward them. The tiger glanced at Marta and Snow White, then looked upward.

Time halted.

The tiger seemed confused by the noisy heavens, the fires, and shouts from the ledges.

"Jesus, save us," Marta murmured, then let her head sink.

All around her, flames crackled. She felt their heat and thought it might be the breath of the tiger. She heard the sound of Trimble's boots as he crossed before her to keep it away and heard him run the other way toward Gaspar and Thomas. Sobbing, Snow White gripped Marta's hand so hard it hurt.

A silence fell in which only the fire and thunder spoke. From afar, another sound issued—a sound like a trumpet marshalling troops. Was she only imagining this?

She raised her head.

Sword in hand, Trimble was stationed before the tiger. His thinning hair had fallen into his eyes, and he shook it back. One of his hands began to inch toward the pocket where the pistol was, but he seemed to rethink this scheme, for he quickly brought this hand back to the sword to grip it with both.

The tiger uttered a hellish cry, its ears back and whiskers fanning. Its moist teeth and exquisite fangs glistened with the light of flames. It began to pace, its muscles and sinews tightening and loosening, its long tail out behind, and its ears up. At last, it stopped, trotted toward Trimble, and stopped again, the sword gleaming in its eyes. It moved off but circled back, then shot away to lope around the perimeter of the enclosure.

Trimble stumbled as he ran, trying to stay between the tiger and his charges, and got up again and hurried.

The tiger slowed, keeping him in view and complaining in a throaty rumble.

Snowballs—hard-packed missiles that stung—began to rain from the ledges.

The tiger roared and crouched, gazing upward toward those gathered there. It stamped a great forepaw over a snowball that bounced across its path. Its heavy coat and luxuriant ruff were beautiful in its fury.

Trimble stepped between it, and Marta and Snow White.

It stood, head low as it measured him, and then charged.

Trimble was ready with a stroke of the sword and wounded it, but as he did, it rose onto its powerful hind legs, clamped its jaws around his shoulder and raked a claw down his hip and thigh.

Balancing on his good leg, Trimble beat it off with the flat of the sword. His face, lit by fire, seemed like the face of an angel struggling against a fiend.

The tiger backed off and lowered its haunches to lick its flank, then cowered under sudden cracks and flashes from the storm clouds now overhead.

Swiftly, Trimble pulled the pistol and, when the tiger glanced heavenward, fired.

There was a sharp report, flash, and puff of smoke.

Drugen's company jeered as the tiger went down.

But the tiger stood again, bared its fangs, ran, and leapt upon Trimble so that he fell backward with it over him while he gripped the sword. The tiger groaned as the sword entered its chest and broke out through its shoulder. Trimble lay motionless beneath it.

Marta sobbed, fretting at her confinement, and screamed his name.

Thomas and Gaspar shouted as they tried to get free to go to him.

Then a trumpet blared: loud, near, certain, with a long and silvery sound, as if a star had been given a voice. The voice quavered, expanded, melded with one long, final, snapping crack of lightning as the storm clouds fled over and onward by divine appointment.

Hooves were heard pounding snow as riders arrived. Voices cried out, harsh and ringing—some of them in alien tongues. A clash of arms resounded. Archers could be seen scaling the ledges.

Part of the flaming wall was dragged aside, and the hosts of Cazmarya—Faerie's hosts—rode in upon dappled steeds, holding reins of silver-struck leather in panoply of a gorgeous color. Ladies on palfreys accompanied warriors whose hands gripped lances that were darkly stained.

Next appeared the mounted knights of Sapore caparisoned in scarlet and gold, their bloodied swords held high.

Last, the few stalwarts of Zuphof thundered in upon their heavy destriers.

Bartolo leapt from his horse, Piers and Elda dismounted, and Gurnemanz jumped down. All saluted Marta.

Bartolo reached her. His well-loved face was covered with a beard of many weeks. As he cut her bonds, he said, "Thank God, Marta! I'm not too late!"

"My wonderful friend, thank you!" she said. "But we must help Trimble now!"

As Thomas, Gaspar and Snow White were being freed, they cried out with one voice about him.

Gurnemanz and his squire moved the tiger's carcass aside then crouched over him.

"He lives, Your Majesty!" Gurnemanz cried.

"I must go to him!" Marta said to Bartolo.

Bartolo smiled. "Let me help you!"

He put an arm around her and walked her to Trimble. Soldiers were carrying him to safety. They halted. Trimble opened his eyes, saw Marta, and smiled with swollen lips. She kissed his cheek. He was carried away. For a moment, she leaned against Bartolo, who held her tightly and kissed the top of her head, despite her filthy hair.

He led her to his mount, climbed to the saddle, then drew her up behind him. She clung to him, and they cantered out of the enclosure to where the fight was continuing.

The unicorn had joined the battle. Ghenter, shot through the heart with a silver-barbed arrow, pitched headlong from a fiery ledge.

Lances flashed, and shots exploded. Cries sounded, and trumpets shrilled.

The enemy fell back, pleading for their lives, and the riders of the delivering armies encircled them. Some of Drugen's minions lay beneath the horses' hooves. Without a weapon, Drugen was held at bay by the unicorn.

While Bartolo, Piers, Gurnemanz, and a silver-haired nobleman and his lady conferred, Marta rested her head against Bartolo's back, on his soiled and wayworn coat.

Soon he looked over his shoulder to say, "Beauschante, king of Faerie, and Fleurdamour, his queen, say there is a place close by where you may rest before you journey on—caves known from former days of trouble. Shall we go there?"

Marta nodded.

Beauschante and Fleurdamour came to her, doing homage. Their eyes were bright and fierce with exultation. Despite their silvery hair, their faces looked smooth and young.

"How...how did you know?" Marta murmured.

"Piers and Elda brought news of Imane's death," Beauschante said. "As we rode to avenge her, we met this necromancer coming to seek help for our cousin, Schoya."

Beauschante gestured toward a tall, gangly man astride a lady's light-boned horse. His head was hanging, and his wrists were bound. The man looked up at Marta—Merl la Corneille.

Beauschante went on. "His desire to help Schoya was greater than his fear of punishment. For long ago, we banished him upon pain of death. This is his moment of redemption—his one selfless act. We met the Duke of Soggiorno and your own contingent riding to rescue you, and all joined forces."

Preparations for a march began. Corpses of enemies, among them Ghenter and Falconier, were thrown onto the fires. Gaspar, Thomas, and Snow White were helped up behind riders. A bed was laid for Trimble in one of Drugen's sleighs; and the rest of the wounded, both friends and enemies, also rode in sleighs. The tethered horses were taken from the cave and put in harness, while infantrymen took on the job of driving. Those enemies strong enough to walk were rounded up and bound one to another. Drugen and Rose Red were made to walk like any common felons, but were bound only to each other with a strong cord of fairy make, and were under special guard.

The troops headed off. The unicorn rode along the line for a time, tossed his mane when he saw Marta, then galloped wide, off into the wilds that were his home.

They passed by the corpse of Altamente lying face down in the snow with a crossbow dart in its back. One of the knights threw a blanket over its awful legs.

Beauschante and Fleurdamour, and Bartolo and Marta were in the vanguard. Trimble's sleigh, with Piers and Elda riding on either side, followed just behind them, along with the sleighs with the rest of the injured. The prisoners came last, with Gurnemanz and his men as rearguard.

The sky had cleared, and the sun was rising like a great, spherical lamp set in the heavens to light their way. They were approaching a pass that led down into the Vale of the Nameless Mountains, an immense forested valley fenced by peaks and cliffs and falls of such grandeur that no one had dared to name them.

Marta overheard Piers and Elda discussing Trimble, and turned her head to listen. Elda had drawn her mount alongside of Piers's warhorse.

"Do you know if the caves are far, my love?" Elda asked. "He's barely breathing."

"We still have some distance to go," Piers answered. "Why not ride with him? Give him a little more of this." He held out a golden vial that looked dazzling in the sunlight.

"I must *go* to Trimble," Marta said weakly.

"Piers and Elda are watching over him," Bartolo said.

He laid a hand in its gauntlet over her arm, which gripped his chest, and again, she rested her head against him. She wept, thinking of Tinka and Timka...of Trimble tossing a potato...killing a wolf, a tiger...

The company started into the pass. There was the sound of a commotion in the rearguard. Gurnemanz appeared riding his stallion forward, with Drugen and Rose Red stumbling behind him under guard. Beauschante and Fleurdamour rode back to join Gurnemanz.

Drugen dug in his heels and cried, "As I've said, I won't go there!" Rose Red stood close to him, as if biding her time like a cat getting ready to escape restraint.

Gurnemanz turned in the saddle with his hand on the hilt of his sword, and Bartolo gripped his own weapon.

Gurnemanz looked down at Drugen and said, "You *will*, my enemy!"

Beauschante added coolly, "Or be executed without a trial where you stand, sorcerer."

Fleurdamour said in a haughty tone, "Perhaps, *wizard,* you think yourself safe from such a fate as Clinschor met. You would do well to remember him and Siglorel!"

Drugen lowered his head, hiding a look of fear and hatred. He and Rose Red were brought forward into the vanguard by Gurnemanz and his men.

Again, the company moved along the narrow defile. Marta glanced over her shoulder and saw Piers hang back to let Trimble's sleigh clear the walls of rock. The vanguard passed beneath an archway to a broader trail beyond. Wind whipped up the snow and icy crystals stung Marta's face. To their right, a snowy slope, strewn with boulders, soared toward a high pass between peaks. On the other lay the vale—vast and deep, with precipitous slopes. Above and beyond the vale, titanic alps marched in a heady ascent of blue and white toward the rooftop of the world.

Vertigo assailed Marta. She closed her eyes and clung to Bartolo. After a moment, she looked again—out, not down. Treetops pierced low-lying clouds heavy with snow. Through breaks in the clouds, streams and lakes appeared, bordered by thickets that glinted with hoarfrost.

She raised her thoughts to the One who had made all this. Who had stooped from his throne in heaven to become a man, to die and rise again and thus save his wayward children. Once again, he had come to their rescue. He could—he *would*—heal Trimble.

She looked behind her and saw an infantryman driving Trimble's sleigh, Elda tightening a blanket around Trimble, and Piers riding beside them. At peace, she closed her eyes, lulled by the closeness of Bartolo and the gait of the horse.

A woman shrieked. The shriek went right through Marta. Shaking with shock she raised her head.

Then came the sound of Gurnemanz crying, "Drugen and his wench—they've *vanished!*"

Solace

The vanguard stopped on an overlook and encircled Fleurdamour and Beauschante. Shouts went down the line to tell the rest of the troops to halt.

Fleurdamour moved her hand from the scabbard at her belt to her long silver hair that tumbled from her hat of snow leopard to her hips. "He stole my knife! And cut off a lock of my hair!"

As she began to panic and her horse became skittish, Beauschante took the reins from her. "He cannot have gone far, my queen." With his other hand he slid a lance from the quiver on his saddle and hefted it. "We shall find and *slay* him!"

"No!" she cried. "He shall kill me with *magic*, for he now has something of mine with which to weave a spell!"

With a shudder, Marta surveyed the scene. Bartolo had raised his sword, and a forest of weapons bristled and tossed as knights and squires wheeled their mounts to discover the enemy.

A voice cried: "Up there! The *enemy!*"

As one man, the riders turned to look. Drugen was standing a stone's throw away on the slope overlooking the pass. His knees were flexed as he balanced there. Beside him, Rose Red stood, her tresses billowing in the wind like Medusa's vipers. Drugen's hair blew across his eyes, and he brushed it aside with the back of the hand with which he clutched the knife. In his other hand, he held Fleurdamour's silver lock. He waved it—the wind tried to snatch it—while Rose Red stared at it greedily.

Overcome by the power of sympathetic magic, Fleurdamour slumped forward against her horse's neck. Part of her life was in the lock of hair.

Her men-at-arms and ladies rallied to her.

Beauschante threw his lance with a mighty throw, but it veered aside.

Taking a backward step, Drugen smiled, raised his hands with the knife and fetish, and began to chant strange words in a voice as cruel as a priest of Nimrod. Rose Red crouched at Drugen's feet as if worshiping him, and whatever it was he really loved. He stared hard at the lock and laughed when it began to fizzle.

Archers fired, lances shot forth—all of this futile.

The fetish vanished in smoke.

Drugen gripped the knife like a dagger and drew Rose Red to her feet. He said in a voice that was louder and stronger, though he was farther away, "As I've said, *fools,* I won't go! No one commands me!"

The two climbed more swiftly than humanly possible, disappearing and then reappearing higher still amid the snow-clad boulders.

Without a word, Thomas got down from the horse he shared with a squire. Feeling for the saddle quiver, he withdrew a lance. He started up the slope with it, his coat flapping. He tripped and nearly impaled himself but put a fist to the snowy ground and straightened.

Then his voice rang as he shouted, "Stay your spell, sorcerer, or die!"

In a voice that was strangely weak, Beauschante urged him on. "Steady, knight, steady as you go."

The troops watched. Their weapons were seemingly at the ready, but their faces showed doubt and confusion. Bartolo's right hand, the hand that held his sword, started to shake.

Magic was in the air. Marta could feel a spirit of unnatural restraint and terror and, in her heart, cried out to the LORD.

Gaspar shook his head as if to clear it, dismounted, snatched a spear from a Saporian knight, and then started up. Gurnemanz followed, gripping the broadsword, "Bane of Wizards," which had been his father's. They hurried toward Thomas. Outstripping him, they could then deal with Drugen.

But Thomas was gaining speed. And Drugen, with Rose Red, continued to ascend, now without seeming to move a muscle, disappearing and reappearing as if to taunt his enemies. So near the top of the slope, the two would soon be over and beyond reach.

Halting, Thomas felt forward with the lance along the ground as if to make sure his path was clear, then he suddenly charged. He stumbled and then stopped and shouted, "Where?"

"Left!" yelled Gaspar. He then bent over, his hands on his knees, to catch his breath.

As Thomas made way, the wind lifted his cap away. It landed then cartwheeled downward. While Drugen mocked Thomas, Thomas continued his blind climb, groping at times. At last, he went far enough—he seemed to think—for he stopped short and held out a hand. He raised his other arm and drew back the hand with the lance. The lance was supremely steady.

Drugen's voice, powerful with magic, descended. "You utter, complete *fool!* Your eyes were destroyed! Leave the fight to us who can see!"

Thomas's lance—a dark line from Marta's vantage—lowered in his grip as he swayed.

She cried, "LORD Jesus, help him!"

Gurnemanz and Gaspar had almost reached him. Gaspar began to raise his spear but immediately lowered it, grabbing his shoulder as if in pain. Gurnemanz ran up against him, his own ascent blocked.

Thomas recovered and again raised his weapon but didn't throw.

Drugen stretched forth a hand and cursed him, every word of cruelty and every dark word gushing from his heart to stain the world. He cursed all of his enemies, but especially the God of heaven and earth and his beloved Son. The heights, so innocent-looking in their robes of purist white, echoed with his blasphemies.

Thomas turned toward Drugen's voice. When the echoes began to die, he cried, "Sorcerer, your voice betrayed you!" He threw the lance.

It sailed—as if forever—glanced off rock, changed tack, and impaled Drugen and Rose Red, who stood behind him.

As one, the troops drew in their breath in an audible gasp.

Drugen groaned and dropped to his knees with Rose Red against him. He took the lance in his hands and bent his head to see it, looked down the slope for a moment as if seeking someone, then fell forward.

Marta hid her face against Bartolo's back, then looked again.

Face flushed with zeal, Gurnemanz pushed past Gaspar and Thomas, reached Drugen and Rose Red, seemed to study them, then raised Bane of Wizards and struck off their heads swiftly, one and then the other.

The heads tumbled.

Marta shrieked. Her hold on Bartolo loosened as she sank into oblivion. Quickly she was drawn up from blessed forgetfulness when Bartolo tightened his arm over hers to keep her from falling. She clung to him, the vision of Drugen and Rose Red's terrible demise seared upon her mind.

Fleurdamour, who had cried out as if startled out of sleep when Drugen died, struggled to sit up. Beauschante steadied her in the saddle, climbed behind her, and held her.

Gaspar, leading Thomas by the arm, covered the last few steps to Gurnemanz and the bodies.

The troops—some standing in their stirrups, some dismounting to fall on one knee—gazed at the men high on the slope. Gurnemanz and Gaspar knelt so that Thomas was left standing alone. A cry rose to the heavens as everyone except a few prisoners saluted him.

"Thomas of Fredersberg!"

Marta dashed away her tears to echo, "Thomas!"

Thomas's voice carried on the wind. "Christ alone is victor!"

Far below, over low-lying clouds, firebirds glided the winds.

The Caves of Refuge, an old hideout of Wolfram of Bettensberg—a man of God and man of war who fought in the days of the Reforms—had a stream that rushed through, luge-like, on a bed of solid rock. It sang and rang as it swept onward, and its music poured through Marta's ravaged mind and heart, cleansing and healing her.

Comfort dwelt here. It received her and the others like long-awaited guests, providing safe haven, refreshing sleep, simple fare, and fellowship—even baths in secluded hot springs. Fairy lanterns, which made the rocks sparkle, hung in a lofty central space and in alcoves and smaller caves made cozy with furs and fairy furnishings.

Marta lay as if in a dream, soothed by fairy teas brewed from herbs that grew in Cazmarya alone, and reclining under the softest of coverlets upon a linen cot set by a banked fire surrounded by heated stones.

Everyone gathered around such gentle fires to talk, weep, and laugh but soberly, and to rehearse the tale of deliverance or pray for Trimble and her and others. She often heard Thomas's rich laughter and Gaspar's thoughtful tones.

Bartolo kept watch over her. He rarely left her side. King Beauschante, who was a skilled herbalist, attended her, Trimble, and others, while Snow White and Elda saw to their humbler needs.

Marta slept and cried—once for Drugen and Rose Red. One of her prayers, she realized then, had been answered: it no longer lay within his power to harm others. She calmed herself, listened to the conversations going on around her, and prayed silently when others prayed aloud.

During her recovery, those guards of Drugen's who were among the prisoners of war entreated her for an audience. How strange it seemed to be *entreated!* She received them graciously. The guards, whose hats and coats were splattered with dried blood, knelt with their foreheads to the stone floor.

"Your Majesty," murmured he in the tallest hat.

She leaned up on her arm. "Please don't grovel! I'm not like he whom you served for far too long."

The guard looked up. "What will you do? Order our execution? Imprisonment?"

"I haven't decided."

"May we...serve you?"

As she studied him and his comrades in their torn and soiled uniforms, their dark eyes huge with seeming sincerity, the answer came to her suddenly.

"Yes, you may serve me if you do this with a true heart," she said. "You shall serve as water and wood bearers for my troops. And remember, I grant this not for your own sakes but for the sake of him who passed the pistol to Trimble and him who died when he hesitated to execute Drugen's order."

The guards backed away, bowing deeply and thanking her, a few with streaming eyes.

Bartolo and Beauschante looked at Marta, then at one another, as if in wonder.

Beauschante said, "Majesty, is this the wisest course?"

"I'm following my father the king's example." She rested her head on her pillow again. "He failed in some ways, but not at being merciful."

Gurnemanz also sought her forgiveness. As they spoke of his failure, he went on to break some news to her. Before he had left Stootna to ride to her, he had learned that Droopsk had conquered

Zuphof in a single night, unexpectedly in winter, through the perfidy of the Earl of Ester.

She swallowed hard and at last asked him with quivering lips, "And the cost in lives?"

"Two of the older guards," Gurnemanz said. "Men who couldn't be seduced to treason, died."

"And my mother?"

"The Queen Mother sought refuge in Madrigal and is safe there." Marta had more questions, but Gurnemanz went on.

"Those knights who opposed Ester's plan fled into the countryside," he said. "I met a few in Stootna. After making sure that my wife and daughters were safe in her father's home, I set out with the knights loyal to you to find you. On the road, we joined the troops from Sapore and Cazmarya."

Marta nodded slowly. Her heart felt like a blank. Torn clouds of anger raced across its skies but were lost to this blankness.

She nodded once more while Gurnemanz knelt before her with downcast eyes. At last, she prayed and felt her heart live again. *So this is how a kingdom falls,* Lord! *If a gift isn't treasured, it is stolen. Oh why, oh why didn't I heed the wisdom of my dear mother and truthful bishop? Jesus, forgive me! So many have suffered and will suffer because I was foolish! No matter that Zuphof was a gift I didn't want. It was your gift, and I held it so cheaply!*

Ashamed of herself and her father, she returned to the present and Gurnemanz. "Thank you for your loyalty, for leaving those you love to find me."

He looked at her.

She said, "I now understand, friend, why you abandoned the king. I have faced the same enemy."

He bowed over her hand. "Though I acted from necessity, it is still hard to know I am forgiven."

She rested her hand on his shoulder. Again, he met her gaze, and she noticed, in his face, changes and tiny lines imposed by his grief and guilt.

"I forgive you," she said.

She soon grew strong enough to help take care of Trimble, sharing this loving burden with Elda and Snow White, who were both especially tender with him.

Gaspar and Thomas kept constant vigil at his side praying or, when he was conscious, attempting to make small talk. Rarely did they refer to the glorious deeds that had been accomplished. Sometimes they spoke of Christ's sufferings or of heaven's bliss.

One day, when Trimble's fever broke for a time, he was able to speak more than a word or two to Marta. She was changing the dressing on the wound on his shoulder—the great, bruised piercings from the tiger's bite.

"You must tell Tinka," Trimble began.

"Tell her what?" she asked, but he lapsed into silence.

"Perhaps he should lie quietly," said Bartolo, who was seated on Trimble's other hand while she waited on him.

But Trimble went on. "Write to Tinka...all you think best, my queen, but...especially that Timka must go to school."

His eyelids flickered, then his gaze focused on her hands as they tied the bandage. "Afterward, he must go to Gurnemanz for training in arms. I must speak with Gurnemanz—"

He tried to rise from his cot, but she put a hand to his chest and restrained him.

"I'll let Gurnemanz know that you want to speak with him," she said.

"And why not write everything in a letter to Tinka?" Bartolo suggested.

Bartolo fetched his reading spectacles, paper, ink, and a quill, and Trimble dictated letters to Tinka and Timka.

When Trimble had finished, he thanked Bartolo, addressing him as "my prince," then quietly wept, staring at a lantern fashioned from colored panes of glass, which told the story of a dragon attack on a castle.

"The knight seems about to walk off history's stage," Trimble said and sighed. "Timka may be he who takes the final bow."

Thomas nodded. "Yes, somehow I sense that there will be changes."

"There will always be work for a loyal man-at-arms," said Gaspar. "Timka may come to me at Beaubois. I will honor his service."

Bartolo removed his specs. "Or to Sapore to serve the House of Piccolo."

Trimble smiled and closed his eyes.

Marta clipped the ends of the bandage. "Yes. This must be so, now that Zuphof is no more."

She sighed, then smiled wryly. She was no longer queen apparent—her own doing, the typical Happstein *blunder*. She bit her lip. No longer queen apparent, and—selfish and foolish thought—she hadn't yet worn her crown of sapphires set in several pounds of gold. It was bulging the coffers of Droopsk. And should she return to Zuphof, she would be arrested, her knights informed her. The warrant had been issued.

She recalled her rebuke of Ester and wondered if he had turned traitor because of this personal affront. No, he must have *long* been contemplating treachery against Zuphof and its Royal City. Tiny, lovable, simpleminded, ever-drizzling Zuphof-on-the-Zonderzee! Seat of her father's throne. Her home and Carissima's.

Carissima was now at her family's ancestral estates in Madrigal. According to one knight—a man who noticed such things—she had remembered to bring Keyah. Marta planned to return briefly to Drugen's lodge with the others, then to join Carissima in Madrigal.

Tinka had taken Timka to her father's cottage on the River Zilp in Blikstein, and Kikki and Betsy had escaped with help to their own residences. The bishop had refused to acknowledge the usurpers and was jailed, along with Cami and the children. What would become of them? God help them!

Trimble interrupted Marta's thoughts. "And you, my queen—"

She started.

"—must fight. Don't give up!" His hair was streaked with white, and his hand shook as he raised it, but his eyes were filled with the old intensity. "You're the true sovereign and have many loyal subjects who will help you."

She lowered her gaze. The future would be difficult, but she would fulfill her obligations.

He took her hand. His hand was cold. She looked at him.

Tears slid from the corners of his baby blues. "I'm glad—" he said in a faint voice.

She bent closer.

"Glad it was me the tiger took," he said.

She pulled back. "I'm not!"

"Think of it this way." His gaze showed some of the old merriment, but his grip was firm. "I'll be taking some news to your father. News he's waiting for."

She smiled but wrinkled her brow.

"That his prayers were answered," he said. "That you grew up to be a woman of virtue."

He shivered as the fever returned, and she tucked the covers tightly around him.

She began to write again, hoping her journal hadn't been destroyed and that she could include these words:

Fleurdamour, queen of Faerie, was made ill by Drugen's spell, which somehow survived his death for a time. She would tremble at sudden sounds and cry out in her sleep. I've heard Beauschante comforting her and heard her weeping, probably in his arms. And in the evenings, when the warmth and light of the sun departed the world, her wings would appear, sheer but darksome and quivering as if with distress.

Last night, she slept peacefully, and this morning, her smile returned. Though, like all fairy smiles, it's still a little odd, as if painted or pasted on, and her expression is still incapable of all but the tiniest alterations. This evening, when the sun sank and night covered the world, she seemed unaffected. Piers toasted her and Beauschante and a brighter future for Cazmarya, and she and Beauschante drank from the same cup with their arms entwined, then kissed.

Trimble's health is failing swiftly, as if death is a rider who is riding hard and shall soon overtake him. He has a high fever and is in a great deal of pain, which we ease with the fairy teas. I'm glad he has written his letters, for there's little hope. Beauschante says the wounds are putrefying. I pray all the time but know I will lose him, and I suffer too knowing what Tinka and Timka will have to endure. In their world and mine, there will be a huge, Trimble-sized hole.

But at all times, in everything, Bartolo is my consolation, though a consolation mixed with further grief. Today, we walked out for fresh air to an eminence that overlooks a falls higher than any I've seen. The waters, freed by approaching spring, thunder down and down into mists overspread by rainbows. When we turned to go and I became lightheaded and stumbled, Bartolo caught me.

"Marta, I have something to tell you," he said.

His expression forewarned and forearmed me. "Yes?" I asked in a small voice.

"I am going to marry." He drew apart while keeping hold of my hand. "It is not what I want but what must be."

Not wishing to bring him pain, I didn't allow myself to cry. "Who is she?"

"Lacrima, the eldest daughter of a distant cousin, the Duke di Dolere."

Besides shock, what was uppermost in my thoughts was amazement at his selflessness. "Bartolo, forgive me for having asked you to risk everything in this venture!"

He squeezed my hand. "But, my darling friend, I was already on the road to come to you when your letter reached me. Whenever you need me, call upon me. Your friendship is of the greatest importance, and Sapore will continue as your ally and assist you in regaining your rights."

"Perhaps the people of Zuphof will be better off without me."

"Never."

As we spoke, I felt feelings that couldn't be indulged if he were to happily marry, and I were to obey the Lord. I withdrew my hand.

Bartolo lowered his gaze, then looked up with tears. "Before we part, would you kiss me?"

I wanted to but shook my head. I had refused him for reasons of conscience; he had been refused, then done what he had to—a prince must marry. He had remained my true friend; I would remain his by protecting him in every way I could.

He nodded, then offered me his arm.

Trimble died during the night with his friends around him. He had already left the world, it seemed, for he stared at something no one else could see, reached for this, and smiled like a delighted baby. Then he closed his eyes.

The fairies tore their hair and rent their clothes. Marta kissed his hand, then helped Snow White prepare his body for burial.

The next morning, the troops rode back up the pass. Gurnemanz drove the sleigh in which Trimble lay, resting on furs and partly covered by them, his hands crossed on his chest and the sword beside him. The great garnet in its silver cross shone with quiet splendor.

As Gurnemanz drove by the spot where the bodies of Drugen and Rose Red were, he frightened off birds of prey. They were firebirds of a vivid blue with curling crests and long, shimmering tail feathers, and Marta recalled how Trimble's fingers had fidgeted with the lock on the cage, and she wondered about this.

As the troops came out of the pass, they separated into their companies; Beauschante and Fleurdamour, and Piers and Elda were at the head of the fairy hosts going northwest toward Cazmarya. Merl la Corneille went with them as a hawk on the arm of a squire. Since he liked to be a bird, Beauschante had said, and since he seemed sincere about wanting to go home and wanting to change, he would go hooded and tethered before being completely forgiven. Such was the power of Beauschante's fairy magic that he only had to command this. The prisoners of war went as crated pigeons with the smell of the hawk in their nostrils.

As Marta reined in to watch the Cazmaryan troops move into the distance, she noticed a crocus pushing up near the dainty hooves of her palfrey. Its hooves were very unlike Toivo's sturdy ones, and she felt another keen pang of loss. Would she see him again? She silently prayed about this, then, with Bartolo, the Saporian knights, and the small Zupian contingent, headed toward a valley below the Zelhorn, where the village of Nobya-tolonya lay as if napping in the sunshine. There, they would bury Trimble and restock supplies before going on to Isabay and Veronique at the lodge. From the lodge, they would go on to their different destinations. Marta whispered a prayer for Isabay, Veronique, and Royal, then glanced at Bartolo, who looked unhappy but resolute. At her other side, Thomas was riding, deftly managing his destrier, which took its lead from the other horses.

Gaspar urged on his own mount eagerly, impatiently. Snow White, who had been born in Beaubois and had expressed her desire to return there, was riding with him.

The sky over Nobya-tolonya was exquisitely blue, and the onion-shaped domes of twin buildings, hiding behind high walls, glinted in the sunlight. Carriages—not sleighs—were parked at the sides of the road; the piles of snow were negligible; and there were puddles everywhere. Jonquils were bending in a breeze.

As Marta and Bartolo, Thomas, Gaspar, and Gurnemanz rode down Main Street at the head of the troops, the villagers came out to greet them with subdued but heartfelt cheers. The news of Trimble's noble death and Drugen's horrible demise had traveled quickly. Unshaven and battle-worn, Bartolo appeared to be only an ordinary soldier; in her borrowed gown, coat, and scarf of fairy make, Marta felt like a peasant queen. Thomas was sitting very straight in the saddle, with Gaspar and Gurnemanz riding behind him as his honor guard.

Nobya-tolonya seemed a fitting place for Trimble's interment. It was very old, and living artifacts who addressed one another as "thee" and "thou" lived there. Like his birthplace, Brughil, it was humble and out of the way. It had a monastery and convent dating from the period in which he was born. And at the main cross, a statue of bronze stood—a knight holding a spear to the throat of a dragon at his feet.

Bartolo described this monument of a real slayer of dragons, Blessed Waromyr, to Thomas.

Thomas smiled and said, "Trimble would see the irony in this."

The antique mausoleum—its stones were blackened with time— offered by the magistrate and council in gratitude for the part Trimble had played in vanquishing a common enemy, was that of a venerable family with no living descendants. His casket, sandwiched between the tombs of persons of great consequence, bore this epitaph:

Trimble of Uspenska, a bondservant of Jesus Christ, sleeps here. He shall awaken someday to reign with Christ a thousand years.

Necessity

The Firebird & Dragon Inn
Nobya-tolonya
The 16th of April 1622

Dear Tinka,

Enclosed are letters for you and Timka from your beloved husband Gregor, Baron of Brughil, as dictated by him to Bartolo, the Duke of Soggiorno.

On the 13th of April, your "Trimble" died from wounds received in God's service and mine. He always protected me and others, a responsibility he met with the utmost faithfulness. His heart never failed him; he was brave and kind—I need not tell you all that he was! He made my quest possible and, in the end, contributed to the downfall of the enemy who killed my father.

I know your heart is breaking. (Mine is.) Please know that he was longing to get home to you and Timka. I am so sorry for Timka! I hope to see you both when days of peace come and tell you all that happened.

Enclosed is his timepiece with the lock of your hair and Timka's. Please be assured that any concerns for your future will be amply met by his loving friends.

I embrace you and Timka!

Marta Louisa Happstein
Queen of Zuphof

My dearest Tinka—Lady Katinka,

I've botched it again, I guess, though certainly the Lord intended things to happen as they have. I won't be coming home to you, for I am soon to leave this world after finally facing "the beast" after all these years.

Thank you for your selflessness in encouraging me to do what I felt I must in accompanying Her Majesty. You and I knew the risks, though that doesn't make it easier now.

For most people, life is short. For me, it was long and sometimes fraught with hell's pangs, so I don't mind going to heaven, except for missing you and Timka. The Savior is there—my dearest friend, my true King. And my earthly king is there as well, and we have much to talk over. I know the Lord will guard you better than this coward could; I only wish we were going to heaven together, after Timka is grown.

My arms are around you. Thank you for marrying this failure, who loved you with all his heart, and for loving him in return with all of yours. And for turning him into a success of sorts—imagine. So then I've had life's greatest gift, most folks will have to admit: love. But also the "worst fortune," some will still maintain.

I want you to give our son an education, befitting his true station, both at books—it need not be long to be baronial—and at arms, which will be long and arduous. For the latter, I've made arrangements for him to go to Gurnemanz, who is instated as "Queen's Champion."

Be sure to tell our son the whole truth! Hold nothing back, my darling, or you'll destroy his ability to trust! And tell him that, though I waited a long time, I at last killed not a dragon but a tiger—a man-eater who was about to kill Her Majesty. I'm dying from the wounds I received. So then, be sure to say that for a while I was "Queen's Champion." This is his rightful legacy, and he must have it, though he will see that it is best not to boast of all of it.

One final word. This may seem indelicate, but I want you to know that should you wish to remarry—a

Maria Tatham

loving man of faith—it's all right with me. My deep-
est desire is for your complete happiness.

Gregor, Twelfth Baron of Brughil

My lad, Timothy—my Timka!

You're my boy, and I love you. Don't forget that!
And don't break your neck skating, for you have
work to do! It may fall to you to help Her Majesty regain the throne.

Your mother has something to tell you. Be brave
about this, enjoy as much of it as you can, and
never be ashamed! All men fall. What matters is
what they do on rising to their feet again.

Be kind, trust in the Lord Jesus, and hide his
Word in your heart! The world is consumed with
wickedness.

Marry a good Christian girl who has a sense of
fun but is also sensible and who truly loves you!

One word more. Should your mother marry again,
respect the man while contriving to watch over her
from a discreet distance. I'm depending on you.
                              Your loving father

Epilogue: Promise

On a hilltop overlooking a forest in leaf, a young queen paused for a last look at the castle at her back. Beaubois. *Beautiful wood.* Its slender towers looked like a forest of stonework, and its roof tiles shimmered with dew. Far below, glimpsed where it tripped along, a river thundered.

She had accompanied a new friend and his daughter to the castle, took her rest, and was going on. It was the beginning of summer, and her knights were anxious to get on the road. She was fighting the blues, for her champion had died and her beloved had married another. She had also been robbed of her kingdom.

Ahead lay the verdant pass leading into the fabled realm that was her mother's country of birth. Her mother was there, awaiting her. No lies, like bulging walls threatening to topple, now stood between them or between them and the real world.

Her long, wheat-colored hair was neatly tied back beneath a cap of greenest velvet that set off her clear green eyes—eyes that now showed conscious wisdom, meekness, and certainty. She was seated sidesaddle on the stout little Fennish, who had been fetched from an outpost on the brink of a world in which she had almost lost her life.

She raised her chin. Part of that life was mapped with pins of pain marking its fields of battle. The rest of her life was about to be explored and mapped. It would be studded with landmines, she was certain of this—camouflaged pits filled with a hundred-weight of black powder and killing stones that might explode at any moment in a deadly rain. But it would be dotted with watering holes, resting places, and heart-stirring vistas.

There was the certainty of ultimate good beyond her pilgrim world.

There was the small promise, as faint as the beating of an infant's heart, of *love*...

She leaned to pat her horse's neck and then smiled at the knight she now called *champion*. He was an older man of sound judgment who was back in his appointed place after a time of trouble and misunderstanding.

"Ready, madam?" he asked.

"Ready!"

Glossary of Names, Beasts, and Places:

A word about names: Four proper names were borrowed from Wolfram von Eschenbach's *Parzival;* they appear below with an asterisk (*). One proper name was borrowed from *The Song of Roland;* it appears with a double asterisk (**).

CHIEF ACTORS:

Marta Louisa Happstein, queen apparent of Zuphof
Trimble of Uspenska, her father's former valet, now the palace handyman

Peter Happstein, King Peter Josef Michael, Marta's father
Carissima, the Queen Mother, Peter's wife and Marta's mother

Kikki (Francesca di Sapore) and *Betsy (Lizaveta Tribotski),* Marta's ladies-in-waiting and confidantes
Jerome and Cami (Camila) Wenzel, the Bishop of Zuphof and his wife
Bartolo di Sapore, Duke of Soggiorno, heir apparent of Sapore, Vincenzo's son and Kikki's brother
Lord Alexander Montanus Drugen, outlaw overlord of the Eastern Wilds
Lady Schoya, Drugen's wife, *a fairy*
Isabay, his mistress
Royal, his son by Isabay

Gurnemanz*, the king's former champion, now a hostler at the livery in Stootna
Gaspar, Count of Beaubois, Isabay's father
Thomas of Fredersberg, a king's knight who was blinded

SUPPORTING CAST:

The Earl of Ester, chancellor of Zuphof
Countess Gallina, one of Marta's courtiers
Matthew of Maiberg, Abbot of Blessed Philip the Bold's in Madrigal
The innkeeper and *a maid* at the Bucket & Ladle Inn
Piers and Elda of Cazmarya, newlyweds who flee from Drugen on a unicorn, *fairies*
The Abbot of Blessed Waromyr's Abbey in the Forest of Zwipplenitch
A brother who operates the elevator basket there
Brother Mikhail of Blessed Waromyr's
Brother Waclaw of Blessed Waromyr's
Brother Segird of Blessed Waromyr's, a former king's knight
Brother Edelbert of Blessed Waromyr's, once the king and Drugen's teacher
Glaber, a shepherd, Royal's comrade
Baron Ghenter and *Lord Falconier,* Drugen's knights
Merl la Corneille, Schoya's uncle, a necromancer and changeling
Drugen's guards
Gypsy dancers at his castle
A dwarf king and *a lordly personage,* characters portrayed by actors in a play enacted there
Chief cook and *chief baker,* cook's and baker's assistants, *a contented servant girl,* and a troop of servant girls, pages and footmen
A compassionate Gypsy man in the Forest of Zohemia
A beautiful Gypsy fortuneteller
Veronique, Drugen and Isabay's little girl who lives with her mother at his hunting lodge
The matron, Isabay's attendant at the lodge

Albert, Drugen's gifted, handicapped brother who lives in seclusion on the lodge grounds

Dame Anna, Drugen's aunt, who takes care of Albert and who took care of the king when he was mortally wounded

Rose Red and *Snow White,* Drugen's courtesans

Meljahkanz*, Drugen's courtier, a man of tremendous physical strength

Altamente, a satyr who lives in the wilds near the Zelhorn

Beauschante and Fleurdamour, king and queen of Faerie, that is, of the Realm of Cazmarya in Madrigal, *fairies*

Persons Alluded to:

Tinka (Katinka), Trimble's wife

Timka (Timothy), Trimble and Tinka's young son

Trimble's deceased relations: his godly *mother* and sister, *Hulda*

John Kolpos, former Bishop of Zuphof, Cami Wenzel's deceased father

Vincenzo, Prince of Sapore, Kikki and Bartolo's father

Mademoiselle Polinard, mistress of the finishing school Marta attended

Gurnemanz's wife and daughters from Stootna

Borg de Lanz, a shrewd statesman, an adulterer

Ferdy (Ferdinand) de Lanz, Borg's son and heir, Betsy's fiancé

Ottwig de Lanz, Borg's illegitimate son

Don Ricardo Alvarez, a nobleman whom Marta calls "a scoundrel"

Ariel, a Jewish physician who fled from persecution into the Eastern Wilds

Reba, his young, unmarried daughter

The dancing prophets, bands of ecstatic prophets who rove the country-side, warning of the End of the Age

Vlad Ostreich, a Count from the Eastern Marches

Bellefleur, his wife, *a fairy,* mother of his daughters, Schoya and Imane

Imane*, Elda's mother, who is believed to have been killed by Drugen's enchantments

Queen Wilominna, Marta's paternal grandmother

Basilides Drugen, Count of Mortomyr, Drugen's grandfather, an apostate and mad scientist
The prince, the king and Carissima's son who died in infancy
Guyon, Gaspar's champion, who was killed in single combat with Falconier
Clinschor*, a sorcerer who was castrated by his lover's husband
Siglorel**, a magician who, upon his death, was "taken straight to hell"
Lacrima, eldest daughter of the Duke di Dolere
The Duke di Dolere, a nobleman of Sapore, Bartolo's distant cousin

The Blessed:
John Calvay, sixteenth-century Reformer of Zuphof
Wolfram of Bettensberg, a man of God and man of war who fought during the days of the Reforms
Blessed Philip the Bold for whom the abbey in Madrigal was named
Blessed Gregor of Brughil, the patron saint of Zuphof
Blessed Waromyr draconemesis for whom the abbey was named; he slew the dragon Uxondyne.

Dragons and Other Beasts:
A white tiger, a man-eater captured by Drugen
The unicorn captured by Drugen but freed by Piers and Elda
Wolves who attack Toivo, and others who pull Drugen's dogsleds
A bear captured and mistreated by Drugen
The werewolf, Baron Ghenter
Valkynde, emperor of dragons
Uxondyne, his consort who was slain by Blessed Waromyr
A dragon slain by the king and his knights as they rode to Drugen's lodge
Hexglendyia, the fiery wyrm who burned the village of Spoot to the ground

Inmates of the menagerie: firebirds, koi, hummingbirds, songbirds, a chameleon, dragon eggs (species: draconis cappadociae[1]), vampire bats, an ogre, white stag, and griffins
Toivo (Finnish for "hope"), Marta's Fennish mount
Nostratu, the king's warhorse

Places:
Kingdom of Zuphof
Royal City of Zuphof, its capital on the coast in the west
Zonderzee, western ocean
Sapore, a sovereign princedom far to the south and east
Madrigal, a rebellious duchy to the north of Zuphof
The passes that lead into that fabled realm; close by there is said to be the den of a dragon.
The Abbey of Blessed Philip the Bold's in Madrigal
Cazmarya, the king and queen of Faerie's realm hidden deep in the forests of Madrigal
Alvanay, a city and a province of Madrigal
The Fens, Zuphof's lowlands stretching from the Royal City to the Forest of Zwipplenitch
Stootna, a village on the fens where Marta went to school
The Bucket & Ladle Inn in Stootna
Beaubois, Gaspar's domain, a forested realm located along the borders of Zuphof and Madrigal
Spoot, a village unsuccessfully defended by Blessed Gregor against Hexglendyia
Uspenska, a northwestern island province of Zuphof
Droopsk, a rebellious duchy to the south of Zuphof
Ittyohobonetska (City of Scholars), *Blikstein* (City of Churches), and *Brughil* (birthplace of Blessed Gregor): cities of Zuphof that were annexed by Droopsk
The Brothers' School in Ittyohobonetska, where the king and Drugen were taught by Brother Edelbert

College of the Knights of Marcion in Ittyohobonetska, an institute infamous for its secret rites; Drugen completed his education there.

River Zilp, on its banks Blikstein was built

Zogtromp-on-the-mere, a lakeside town near the Eastern Wilds

Forest of Zwipplenitch near the Eastern Wilds

Abbey of Blessed Waromyr on a hilltop in the Forest of Zwipplenitch

Tavern and *sheepfold* near the Eastern Wilds

Biklava, the last outpost on the edge of the Eastern Wilds

The Eastern Wilds, wilderness many leagues due east from Zuphof

Drugen's castle in the Eastern Wilds

Forest of Zohemia in the Eastern Wilds

Drugen's hunting lodge in the Forest of Zohemia

The menagerie at the lodge

The Keistrel Pass, a northern pass that leads up to the lodge; from Zuphof the only way into the Zelhornish Range on horseback

Zelhornish Range, alps of the Eastern Wilds

The Little Kapstein, mountain whose lower slopes are blanketed by the Forest of Zohemia

The Zelhorn, a cloud-capped peak whose cliffs are the legendary breeding grounds of dragons

The glen at the foot of the Zelhorn

The Vale of the Nameless Mountains, a deep valley surrounded by the highest peaks in the range

The Caves of Refuge, an old hideout of Wolfram of Bettensberg in the Vale of the Nameless Mountains

Gupenstock and *Nobya-tolonya*, two villages in the Zelhornish Range

The Firebird & Dragon Inn in Nobya-tolonya

The Eastern Marches, steppes east of the Zelhornish Range

Terms:

Fennish, a hardy, cold-blooded breed of horse

Zupian, something pertaining to Zuphof, e.g., the Zupian calendar

Zupish, the language spoken in the greater part of Zuphof

Zelhornish, the language spoken in the Eastern Wilds of Zuphof, in the environs of the Zelhorn

Saporian, having to do with the princedom of Sapore

Cazmaryan, having to do with the realm of Cazmarya

Endnote

1   *draconis cappadociae*: according to Page and Ingpen's *Encyclope-
dia of Things That Never Were*, Penguin Studio, 1985, this is "the
Mediterranean or Levantine" dragon.